First Christmas at Muddy Creek

By

Richard A. Bartlett

✳ 5-13-08

ISBN: 1-4196-8201-6

ISBN-13: 9781419682018

Visit www.booksurge.com to order additional copies.

FIRST CHRISTMAS AT MUDDY CREEK

I

People were puzzled when, in 1995, the Catholic Bishop of Montana announced that he would celebrate Christmas Midnight Mass at the Church of the Mountain Madonna in Muddy Creek. After all, Muddy Creek was off the beaten path, could boast of barely a thousand inhabitants, and some claimed the number included their cats and dogs.

True, a hundred and thirty years ago, in December 1865, Muddy Creek had been one of the wildest, most boisterous, not to say sinful boom towns on the Montana mining frontier. Even before the placers had given out, valuable veins had been discovered. Hard-rock mining, with Eastern investors bringing in heavy machinery, was taking over. Whatever the population in '65—and some claimed it at nearly three thousand—Muddy Creek was so crowded that every storefront was occupied on that Christmas Eve.

And yet, from this particular Christmas Eve experience at Muddy Creek, there arose within six months one of the most beautiful little Catholic churches in the American West, the Church of the Mountain Madonna.

The thousand residents of Muddy Creek in the 1990s, eking out a living from tourism, trout fishing, and a long hunting season, were so proud of their little church that they applied for its inclusion in the National Trust for Historic Preservation. In the late fall of 1995, the Commission came through. So overjoyed were they that they invited the Bishop of Montana to say Christmas Eve Mass there in celebration of the church's founding. When he heard the story of how the Church of the Mountain Madonna came to be, he graciously accepted the invitation.

This is the story he heard.

When he first started east from Oro Fino, Pierce City, and Bannack City, Jesuit Father Demetrius de Mara was alone astride his big, black riding mule, Gabriel. His smaller, meaner, gray pack mule, Lucifer, followed in tow. The padre was alone with them and his thoughts.

For much had happened since his departure from the seminary in Florence, Italy, for St. Louis, Missouri, in the United States barely two years ago. Sometimes, for the life of him, he could not comprehend the Lord's wishes as interpreted by his superiors at the Jesuit House in St. Louis. Hardly had he arrived from Europe when he was ordered up the Missouri River to Fort Benton and on, still deeper into the mountains, to the new gold mining camps of western Montana and eastern Idaho. Along the way he was to convert Indians, trappers, buffalo hunters, gold seekers, gamblers, prostitutes, ranchers; in fact, just about anything on two legs, and he was also to read Mass every morning and, on Sundays, several times, if needed. Plus baptisms, christenings, first communions, confirmations, marriages, and the administration of extreme unction followed by Catholic funeral rites. He sighed. There had been two christenings, one marriage—of a mountain man to a Blackfoot squaw—and (he paused to count them on his fingers) he had administered extreme unction eleven times and performed fourteen burials. Most disappointing of all, he had made no conversions.

The padre sighed. Now, having done as much good as he could do in such godless places as Fort Benton, Last Chance Gulch, Bannack City, Gold Canyon, and Pierce City, he was headed for Muddy Creek. It was said that there were at least three thousand souls hard at work there. Just as the placers began giving out, veins of gold had been found in the mountains nearby. Hard-rock mining was setting in, and the gold camp was taking on the aura of permanent habitation.

But the slim yet sturdy young man had not been alone with his mules and his thoughts for long. Following the muddy wagon tracks that constituted roads linking the gold camps, and from trails leading to lonely sluices and mines along the way, miners joined him until by the time the padre reached the western ridge overlooking Muddy Creek, there were perhaps a dozen men in the party. They were a motley crew: Yankees and Southerners who had chosen to go West instead of fighting on the battlefield; Irishmen fresh from the Emerald Isle; Cousin Jacks from Cornwall; and yonder-siders from California. They were dressed as alike as peas in a pod, with oversized flannel trousers tucked into boot-tops, flannel or woolen shirts, and heavy woolen or sheepskin coats. Some wore floppy pork-pie hats. All their clothing had seen better days.

The men were in a festive mood. A chinook wind had blown in the night before. To awaken after weeks of below-freezing weather to the sound of melting snow and to feel a breeze wafting seventy degree air was in itself enough to raise one's spirits. But besides that, it was Christmas Eve. The lonely men were cheering up each other, looking forward to revelry at Muddy Creek, hoping to forget memories of homes and loved ones left behind.

Of course they noticed the bespectacled padre. He was of average height and sat well on Gabriel, thanks to months riding the big mule. He too wore the usual boots and heavy woolen trousers, but they were black, not gray or brown. This would hardly have attracted attention, nor would the heavy black greatcoat he wore, its tails flapping in the breeze. But the coat was open at the throat, exposing his soiled white clerical collar. And his hat—it really set him apart, being the round, black prelatic headpiece one saw priests wearing in the Old Country or in the working districts of American cities. The hat and the collar marked him: he was a padre, a Catholic priest. It gave strangers who knew not his name an instant handle upon which to address him and get acquainted: padre.

At the crest of the ridge the men halted to gaze down upon Muddy Creek. It was hardly a beauteous site. Beyond the town they could see how the canyon widened just enough for a gold camp to sprout along the creek (or "crick," as the locals called it). In the widened area, perhaps three-quarters of a mile from end to end, a street careened more or less from east to west, according to the contours of the stream. Then the creek curved to the south and around a ridge, and the town abruptly ceased.

"How'd Muddy Creek get its name?" asked a bearded miner.

One of the men leaned over his horse's neck to better scan the town. "Story is," he replied, "that a party of prospectors arrived here after a cloudburst and found the crick roily and muddy. All but two of 'em passed off the stream as havin' no color, and went on. But two stayed. Next mornin' when the sun come out and the water cleared and went down and sand bars came up for air, they worked the sands and—Eureka! Gold! Gold at Muddy Creek!"

From the crest of the ridge they could make out Muddy Creek's Main Street, crowded with people. The buildings were mostly of sawed timber, single storied and false fronted. Some had received a coat of paint, now chipping and fading. A few were built of logs. Two or three two-story buildings stood out, one of them with fresh paint.

"That two-story building with the fresh yellow paint—that's Reece's Music Hall," volunteered another. "I hear they have taxi dancers what can do the can-can. They'll dance with you, too, for a price. And it's got gamblin', and pretty good likker."

"And that other two-story?" asked another.

"That's the Sanborn House, Muddy Creek's only hotel."

"What interests me," another said quietly out of the padre's hearing, "is the whorehouse."

"Madam Dahlia's?" volunteered still another. "She and her girls are in those funny lookin' log cabins up 'A' Street. That's one of the streets runnin' at right angles to Main. You can just make out the cabin with a front entrance and what looks like two cabins connected on either side. The girls occupy those cabins. Behind them is a stable. Maybe she's got some new whores," he commented. "The ones I last saw were overworked, to say the least."

"On Christmas Eve, you goin' to a whorehouse?" chimed in another.

"Damn you," was the reply. "Now you've pricked my conscience." He paused a few moments, his thoughts on his childhood in Iowa. "I guess not," he replied, glancing at the padre, who pretended not to hear. "I'll wait till the day after." Then he added quietly, "I didn't know Christianity had got to Montana yet."

"Seven…eight…nine…by golly," said the miner who had described Muddy Creek's beginnings. "There's two new saloons since I was here last month. I'm goin' to hit every one of 'em."

"Me for a barber shop an' a shave an' a bath first," said his partner. "Gawd, I need all three afore I'd want any gal to see me, let alone smell me, even a whore."

"I agree," said the miner, laughing and holding his nose.

"I need bullets for my rifle," volunteered the Southerner. "Hope the shebangs are still open."

"Those are our general stores," a miner whose horse was close to the padre said. The padre already knew it.

As for Father de Mara, he leaned forward again on his black mule and studied Muddy Creek's layout and buildings with other considerations in mind. Suddenly, someone in the group let out a loud "Ya-hoo!," spurred his horse and started at a gallop down the road toward town. The others joined in, waving their hats and yelling and running their mounts. Father de Mara had no choice but to follow more slowly, his mules trotting along behind the carousing miners, who entered the town at a gallop, whooping like cowboys just off the range. One or two fired pistols into the air.

Their exuberance may have lasted, but their speed did not. The street was filled with wagons, horses, buggies, booted men, and a few calico-clothed women with shopping bags and shawls. Worst of all, Muddy Creek's Main Street was a morass—if one's boots sank into the muck just to the calves, one felt lucky. The next step might not be so shallow.

Arriving at the head of the street, Father de Mara realized at once that it would be easier to make headway afoot. Moreover, he had questions to ask. So he dismounted and began picking his way up the right side of the busy thoroughfare, leading his mules. He advanced past the barber shop and bath, wherein several of the party had disappeared, and past Tigh's Saloon on the other side of the street. He observed others of the group dismount, hitch their horses, and disappear through the swinging doors from which came the brassy tones of an out-of-tune piano.

He trudged on up the street past a vacant lot, past Webster's Miner's Supply—one of the miner's shebangs—and had just passed a narrow storefront office with a faded sign hanging outside:

William J. O'Bryan

Register of Claims

when he heard a gruff, authoritative but not unpleasant voice of a mounted man behind him ask, "Stranger, can you get your mules out of the way?"

Hardly had the padre responded before the tall rider brushed past him on a fine sorrel horse. At the same moment the door of the Register of Claims office flew open. The padre turned to see a shirt-sleeved, balding, black-bearded man appear. In his right hand he held a Smith and Wesson revolver.

"Jack Langford, you lyin', stealin' sonofabitch!" he shouted at the rider.

To Father Demetrius de Mara the next few moments seemed like a terrible dream. He watched as the black-bearded man raised the revolver and aimed it at the horseman. "No!" the padre blurted out. "No!"

For a split second the gunman glanced in the direction of the man who had shouted those words. Then he fired. A bullet creased the rider's coat in the right shoulder, exposing threads and leaving an ugly crease exposing the inner lining, but apparently it had not touched the rider's body.

The horseman's reaction was lightning fast. Even as the sorrel reared, the horseman's free hand reached for a pistol. As his horse came down and pranced nervously in the muddy street, the rider methodically lifted his revolver and took aim at the black-bearded man in the doorway, who was once again aiming his pistol at him.

"Stop!" shouted the padre again. "Do not shoot!"

But it was too late. Father Demetrius de Mara heard two shots, one from the rider and, a split second later, one from the bearded man—only his shot went high in the air as his body fell with a thud onto the boardwalk in front of his office.

For long seconds all movement stopped. Then men ran to the prone form. They gently turned William O'Bryan on his back. From his breast a red patch of blood was slowly widening on his white shirt. From the way the man's chest heaved as he fought for breath it was clear that he still lived, but was badly hurt. As tenderly as possible the men picked him up and carried him inside his office. They laid the Register of Claims on a long, wide, unvarnished table after first brushing survey plats onto the floor. A crowd pressed into the little office and blocked the doorway.

"Get the Doc!" someone shouted.

"Didn't you hear? The Doc's done left for Salt Lake City. Muddy Creek ain't got no Doc."

"Then get the alcalde," suggested someone else. Immediately one man pushed his way through the crowd to fetch the man chosen as Muddy Creek's combination mayor, sheriff, coroner, and justice of the peace: the alcalde.

The padre, meanwhile, had tethered Gabriel and Lucifer to a hitching post, worked his way through the crowd, and now looked at the wounded man on the table. He had observed the results of violence eleven times since leaving St. Louis, and it was clear that this would be his twelfth: the man was dying. Hastily the priest returned to Lucifer and from his pack grabbed a battered Bible, the requisite cloth to place over his shoulders, and a small vial of holy oil. As he reached the doorway he heard a voice ask the dying man, "Mr. O'Bryan, you're a good shot. How come you missed?"

The wounded man's chest heaved as the patch of blood widened. A streak of red fluid appeared at one corner of his mouth. His eyes moved slowly from one side of the crowd to the other. He gasped. "I—thought I saw a—priest. Christmas Eve…" His voice trailed off.

Father de Mara had reached the table in time to hear the man's words. The padre blanched. In a flash he realized that if William O'Bryan had not caught sight of the clerical collar and hat and thus diverted his aim, he might still be alive. The padre frowned in thought. But another man would be dead. Either way, he would be performing ablutions on a dead or dying man. The priest looked down upon the cherubic Irish face, small nose, blue eyes. O'Bryan looked at him. "So I did see a priest," he gasped. "And, begorra, just in time."

The padre made the sign of the cross over the dying man. He began uttering prayers, anointing O'Bryans' eyes, ears, nostrils, and lips, even his booted feet. Silently, men in the room removed their hats and crossed themselves. Suddenly O'Bryan's chest heaved twice, struggling to retain life. The face, which had been twisted in pain, relaxed; his head turned to one side, and a death rattle came from the open mouth with the blood trickling down one side. The padre completed the anointment. For seconds there was a still life montage. No one knew what to say.

Then spurs jingled in the doorway. The crowd separated, making room for the rider, the man who had just killed William O'Bryan. "He's dead?" he asked.

All eyes turned toward him, this man who had just killed Muddy Creek's Recorder of Claims. "'Fraid so, Mr. Langford."

The tall, well-dressed man removed his hat, lowered his head, and shrugged his shoulders in a sign of hopelessness. Then he looked at the crowd. "I hope you all saw it," he said. "He called me a name and then fired the first shot. I was lucky." Langford tilted his head toward the shoulder of his sheepskin coat. A tattered groove a half-inch deep and a half-inch wide cut across the top of the right shoulder. "I'm going to have to get this sewn up," he said, suddenly aware of how thoughtless his statement sounded. Then he frowned. "I'm surprised he missed. Bill O'Bryan was the best shot I ever knew."

"You can thank the padre for that," a miner said. "O'Bryan caught sight of the priest's hat and collar and it diverted him for a split second, just enough to make him miss and give you a chance to fire back."

Langford, his clean-shaven face revealing the fine features of a man of perhaps forty years of age, tilted back his well-contoured pork-pie hat. "Oh?" turning to the padre. "I have you to thank?" He bowed. "Thanks a million, Padre. Jack Langford's the name. I am indebted to you." Quickly he surveyed the crowd in the tiny office. "By the way," he added, "I hope you'll all attest that I fired in self-defense."

There was an undercurrent of agreement.

"William O'Bryan was a bit teched in the head," Langford added. "I bought the Sunnyside Mine from him fair and square. By sheer luck it turned out rich. O'Bryan decided I'd known it was rich. He thought I'd cheated him. Boys, on my word, I hadn't. But O'Bryan brooded and threatened me—several times—and," he swept his hand toward the table where lay the dead man, "this was the outcome."

All was quiet. For a few seconds Langford stood still, contemplating the terrible event that had just happened, his own good luck resulting in another man's death. Then he swung on his heels, cut a path through the crowded doorway, and was soon astride his horse and riding down the street. Before the crowd had the opportunity to disperse, a horse neighed as a paunchy little man with a swarthy complexion and a sensuous mouth dismounted from a nondescript mare, hitched it to where Langford's had been next to Father de Mara's mules, and appeared in the doorway.

"It's the alcalde, Luke Bassett," said someone. "Let him in."

Standing straight as his big belly would allow, and appearing authoritative as possible, the alcalde appraised the situation. He heard the details. Quickly he absolved Jack Langford, clearing him of all charges. He added that this was Christmas Eve and "by God, we don't want any more shootings here until the day after Christmas." Then he assigned a committee of four to obtain a pine box coffin from Jesse Tinsley's furniture store and prepare to bury William O'Bryan at the cemetery begun on the treeless hill overlooking Muddy Creek. "And dig the grave quick 'cause this chinook won't last long and the ground'll get hard frozen and there's no place 'cept a grave for a dead man."

"When the grave is dug," Father de Mara announced, "contact me and I'll conduct graveside services."

The alcalde started to leave but the padre clutched his arm. "Pardon me," he began in slow, correct English. "I am Father Demetrius de Mara, of the Society of Jesus. I—"

Luke Bassett looked him over then held out a plump hand. "A Jesuit, eh? Father de Mara, you say? What in

God's name—I mean, well, stop and think of it, that is what I mean—what in God's name are you doin' out here in western Montana, Padre? I'm afraid Christianity's a bit tardy in gettin' out here. Any kind of Christianity. I'm a Methodist, myself; we've got Baptists and Presbyterians and Congregationalists and a few Mormons and a whole lot of Catholic Irishmen here, even a Chinese laundryman, whatever his faith might be, but nary a preacher nor a priest for any of 'em. Glad to have you here. Make yerself at home. Maybe you can keep the Irish from gettin' drunk and fightin' and tearin' up the town." He pumped Father de Mara's hand, then released it and turned to walk out the door.

"Wait," urged the padre, stepping in front of the alcalde and barring his exit.

Luke Bassett paused, reflecting impatience. But when he looked into the face of the young priest he liked what he saw. The padre stood about five feet ten, figured the alcalde, was slim, and aged about thirty. He showed dark hair under his hat, a high brow denoting intelligence, blue eyes behind his silver framed glasses—blue eyes that had been soft when first observed, but were now hard, denoting determination. The nose was straight and aquiline, the face clean shaven, the teeth even and white, and the jaw chiseled square. The handshake had been firm, very firm. Here, mused the alcalde, was a man of the cloth who was also a man among men. Methodist though Luke Bassett was, Methodist that he vowed he would be unto death, he had to admit that he liked this lone man of the faith, Catholic Jesuit that he was.

"I need a place to worship here in Muddy Creek," began Father de Mara, "someplace to set up an altar and have Christmas Midnight Mass."

Alcalde Bassett rubbed his bearded face thoughtfully. Slowly he shook his head. "Padre," he said after a few moments, "I don't know where in this boom town you'll find an empty space for church services. Muddy Creek was just settling down with the placers slowly giving out when Jack Langford's Sunnyside Mine struck rich ore, and that started a new rush. Now everyone for miles around is sinkin' shafts and tryin' to find veins in the hard-rock. All of a sudden people are comin' to town and more buildings are needed. I swear, Padre, there's hardly a square foot of empty space in this whole town. And Christmas here, in 1865, means the saloons and music halls and eateries and barber shops and shebangs will all be open well into the night." The alcalde tilted his hat and scratched his thinning gray hair. "I just don't know what to tell you, Padre. You can try, but I can't help you a bit." And with that Luke Bassett stepped aside and strode out the door.

Father Demetrius de Mara, late of the Jesuit novitiate at Florence, working on his first assignment—to establish the Faith in the heathenish gold fields of western Montana—quickly packed his Bible and religious paraphernalia, strode outside, unhitched Gabriel and Lucifer and trudged down Muddy Creek's Main Street. His silver pocket watch read three-thirty, and, he reflected apprehensively, in December it got dark early in Montana.

He did not have much time.

II

Dejectedly, Father de Mara sat on a wooden bench outside of HARDY'S BOOTS, SHOES, AND NOTIONS. The parade of humanity passed him by, all in a hurry. Catching snippets of conversations made him realize where he was: For each person talking of Christmas gifts there were three talking mines, claims, liquor, gambling, or wenching. There were many more men than women. He heard nothing of church services, and Christ's name, when mentioned at all, was taken only in vain.

Absently he stared across the muddied boardwalk at his two companions of many a lonely Montana mile: Gabriel, his big, black riding mule, and Lucifer, his pack mule, eyes half closed, placid and still. Tethered and patient, they awaited his next decision. Father de Mara began talking to them, as he had on so many lonely occasions, but thought better of it when two shabby miners, quite drunk, loud, and boisterous, came weaving down the boardwalk toward him, one holding a whiskey bottle half full (or half empty). The padre was glad they paid him no attention as they passed by.

At a loss at what to do next, he sat back and reminisced silently.

Indeed, it had been a long, lonely journey. It had begun with his decision, when he was eighteen years old and still living with his parents in Florence in northern Italy, to take Holy Orders in the Society of Jesus (the Jesuits). After more than a decade of study he was ordained and sent to St. Louis, in America. He had expected an assignment teaching at a Jesuit boys' school, or possibly even in a Jesuit college. Instead, the Order sent him to proselytize in the new mining communities of Montana and Idaho territories. Up the Missouri River on the steamboat *Yellowstone* he had made his way. At Fort Benton he had learned to shoot a rifle, hunt, and butcher a buffalo. He also learned enough sign language from an old mountain man to be understood by the Indians.

It was at Fort Benton that he had purchased Gabriel and Lucifer and had the good fortune to join a group of argonauts bound for the Montana and Idaho mines. They would be passing by the Sun Mission, west of Fort Benton, where his superiors at St. Louis had suggested he contact Father Francis Xavier Kuppens, the Jesuit missionary there. He could give the young priest good advice on surviving on the wild frontier.

It was at Father Kuppens' lonely outpost of Catholicism that Father de Mara realized how lucky he was that his orders were primarily to convert the white heathen, not the red ones. Father Kuppens lived in constant peril of his life. His converts were Blackfeet–Piegans, Bloods, and Gros Ventres—who numbered among the most warlike of all Indians. Somehow the Jesuit had gained their respect. The good Father had mastered their language and at least had a few loyal converts who attended Mass. To Father de Mara, the Indians seemed more fascinated than moved by the ritual. One did not inquire of Father Kuppens how much the Indians understood.

After a week at the Sun Mission, the padre joined still another party of gold seekers. He held Masses at Last Chance

Gulch (present Helena), then headed alone, save for Gabriel and Lucifer, into the mountains of northern Idaho. He preached and read Masses at Oro Fino, Bannack City, Gold Canyon, Pierce City, and many other small mining camps that arose overnight, prospered briefly, and disappeared just as fast when the color gave out in the sluices. Hard to believe, he mused as he sat on the bench soaking up the last warmth from the winter sun, hard to believe all his adventures since his arrival at the camps last April.

Once, making his way from one gold camp to another, he with Gabriel and Lucifer, had rounded a curve and trotted into the midst of a Bannock war party. They were in a surly mood. Two years before, in 1863, General Patrick Connor and his California Volunteers had defeated them in the Battle of Bear River. Two-thirds of all the Bannock braves had been killed. Only the padre's crude knowledge of sign language—plus God, of course—had got him out of the chance meeting alive. Once, he and the mules were almost washed away in a flash flood. A few times Protestant miners let him know that he was *persona non grata,* and "take yer stinkin' mules and git!" But if Irishmen were around, then his problem was getting away. This he did by always promising to return soon. And he meant it, but "soon," he always reflected, had a meaning all in the mind of the speaker.

His reverie was broken by the sudden realization that he was wasting time. What should he do now? He scanned the muddy, busy street. A big J. Murphy freight wagon pulled by a team of twelve oxen, the teamster, walking alongside and commanding them in German, was struggling through the quagmire ahead, blotting out the padre's view. Already the padre had inquired at five saloons (or music halls, tasting houses, or emporiums, as they were also called) where his reception had ranged from welcome, to we're sorry, to "better git outta here, stranger. This is no place for a man of the cloth."

Jesse Tinsley's furniture store had intrigued, for it had substantial square footage, but Jesse had just received off of the big freight wagon a new supply of furniture and crude, wooden caskets. Jesse was the town mortician as well as its merchant of tables, chairs, and beds. He had no empty space.

Father de Mara had also passed two livery stables, a tiny lawyer's office, and walked under a modest, weathered sign hanging on one hinge over a chicken coop-sized shack entered by a crude door, soundly padlocked. The sign read: T. LAVERNE M.D. The padre wondered why the doctor had left. It certainly wasn't for lack of patients. He shuddered as the breeze became noticeably cooler. Was the frontier making him callous? In his concern over finding a place to hold Christmas Midnight Mass he had forgotten the dead William O'Bryan.

He had a mother, he mused. He was raised somewhere and learned to read and write, otherwise he wouldn't have been the Register of Claims. He was a Catholic. He had a soul. Father de Mara crossed himself. "May he rest in peace," he whispered. Then his thoughts turned to William O'Bryan's killer, Jack Langford. An intelligent, authoritarian kind of man. His face was not all that wicked. He was clearly shaken by the incident. Which of the two, O'Bryan or Langford, had most deserved to die? The padre nodded his head in the way of one who faces insoluble problems.

His thoughts were broken by unusual commotion beyond the freight wagon which had just passed by. It blocked his vision but not his hearing. There was a scream followed by the crack of a whip, then obscenities, cheering, and men running down the boardwalks and even down the muddy street to observe the action. Priest or not, Father de Mara could not resist the attraction of curses, screams, and the crack of a whip. Leaving Gabriel and Lucifer tied at the hitching rail, he hastened down the muddy boardwalk, past the freight wagon, to a crowd circling what he assumed were two men fighting.

On one side of the street was the false-fronted REECE'S MUSIC HALL AND LIQUOR EMPORIUM; on the other side was Muddy Creek's newest, most imposing establishment, the Sanborn House, a two-story hotel. And in the muck of the street, surrounded by shouting men, were two combatants. Both were so mud-covered as to be nearly indistinguishable. One, a burly giant whose fellow employees from a nearby mine were yelling encouragement, held in his hand a bullwhip.

As Father de Mara arrived, he first watched the mine worker yank it from the mud, swing it in back of him with a whoosh! and then, with the dexterity of an experienced bullwhacker, send it singing through the air at his opponent.

That individual, on his hands and knees in the muck, tried to dodge the whirring line. The padre could hear the leather singing through the air. It struck the victim squarely across the back, slicing his coat. But as the burly fellow swung his arm to bring back the whip, the man on all fours made a quick leap and caught it with his bare hands.

At first his fingers slid along the smooth leather, but he quickly twisted it in his hand, kinking the long leather line. In another split second he yanked it.

The husky man lost his balance and fell into the muck. Instantly his opponent leaped through the mud and fell on him. The tall, lithe figure covered with mud and animal manure now had the upper hand. The two wrestled, rolling over and over in the muck.

"Stop it! Stop it, you two. I hate you both!" screamed a young woman in the front line. "I want nothing to do with either of you!"

No one paid attention, least of all the two men fighting so desperately in the muck. Suddenly the lithe one released his hold around the other's neck and, quick as a striking rattlesnake, grabbed the whip handle. It was unexpected. In an instant he had wrested it from its owner. Now he was free and leaping backwards while his opponent remained on his hands and knees, shaking his head.

The crowd watched with anticipation as the tall, slim figure dragged the whip from the muck. It slithered, then rose in the air and snapped backward as his body twisted to the right, as if it was a part of the whip. Then his arm shot forward. The whip whirred through the air too fast to follow. It struck the burly one across the shoulders, just below the neck. It popped!

The victim screamed in pain and fell flat on his stomach as the whip came back again, and fell again, this time on his back, ripping his muddy flannel shirt and cutting a red, searing streak across his flesh. Back came the whip again.

The girl again screamed and lunged into the muck across the open circle of shouting spectators and grabbed the young man's arm holding the whip. "No more!" No more! Let him be!" she wailed.

The gladiator paused, his eyes never leaving his adversary, who lay still in the mud. "Had enough?" he shouted at the prostrate form.

When there was no reply he jerked his arm free of the girl and began the swing. "No!" screamed the girl, again grabbing at his arm. "He's had enough, Barry. He didn't mean no harm. I—I have to take these things. You know that!"

Barry, coated in muck, paused. He glanced down at the girl, her blond hair disheveled, strands across her face. He saw her fear and the tears in her eyes. Then he looked at his opponent. The burly one was rising to his hands and knees, shaking his head. "You leave her alone, mister. Understand? You leave her alone or I'll whip you til yer backbone's showin'."

He threw down the whip, turned, and marched through the crowd toward the right side of the street, the girl trying to follow him. It was difficult keeping up through the muck, which had dirtied her shoes and muddied her black stockings—but not her dress, for she was in dancer's costume, with skirts just to her knees. "Please, Barry. Please stop and listen to me."

By this time they had reached the boardwalk. Barry stomped his boots, trying to get rid of the muck. He tried to brush the dirt from his coat. "Julie Montgomery," he began, "you lied to me. You told me you were a dance-hall girl who charged for dances, and that was all. I walk into Reece's and there you are, going up the stairs with a common mine worker. You're just a common little whore like all the rest."

Her face blanched. Anger flashed in her blue eyes. Julie's hand shot out, delivering a resounding slap to the young man's face. It stung almost as much as the whip lashes he was nursing across his shoulders and back. She began to swing again, but he caught her arm. "Stop that," he ordered. "I've had enough hurt from you, what with you whoring and my fighting with the fellow you were going to…entertain."

Suddenly Julie burst into tears. "Barry, please. Believe me. He grabbed my wrist and pulled me. I tried to get away from him and at the same time not make a scene. I'd have got rid of him somehow. But tactfully. Otherwise I'd lose my job and then I really might have to become a—"

"Whore."

She stifled a sob. "I'm a taxi dancer, Barry." She looked down at the boardwalk. "I'm not a whore. I meant it when I said I'd stay away from other men. But I have to make a living."

Barry Millard hated to see a girl cry, and try as he might, he realized he would never get enough looking at her lovely face. His countenance softened; even his physique seemed to relax. "Best get back to work, then," he said. "Leave me be, Julie. I've not forgiven you, but— I'll think about it."

"Please believe me, Barry."

The two stood awkwardly, facing each other. The crowd had dispersed; passersby gazed at them with curiosity, but strolled on. The ox-drawn freight wagon was passing them now, the teamster turning the air blue with German words that may or may not have been curses.

"I'll think about it," Barry repeated. He turned on his heels and stepped toward the entrance to the Sanborn House, where he had a room.

She watched until he disappeared. Then she slowly, reluctantly, headed back across muddy Main Street to Reece's Music Hall. Her eyes were clouded with tears. It seemed she had lost the one man she felt she could really love. By now she was outside the establishment. She heard the tinny sounds of the piano and the crystal notes from the cornet within. The words MERRY XMAS were pinned across the front of a garish yellow and black double-life-size figure of a can-can girl, propped up at the side of the entrance as a come-on.

Julie paused, breathed deeply, and entered her place of work.

The huge room was full: men were playing cards—poker or faro—and drinking at every available table. A roulette wheel was turning while the operator barked out "place your bets, gentlemen." She was relieved to see that extra tables had been added, covering the dance area; at least she wouldn't have to dance with these men tonight. Miners were standing two deep at the long bar to the left. She observed the lonely men ogling the paintings of the reclining, overweight nudes hanging on either side of the big mirror behind the bar and the three other similar paintings embellishing the opposite wall. Everyone said the art was above average, and Julie had to admit they were pretty good renditions of the female body. (She was glad she had refused to pose for the artist. It was bad enough just working at Reece's.)

Gus Logan, the head bartender, welcomed her back with a friendly nod. He treated Julie as if she were a cut above the other three girls, all of whom worked the mining camps as taxi dancers under the mercenary control of Professor de Lattiere and his pudgy, powdered wife, Camille. Julie had been at Bannack City and Gold Canyon and Last Chance Gulch, and was finishing up her fourth week at Muddy Creek. She was not sure where they would be sent next. The girls were not prostitutes, strictly speaking, although some slipped into the oldest profession. Most hoped for a decent man who would take them from the sleazy world of frontier music halls and saloons. Julie was alone at Reece's now, for two of the girls had run off with men and the third had accompanied Professor de Lattiere and his wife back to Salt Lake City to recruit more girls.

Straight ahead, past all the tables, was the small stage, hidden by a curtain embellished with paintings of flimsily-clad dancing girls doing the can-can. To the left, at the side and in front of the stage, was the piano; it was being played, as was the cornet, although it was stretching things a bit to call the production music. To the right of the piano was the stairway toward which she was headed. It led to a balcony which fronted several rooms, one of which was assigned to her.

By the time she reached the stairway she had been pawed and pinched and propositioned several times. Quickly she ran up the steps, relieved that she was not being followed, and into her flimsy room. There she changed into clean shoes and stockings. Sitting before a small, wavy mirror, she fixed her blond tresses. With rouge and cornstarch she tried to erase the signs of tears from her pretty face. When the signal came for her to come down and do her dance routine, she was ready.

Meanwhile, Father de Mara had watched the husky miner helped to his feet. He noted that he was unhurt save for some whip lashes that would be supersensitive for several days. The young priest slogged along the boardwalk back to his mules, passing the offices of the Muddy Creek *Weekly Herald*, noting that it had already closed for the holiday. He unhitched the mules and led them across the street to REECE'S MUSIC HALL AND LIQUOR EMPORIUM, hitched them again, and scanned the establishment. Certainly he took note of the double-sized can-can girl. He heard the cornet and the piano, and the sounds of men's voices. The swinging doors gave brief glimpses of a large and dimly lit, smoke-filled room.

Something led him to enter. After all, he thought, as a Jesuit he was supposed to be a man among men, knowing well the ways of the world and showing the way to salvation to those who would listen. Something told him that Reece's would make a good chapel for Christmas Mass.

He saw what Julie had been forced to make her way through. Reece's was indeed the ultimate frontier saloon. Now it was filled with revelers in all stages of inebriation. At one table were bottles and glasses and two men sitting across from each other, heads on the table, sound asleep in spite of the din. He was amused to observe that there really was that ubiquitous subject of mirth: a drunk passed out under a table; above him, their hats tilted back, were four men playing cards and drinking whiskey, their feet resting on the drunk. The padre also took in the garish paintings of buxom nude females, the long bar, a narrow hallway beyond the bar extending past the stage to a rear entrance, and a side exit on the right side of the room, next to which was a huge, pot-bellied heating stove.

Behind the bar he counted four bartenders dispensing wine and whiskey—lots of whiskey. Surprising to the padre, they were also mixing an assortment of cocktails made of gin, rum, vodka, applejack, brandy, and other exotic liquors. He noticed the big kerosene lamps hanging from the high ceiling, rather unusual for an establishment in the Far West. They cast shadows over the scene, made foggy by tobacco smoke. "A sight out of hell," mused the padre.

He frowned, taking measure of the music hall's potential. He noted that, if the tables were removed and chairs set up in rows, Reece's would make an excellent temporary church. The stove would furnish the heat. The altar and the pulpit could be set on the stage. Of course, that stage curtain with the paintings of kicking dancing girls in flimsy costumes should be temporarily removed.

The padre's imagination led him to take action. True, he had been rejected in his plea a dozen times already, but perhaps God was with him now. He would inquire of the bartender as to who was the owner or manager and make his pitch.

Suddenly, as he squirmed and pardon me'd his way toward the bar, cheers came from the patrons. All faces turned toward the stairway. Down it, one graceful step at a time, her skirt falling just above her stocking-covered knees, was Julie. The wide skirt flounced, revealing crimson petticoats and white drawers with lace hems. Her shoes were high-heeled, her bodice low, and her arms bare. The cornetist and piano player struck a tune, and Julie danced onto the stage in front of the curtain—a dance with high kicks and pirouettes, ending finally, to the cheers of the men, in a can-can flounce showing her derriere. The applause was deafening.

If the truth were told, Father de Mara enjoyed the performance. He was especially fascinated by the young blond dancer, for she was, he was certain, the girl who had been involved in the whip fight on the street. Not only was she curvaceous and graceful, he thought, but her face showed intelligence and character. What was such a young girl doing here? And what was the quarrel she had with the young man who had won the fight?

The padre could not help it. He was puzzled by her. He felt sorry for her. He did not know why.

When her dance ended, Julie ran back up the stairs while men shouted More! More! But her dance was finished. After a few minutes, when the crowd had calmed down again, she would quietly come back downstairs to mingle, getting men to buy drinks. Meanwhile, Father de Mara edged closer to the bar, searching for the manager. He was obviously the big, balding, dark-complexioned individual almost at the center, drying a shot glass with a towel. He wore a white shirt open at the neck, wide black suspenders, a stained apron, and sported an immense handlebar mustache. It was toward him that the padre edged and elbowed his way past the men standing, holding glasses, some to their lips, and conversing. Somehow he got in front of the manager.

"Excuse me" began Father de Mara in his low, resonant voice.

The bartender-manager looked at him with surprise. "A priest?" he commented to anyone wanting to hear. "Good

Gawd. Civilization has arrived at Muddy Creek. A priest! You must be the fellow who administered extreme unction to poor old William O'Bryan. Gus Logan's my name. Glad to meetcha." And Gus Logan put down the shot glass and held out a pudgy hand which Father de Mara quickly grasped.

"I'm Father Demetrius de Mara, of the Society of Jesus. I'm—"

"A Jesy, eh? First Jesy I've seen since leavin' Chicago two years ago. Glad to meetcha," Gus Logan repeated. "What brings ya to these God-forsaken parts?"

The padre smiled. "Isn't it obvious?" he asked as someone yelled "Eureka, I've won!" followed by loud cheers. On the other side of the big room someone shouted obscenities at a player in a card game, others rushed to prevent bloodshed, an argument ensued with more profanity, then a scuffle, commotion edged toward the swinging doors, and someone was thrown out.

Gus Logan smiled, exposing stained teeth save for two covered with gold. "Obvious?" he said, looking around the room. "Right ye are, Padre. Your work's cut out fer ye. I want ye to know we are damned glad to have ye here. What can I get ye?" Without asking, he reached for a bottle of Old Crow and poured three fingers of the bourbon into a sparkling shot glass. "Here, Padre," he said. "A bit of Christmas cheer for ye."

Father de Mara hesitated. He was a teetotaler save for the sacramental wine he took during Mass, but then, as a Jesuit, a man among men, he thought perhaps the Brotherhood would sanction his acceptance of such a libation. It had been a busy afternoon: a death and a vicious fight with a bullwhip, and he felt the fatigue of failure, for no one had been willing to lend a storefront for Christmas Midnight Mass.

"Thank you," he said, bowing his head. The padre took the glass to his lips and carefully sipped some of the Old Crow. It felt hot, yet good as it trickled down his throat. He was afraid his face turned purple—but he hoped not—and at least he did not cough and reveal what a greenhorn he was when it came to straight bourbon whiskey.

"Thank you, Mr. Logan," he said quietly, almost in a whisper, the liquor having weakened his voice temporarily. "I'm looking for a vacant building in which to hold Midnight Mass. Can you help me?" Father de Mara glanced around the big room, hoping by his motions to convey that it could serve as a church.

The manager of Reece's bar read the padre's mind. Gus Logan shook his head. "Sorry, Padre. The owner has ordered that Reece's stay open until the last drunk has passed out. Look at the business we're havin' here," and he waved an arm in an arc from one end of the room to the other. "Muddy Creek was just a Montana crick last April; now we may have three thousand inhabitants here and within twenty miles of here. And ninety percent of them are men. They're lonely men, Padre. They're full of memories of Christmas past, of wives and sweethearts and, yes, I suppose, of churches and mothers. But there's none of that here, so they've settled on the next best thing: come into town and raise hell with others in the same fix. Tell you somethin', Padre, I hope I get some sleep tonight, but don't bet on it."

The padre sipped a bit more of his Old Crow. He had heard, but ignored, Gus Logan's statement. "You know," the padre replied, "this big room could be cleared and made into a fine hall for worship."

Gus Logan surveyed the surroundings again then looked at the young padre. With a twinkle in his eyes, he said, "Father, the Devil's in charge here today. Even if ye cleared out the men and the few women and the paintings of nudes and the liquor and the cards and the tables and scrubbed the floor, it would still smell like unwashed men and over-perfumed women and strong tobacco and cheap whiskey. Aye. Indeed. Reece's Music Hall belongs to the Devil, Padre." Gus shook his head again. "Don't even think about gettin' it for Holy Mass."

But there was something in the way he said "Holy Mass" that caused Father de Mara to see hope. "You are a Catholic?" he asked.

"Yep. Christened at St. Thomas More in Chicago's West Side. Took my first communion there. Got married…" His voice failed. "We won't go into that now, Padre."

"Then wouldn't you like to celebrate the birth of our Savior in the Catholic way?"

Gus Logan frowned and looked a bit sad. "Sure, Padre. But not here. I'm sorry, but there is no way you could get Reece's Music Hall."

"Just for one Christmas Midnight Mass?"

"Not a chance. The owner wouldn't give up a plugged nickel of profit."

"Who is the owner? And where is he?" asked the priest.

"Not Reece," said the bartender. "Reece was killed in a shootout with a professional gambler named Charlton Edwards a couple months ago. The owner is his surviving partner, Jack Langford."

"Jack Langford? Isn't he the man who shot—"

"Quiet, Padre," replied Logan, glancing around. "Yep. Same man. And I don't know where he is. Maybe paying off the men at the Sunnyside Mine. Anyway, that should convince you that there's no hope."

The padre downed the last of the whiskey. His stomach felt warm as a glimmer of hope entered his mind. "You have no idea where I might find Jack Langford?" he implored, looking Gus Logan straight in the eye.

"Nope. He could be at one of his mines—he has several, you know—or at his cabin, at his office, at one of his girl friends', or even here. Sometimes he comes in and sits at a table against the wall and has one drink and talks with some of the boys. No way of knowin'."

Father de Mara placed his empty glass on the bar. "Thank you, Mr. Logan," he said quietly. "I'll look elsewhere. And if I do find a place to hold services, be sure to attend."

"That I'll do, for certain, Padre," replied Gus Logan, extending his hand once again. "And good luck to ye."

Father Demetrius de Mara made his way through the coarse humanity and out the swinging doors of REECE'S MUSIC HALL AND LIQUOR EMPORIUM. He breathed deeply of the fresh air, unhitched Gabriel and Lucifer, and started down the busy street. Now he was passing the office of Gilmer and Salisbury Stage Lines. Looking in the window he noted how small it was, just a baggage room and eight or ten seats for waiting passengers and, of course, a counter. Behind it he saw a young man in shirtsleeves and vest, working on a ledger; the office was otherwise empty. The padre never knew what led him to step inside and inquire, but when he did the young clerk looked up and welcomed him with a cheery, "Howdy."

"Good afternoon," replied the priest.

"That's a fine riding mule you've got hitched out there," commented the clerk.

Father de Mara turned and looked at Gabriel and Lucifer. "Yes, Gabriel is a fine mule. Lucifer, not so good." He laughed.

And so did the young man, but then, suddenly, his countenance changed. "You're the priest who did the honors at William O'Bryan's demise, aren't you?"

"How news flies," replied the padre. Quickly he changed the subject. "I'm looking for a place to hold Midnight Mass. Any suggestions?"

"Sorry," the clerk replied. "I can't help you, Padre. I'm a Lutheran, name of Robert Sungren. That doesn't make any difference. Lord knows this town could use some religion. I'd help you if I could. But I can't. I draw a blank."

"Have any ideas where I can find Jack Langford?"

Robert Sungren blanched. "N–no, sir. I don't know where he is."

"Just thought I'd ask," replied the padre, turning to walk out.

"Wait, Father de Mara."

The padre paused. Robert Sungren looked around the office, then walked around the counter, stepped outside briefly, and scanned up and down Main Street. Then he closed the door. "Padre," he said hesitantly, "could we sit down here?"

They sat down. The padre waited.

The station manager bit his lip, looked around once more, and then said, "As a Catholic priest, Father, you keep secrets, don't you?"

Puzzled, the padre assured Robert Sungren that his lips were sealed.

"Even if the man telling them is a Protestant?"

"Yes."

Father de Mara searched the face of the clean-shaven young man. Mostly he noticed how thin he was, that his cheeks were hollow, but his eyes were bright and his voice firm. He seemed like a decent, nice sort of chap.

"Are you aware of the spate of stage robberies we've had in these parts?"

The padre nodded. All over the mining region news had spread of a gang that knew which stagecoaches carried bullion. Only those stages were held up, and the highwaymen always went for the bullion. Rumors were that the gang had massacred Chinese prospectors who had been working a lucrative sand bar. Some placed the gang's headquarters in the region of Muddy Creek.

The padre's face showed concern. "Are you involved, young man?" (Father de Mara was shocked at his own words, he being just thirty-two himself. But this man was younger, perhaps twenty-five, and the words had come easily off the padre's lips. Moreover, his calm, priestly manner seemed to have calmed the young man.)

For Robert Sungren was visibly uneasy. He brushed his unpressed woolen trousers up and down with his palms. He glanced around again. Then he said, "I don't know how I got mixed up in this mess, Father. I came to Muddy Creek from Denver, and before that from Cleveland, Ohio.

I developed a spot on my lung. I was coughing all the time and losing weight so the doctor told me I had phthisis—that's tuberculosis, you know—and my only chance to be cured was to go West. I sing, believe it or not. I tried to make a living giving voice lessons in Denver. Ever try to sing when you start coughing half way through a song? Of course, I barely kept body and soul together. Then I decided to try my luck in the gold fields. But I lacked the physique for such work. So I took this job as clerk for Gilmer and Salisbury. So here I am."

"But what is your problem. Are you ill?"

"Oh, no. My health has improved. I've gained weight. I almost never cough anymore. It's not that. It's—it's—" His voice trailed off; he stood up and went to the window and looked up and down the street.

The padre said nothing, waiting.

"About a week ago, a gambler name of Charlton Edwards, who makes the rounds of the mining camps, came into this office just before closing. The stage had left and no one else was around. And he said, 'Boy, I'll get right to the point. On the morning before the afternoon stage carries a bullion shipment from the Consolidated Hard-Rock Mines, you go to Reece's Music Hall and come to the table where I'm playing cards. You ask to be cut in, and I'll make room for you. I promise you that you'll win five hundred dollars at stud poker. When you reach that sum, count yourself out.'"

"'What?' I said.

"And he said, 'you heard me. Do that and you'll be five hundred dollars richer. Don't do it and you just might get waylaid on your way home from work. And, boy, even your mother won't recognize you if that happens. Understand?'"

Robert Sungren paused and then added, "Father de Mara, I was so surprised I agreed. I said 'yes, sir,' and before I could collect my thoughts, Charlton Edwards had left the office."

The padre frowned. "I see," he said.

"Lord knows, I don't want to be an accomplice to that gang," the thin young man went on, his voice rising higher and higher as his fears gained control. "But I don't want to be waylaid, either."

"Of course not."

"But it's even worse than that," the clerk added. "About six months ago, some of the miners and merchants here in Muddy Creek discovered that they were all Masons. They formed a Masonic Lodge here in Muddy Creek."

"I don't follow you," said the priest.

"Rumors are that when these men got together in a situation of trust, they began talking about the stage robberies, and they've formed a vigilance committee. They're said to be compiling a list of bad men, and certainly that will include the gambler Charlton Edwards. Do you realize that if I go to the Music Hall on the morning of the bullion shipment and ask Charlton Edwards to deal me in, and that afternoon the stage is robbed, then I'm an accomplice?" Sungren put a hand to his throat. "And I'll be hanging in mid-air."

"Is this Jack Langford one of the robbers?" asked the padre.

"Oh, no. Far from it. Some say he's the vigilante leader. He's a hard-nosed businessman who won't be pushed around."

Father de Mara rubbed his chin. "When is the next bullion shipment due out?" he asked.

"I don't know," answered the clerk, "but probably within a week. That means that one morning soon I've got to cut myself into a poker game or get beat up. If I do play the game then I'll be hanged before 1866 arrives." Sungren slapped his hands on his thighs. "Padre, for God's sake, what am I to do?"

Father de Mara stood up. He turned to the pale young man and placed a hand on his shoulder. "For now, don't do anything," he said. "Let me think about it. Meanwhile, I've got to find a place to hold Christmas Midnight Mass."

They shook hands and the padre walked out onto the boardwalk more troubled than ever. He unhitched Gabriel and Lucifer and paused to look at his watch. It was 4:30. He looked west, down the street from which he had come. The sun showed half of its huge golden ball above the ridge. The breeze was still warmish, but getting cooler. The chinook was about over. He looked at the sky. Clouds were scudding. He shuddered and started down the street. There were just a few more stores, another saloon, a Chinese laundry, and a livery stable yet to solicit. Then, as abruptly as Muddy Creek began in the west, it ended in the east.

III

Slowly Father Demetrius de Mara led Gabriel and Lucifer toward the east end of Main Street. He smelled incense. Looking in the direction from whence it came, he observed a small sign overhanging an entrance: LAUNDRY: SANG LEE. He could see inside through the four little twelve-by-twelve-inch windows, two on each side of the door, that Sang Lee was busy. He watched as the pig-tailed Oriental took a big sip of water from a bucket on a nearby table, swelled his cheeks, and then spewed it out in a fine stream onto the shirt he was ironing.

"I wonder what the shirt will smell like?" the padre thought.

On the other side of the street was an assay office, closed for Christmas. The remaining saloon was not much more than a storefront with a bar and three or four tables. A final mercantile establishment, still called a shebang by the miners, was so crowded with merchandise that clearing it to make a small hall was out of the question. The padre did not even bother to ask. Next to the shebang was what the priest first took to be a livery, but on closer inspection turned out to be Muddy Creek's new fire station. Inside the big entrance was a single water wagon with pumping accessories and hoses. In the stable four horses were feeding. The big freight wagon that had been making its way down the street had arrived there, and the freighter and some volunteer firemen (the padre presumed) had just unloaded a fire bell mounted on a square block of wood.

One of the men looked up at the belfry, just half built. "We'll finish it after Christmas and get the bell hung," he commented. "Muddy Creek needs it."

Then, all at once, Father de Mara had left Muddy Creek. Two wagon tracks led upward into a grove of aspens then disappeared as the tracks curved around a hill. He knew that the "road" led to mines and, ultimately, toward Last Chance Gulch. The priest spotted a log at one side of the two tracks and sat down to contemplate his next move. The wind blew cold against his greatcoat and clouds were scudding across the blue sky; the sun had disappeared behind the western hills and, he observed, night was about to fall. His shoulders slumped. He had failed to find a place to hold Christmas Eve Mass. Nor had he thought of where he would spend the night. What to do?

His thoughts were interrupted by the sounds of tramping men and voices singing "We Three Kings of Orient Are." Looking up the wagon road the padre watched as one, two, three, four miners advanced toward him. As they approached, their voices reached a crescendo.

When they reached him they all bowed even as they continued walking. Their leader, a huge fellow at least six feet tall and with commensurate bulk, a black beard, and sporting a tattered pork-pie hat, said, "May the Lord bless ye, stranger, on this night of the Savior's birth."

The other three, two of average height and the third smaller, almost frail, all with countenances flushed from some early Christmas cheer, bowed likewise. They continued down the two tracks constituting the road toward town, starting all over with "We Three Kings of Orient Are," when the big man in front stopped so abruptly that the other three behind him bumped into each other. The singing stopped.

"Begorra!" said the big fellow, turning his face toward the person sitting on the log. "I swear, sir. Is that a priest's hat I see on your head? Is that a cleric's collar around your neck?"

The dejected priest stood up. He smiled and said, "I am Father Demetrius de Mara, of the Society of Jesus. I—"

"Praise the Lord!" shouted the big man, leading his companions back toward the priest. "Christmas Eve in this pagan land, and the Lord has sent us a priest!"

They crowded around the young Jesuit. "Father de Mara, huh? Sorry you ain't an Irishman, but no matter. We can celebrate the Savior's birth here in Muddy Creek."

And one of his companions added, "Just like in the Old Country."

Said another: "I'm Teague Cosgrove, this is my pardner, Boyd O'Connor, and this little squirt is Patrick Shanahan." They all shook hands with the padre.

"It ain't Christmas without Midnight Mass," added Teague, "but here in western Montana Christianity's scarce. And glory be, here be you!"

"And this big oaf here is foreman of our crew, Big Mike Mitchell," added Patrick, patting Mike on the back. "We all work at the Sunnyside Mine. The boss paid us, added a bonus, gave us a few snorts, and the rest of the afternoon off."

The priest looked crestfallen. "I'm sorry, boys," he began. "There is no church. I guess there'll be no Christmas Mass—"

"What?" roared Big Mike Mitchell. "No Midnight Mass? A priest in Muddy Creek and no Midnight Mass? We'll see about that!"

Father de Mara held up a hand. "Oh, I've tried," he said. "I've scouted every establishment on Main Street. With no success. I've administered extreme unction to a dying man and witnessed a street fight involving a bullwhip, two men, and a girl. I've heard about a gang of highwaymen and about vigilantes. But I haven't found a place to hold Christmas Mass."

There was silence as his words registered. Then Boyd O'Connor asked, "Who died?"

"The Register of Claims, William O'Bryan," replied the padre, crossing himself. "May he rest in peace."

"Oh, oh," said the smaller of the group, "his lunacy finally did him in."

"Who killed him?" asked Big Mike.

"A man named Jack Langford. He—"

"Jack Langford! Jack Langford!" they all exclaimed, looking at each other, shock and surprise on their faces.

Again the priest held up a hand. "He shot in self-defense. O'Bryan stepped to the doorway, yelled an obscenity at Langford, who was riding by, and then shot at him. The bullet grazed Langford's coat but did not touch his body. Quick as a wink, Langford swung around toward his adversary, had his pistol out of the holster, and fired a split second before O'Bryan fired again. The Register of Claims was hit in the chest and died within minutes." Father de Mara did not think it necessary to add that, had O'Bryan not hesitated when he saw the priest, he would have killed Langford.

"That explains a lot," Patrick Shanahan commented. "Mr. Langford seemed depressed when he came to pay us. We thought it was just that it's Christmas Eve, and he was sad like most of us and he made up for it by being generous."

"You know him?" asked the padre, although that knowledge had already been given.

"He's our boss, Father," said Teague Cosgrove. "He owns the Sunnyside Mine where we work."

"He's Muddy Creek's leading businessman," added Boyd O'Connor. "Whenever a miner wants to sell his claim, he goes to Jack Langford, who'll more than likely buy it, payin' a good price no matter how worthless it appears to be."

"And," Patrick Shanahan added, "a few weeks ago, William O'Bryan sold Mr. Langford his claim to the Sunnyside Mine. O'Bryan thought it was worthless. Langford worked it for a week and struck the richest vein so far in the district. O'Bryan decided that Langford knew all along about the vein, and so O'Bryan claimed he'd been cheated."

"Which," Teague Cosgrove added, "explains O'Bryan's reason for calling Langford a—(he looked at the priest and paused)—a so-and-so and tried to kill him. There was always bad blood between them, most of it, I'm sorry to say, on O'Bryan's side."

"O'Bryan was a bit teched in the head," the frail Patrick Shanahan added. "He had power as Register of Claims. Some people suspected him of altering some claims to help his friends."

Father de Mara found the information enlightening, but his mind was on obtaining a place in which to hold services. He was thinking again of Reece's Music Hall, of its owner, and of a possibility, a remote possibility. "I've been told that Mr. Reece was killed in a shootout. Was Mr. Langford involved?" he asked.

"He wasn't involved at all," Big Mike replied. "Reece was a professional gambler. He was playing with another gambler, a fellow named Charlton Edwards. Something happened. Both started for their pistols simultaneously, and Edwards shot first. Killed Reece instantly."

"He had no known heirs," volunteered Boyd O'Connor, "so Mr. Langford became sole owner of the saloon."

"Actually, Jack Langford's a pretty decent fellow," volunteered Boyd O'Connor. "A tough businessman but a straight shooter."

The padre rubbed his chin and looked thoughtfully at the four young miners. "If I could just see this Jack Langford," he mused, "I think I might persuade him to give us Reece's Music Hall for Midnight Mass. It is big enough, well lighted, and has a stage upon which we could set up an altar."

"Reece's!" the men exclaimed. "The devil's own den! Wouldn't that be somethin'? Make Reece's into a church?"

"Begorra, we'll find Jack Langford for ye," Big Mike announced while placing an arm around Father de Mara's slim shoulders. "And so help me, he *will* give us Reece's for services. You come with us, Padre. Now that there's a real Catholic priest available, nothin' is impossible."

"I've tried everything, asked everywhere, including the alcalde," responded the padre as he took the mules' reins and they all resumed their walk into town.

"But where can we find Langford?" one of them asked.

"Could be most anywhere," commented Boyd O'Connor, "but I know he often ends his day by having a drink or two at the saloon. This being Christmas Eve, and his being dejected about what he did, he could quite likely be at Reece's right now, talking with the boys and trying to blot our the events of the afternoon."

"Then let's go there first," suggested the priest. "He owes me a favor," he added, not explaining why. "Let's see if he is willing to pay up."

As they made their way through the Christmas Eve crowds, they picked up more Irish and others of the faith, so that by the time they reached Reece's Music Hall a score of men had gathered, all having been told of the situation. All entered the saloon en masse, so that everyone looked up. The big room went silent. The priest looked around. There, slumped in a chair, his back to the wall, toying with a shot glass, sat Jack Langford. The crowd made room as the padre and his party advanced toward him, and the silence in the room thickened.

"Good evening, Mr. Langford." The Jesuit addressed the sitting man who was scrutinizing the group as it approached him.

The businessman did not stand up but his demeanor was respectful. "Evenin', Padre," he replied, tipping his hat back from his forehead. "I haven't forgotten how you saved my life, inadvertently as it was."

"And now I am about to ask you a favor," said the padre.

"I figured as much. What is it?"

"I would like to requisition the Music Hall for Christmas Midnight Mass."

Jack Langford tilted back in his chair. "My God, Padre. Do you know what you're asking? I could lose a couple thousand dollars."

Father de Mara scanned the smoke-filled room. "Yes, I know, Mr. Langford. But these men here—they give you lots of business. Some of them work for you. And they were raised as Christians. 'Tis a shame that they cannot worship the birth of our Savior here in Muddy Creek."

Father de Mara paused. "Are you a Christian, Mr. Langford?"

"'Deed I am, Padre. Not a Catholic, though. I'm an Episcopalian."

"But as a Christian, won't you commit a Christian act and offer your establishment for Christmas Midnight Mass?"

Before he replied, Jack Langford scanned the room. He was aware of the silence, of all eyes turned on him. He took stock of the roulette wheel, the faro tables, the card games temporarily halted, the liquor being consumed. "Padre," he began, "how would I protect all the liquor I have behind the bar? And the glasses and the bar accessories? How would the gaming fraternity like being shoved out of here? How about the little taxi dancer—you gonna deprive her of a good night's earnings? And look at the paintings. They'd hardly fit into a church. And where would you put the tables? Really, Padre, you're dreaming." He shook his head. "Sorry. I'm afraid I can't do this for you."

The score or more of men crowded about the padre, all facing Langford, muttered words in obvious displeasure. Langford noticed; he was also aware of how quiet the big room had remained and that everyone had their eyes on him and the priest. Just then, coming down the stairs, was Julie, the little blond taxi dancer who had been the subject of the whip fight. She looked as fresh and pretty and out of place as when the padre had first seen her.

Langford turned to her. "Julie," he called, not unkindly, but raising his voice so she could hear, "this padre wants to take over the Music Hall and make a church of it. What do you think?"

"Just for tonight," cut in Father de Mara, turning to face the girl, his expression asking for approval.

And Big Mike Mitchell added, "To hold Midnight Mass, Miss Julie. Catholics always go to church on Christmas Eve."

Her response was immediate. "Oh, how wonderful," she exclaimed.

"Now, Julie," Langford said, "think of what it will mean. Moving all the furniture, somehow protecting the liquor, denying you the chance to earn money..."

"Oh, bosh," Julie replied, quickly descending the remaining stairs. "It would be the nicest, most Christian thing you have ever—you ever could do, Mr. Langford. Bringing Christ to Muddy Creek! And we could do it! By midnight we could have Reece's Music Hall converted into the most beautiful frontier church there ever was." She scanned the big room. "We could—"

Langford held up a hand. "I knew I shouldn't have asked a woman," he said. "Women don't understand business."

Julie walked toward the table. "Oh, Mr. Langford—"

"Enough," he ordered. He paused, scanned the crowd. It flashed through his mind that to do this would constitute a bit of penance for the killing he had committed. Abruptly, he stood up and asked, "All who want the Music Hall converted into a church for the rest of the night say aye."

A resounding "aye" was the reply. Then Big Mike Mitchell turned to the crowd and bellowed, "Three cheers for Jack Langford!" And the cheers came.

Then a most unusual thing happened. Quietly, sedately, all the customers filed out of the Music Hall through its swinging doors. Suddenly the big room was devoid of customers, silent. Chairs, tables, a few half-drunk bottles, glasses, cards, all lay as if their users had vanished. Two or three passed-out drunks were carried out or helped out between the arms of their "pards." The bartenders left, too, except for Gus Logan, who wiped one last glass with a towel and smiled underneath his handlebar mustache. Only the score or so of men who had accompanied the priest and his four Irishmen, and Julie and Jack Langford, remained.

Langford scanned the big room with surprise. Then he looked at Julie, the padre, and their supporters. He lifted his shot glass to his mouth for a final gulp then slammed it on the table. "Well, it's yours until ten o'clock tomorrow morning," he announced. He winked. "Got to satisfy the poor fellows needing the hair of the dog, you know." He stood up. "Padre, Miss Julie, and you fellows. Have a good Mass." He strode out the back way. They heard the door slam behind them.

After the vicious fight over Julie and their exchange of words on the muddy boardwalk, Barry Millard had returned to his room at the Sanborn House. It was a shoddily built, wooden edifice with no ambience. Barry sat on the sagging bed and massaged his shoulders, wincing in pain. Gingerly he removed his blue flannel shirt and in the wavy mirror appraised the several red streaks across his long-john underwear. He winced as he gently stripped the cloth off to his waist. The whip lashes smarted, the blood had dried and, although he at first thought he would clean each smarting wound, he now thought better of it. Let them well alone, he concluded, and they would heal rapidly.

He pulled off his mud and manure covered boots and decided to let them dry before cleaning. His trousers were likewise soiled. "Aw, hell," he blurted out loud. "I'm goin' to take a bath." In that dishabille he threw open the door and yelled to the clerk, "Tell Charlie to fill the bathtub with hot water. And make it snappy."

He finished undressing and pulled on an old flannel robe. Then he sat on the bed and waited for Charlie, the only black resident of Muddy Creek, to get the tub ready. While he waited, his thoughts were dominated by the lonesome little blond taxi dancer who had captured his heart. First thing he knew, in piecing his past together, he was recalling how he came to be in Muddy Creek.

Young Barry Millard was from a good family. He was highly educated. Born in upstate New York, he had early become fascinated by nature, by every living thing from insects to elephants, from dandelions to elms. One day when he was about ten years old, he had picked up a stone that contained a fossilized fish. Suddenly he was in the fields, collecting fossils and unusual stones. His widowed mother, who had been left with sufficient inheritance to live comfortably, encouraged her son's interests. By the time he graduated from a high school academy, Barry knew that he wanted to be a geologist. In a day when

Charles Darwin was still looked upon as a heretic, this was a drastic decision, but Barry's mother encouraged him. He attended the Sheffield Scientific School at Yale and, after graduation, did additional work at the School of Mines in Germany.

Upon his return, still a young man of twenty-five, he had hardly been home a week before a letter arrived from a Wall Street investment firm which had been given his name by one of his Sheffield professors. Impressed with his credentials, he was offered excellent compensation to travel to the west Montana and Idaho mines, particularly those around Muddy Creek, and submit his professional estimate of their potential. He had arrived at Muddy Creek early in November, planning to make his appraisal in just a couple weeks, leaving for the East in time to be home for Christmas.

But business had intervened.

Barry frowned. Business? Better be honest with oneself. It was not gold and silver, it was a lithe, vivacious, blond young woman named Julie. A taxi dancer, she had arrived with several other girls from Last Chance Gulch about December first. They had been hired through their agent, Professor De Lattiere, to improve business at Reece's.

One evening, having come in from a week in the surrounding mountains, Barry ambled over to Reece's Music Hall for a drink and conversation. He did not gamble, nor was he promiscuous—if he was, he would have headed for Madam Dahlia's. But neither was he a saint. As he downed his drink he turned around, leaning his back to the bar to watch the dancers go through their paces. His eyes set on one particular girl. The others were nondescript, but this girl would have stood out among any group of young women. Her dance costume revealed ivory white arms, the décolletage revealed marvelously shaped breasts, her legs showed slim and smooth beneath her knee-length, flounced skirt.

"For God's sake," he thought, "what is such a beautiful being doing here? Or is she just a tough little floozy like the others?" Barry Millard had to know.

He was almost six feet tall, slim, stood straight with broad shoulders, had blondish hair that had grown rather too long, blue eyes, a clear complexion, an aquiline nose, and well-formed, white teeth. Barry did not smoke. And he was an excellent dancer. This was again due to his mother, who was determined that her son would have the social graces even if he did enter the masculine, not quite respectable profession of geologist.

When the dancers finished their routine, Barry was immediately on the floor asking the little blond girl for a dance. For a long instant their eyes met, each sensing something special. Then her reverie broke. "It'll cost you— nothing," she said.

Barry was supremely complimented. He knew the going price for a dance was first a dime for two drinks, hers being colored water. "Thanks," he replied, "but I insist on paying the going price."

They sat at a table and drank without speaking. Then the cornet and piano "band" started up again. The two whirled around the tiny dance floor. They gazed into each other's eyes; their dance steps came naturally. When the music stopped, Barry suggested another drink. They sat down at a table and ordered. Thus began their relationship. They talked easily and at length.

"For God's sake!" he thought. "She's read Darwin. And can talk intelligently about his theories. How can this be?"

And she was interested in his work. In days to come, as their courtship bloomed, she would sit with her face in her palms and listen to Barry talk of geology and paleontology and prehistoric fishes and animals and she would ask questions that were intelligent and germane to make him want to talk more. Sometimes he realized that he had talked, talked, talked, and all she had done was ask more questions. He would stop suddenly and say, "Julie, what about you?"

She parried, always parried, his queries. But her eyes, he noticed, clouded up, her sunny disposition disappeared, she lowered her head, and avoided his eyes. Something, he knew, something unpleasant, lay in Julie's past.

They went for walks in the woods; they climbed mountains; they ate dinners at Robinson's Café. In time, Barry realized that he wanted this strange girl, even as he realized how his mother would be shocked were he to bring her home as his wife. "Mother, meet my wife, Julie. She was a taxi dancer."

He wondered if Julie would find it hard fitting into his professional world. Sometimes he couldn't even believe his love for her himself. "Me, Barry Millard! Falling in love with a taxi dancer!" He would shake his head in disbelief. But he acknowledged that it was true. Or, he thought, was it infatuation? His own loneliness?

To find out he had left town for a week, just returning today. First thing, he had marched over to Reece's—only to see Julie climbing the stairs with that drunken, burly miner. Thoughtlessly he had rushed to the stairway and grabbed the man. "Let go of her!" he had demanded. The miner had resisted and the fight had begun on the stairway. Others pulled them off.

"If you're goin' to fight, do it in the street," ordered Gus Logan. Out onto the street they had fought. The burly man had grabbed a bullwhip from a wagon. Thus they had indulged in a no-holds-barred fight that Barry had won, but with bruises and severe, searing whip lashes across the shoulders and back. Smaller ones were elsewhere. He was just beginning to feel them.

"The water is ready," Charlie announced from the hallway. Barry stepped down to the little room with the steaming bathtub in it. Some fresh towels lay conveniently nearby along with a bar of strong soap. The young geologist slipped into the hot water, gasping with pain as it struck the searing whip lashes. Finally he settled in the tub; the hurt was diminishing, and there, as he luxuriated, he began contemplating his next move. What to do about Julie?

Indeed, he had just about paid a hefty price for his— love? Infatuation?—out in the middle of Muddy Creek's Main Street. But her image stuck in his mind. Her soft blond tresses, clear complexion, pert little nose, sky blue eyes. And if he did not marry her, what of her fate? From taxi dancer to diseased whore and then suicide or death from disease? Or as a tough madam? He could not see her as that. He nodded his head. Nothing so bad must be allowed to happen to Julie.

"That mysterious girl," he mused. "The hours we've been together, and I know nothing of her past."

IV

Reece's Music Hall, which just a few minutes before had been teeming with revelers, was now occupied solely by Father Demetrius de Mara; Julie Montgomery; four Irishmen with first names of Mike, Teague, Boyd, and Patrick; bartender Gus Logan; and a few lingering Catholic residents of the region. The "band" had left via the back entrance. The silence in a place used to raucous noise was strange.

The big Irishman, Mike Mitchell, glanced apprehensively around the nearly vacant room. "Where do we begin?" he asked, holding out his hands in a sign of helplessness. "You tell us what to do, Padre, and we'll pitch in."

Julie found in the challenge a chance to subvert her unhappiness into a project new and exciting. "We can start by rolling up the stage curtain," she suggested. Then, her hands on her waist, she announced emphatically that "we're not just going to remove the tables and line up the chairs, we're going to make this the most beautiful church in Montana."

"Fine," remarked the small Irishman, Patrick Shanahan, "but to start with, where do we store the card tables? Where do we store the roulette wheel, the faro games? And the liquor and glasses? Gus, got any suggestions?"

And Gus Logan, still cleaning up behind the bar, shrugged his shoulders. "Search me," he replied. "I'll help you, but I don't know where to put all the tables and gambling apparatus. There's no room upstairs, and the hallway to the back entrance is too narrow. For that matter, tell me where to pack the hooch and the glassware."

Silence prevailed as all contemplated the initial problems. "Hey," volunteered Teague Cosgrove, "what about that big J. Murphy freight wagon that came in today? It was filled with furniture they unloaded at Tinsley's store, then a fire bell delivered to the firehouse. Now it's empty. If we could just get it over here, it could serve as a temporary warehouse."

Father de Mara remembered seeing the huge rig with the teamster shouting expletives in German. "Why don't you fetch it?" he asked, and Pat Shanahan grabbed at the opportunity to be doing *something*. In a moment he was out the swinging doors. The rest of those present assumed he had already obtained approval and turned to other problems. The liquor and barware, for example: where to store it?

"Gus," asked Boyd O'Connor, "where do you store the extra hooch?"

"We have a cellar under here," he replied, pointing to a door in the floor at the far end of the bar with a huge iron ring sunk flush into the planking, "but it's loaded to the gills. There just isn't any more room down there, not even for a case of Green River Bourbon."

Julie lit up. "Gus," she asked, "what's under the stage?"

Gus shrugged again, casting a glance at the small stage, raised a yard above the floor. "Search me. I always figured it was…heck, I dunno. Never thought about it." He walked around the bar to the narrow hallway and examined the side of it. "Well, I'll be," he said. "Look. There's the outline of a door, dimensions less than a yard by a yard. No lock. No handle. But it sure is an opening."

"Let's try it," said Big Mike. "Stand away, everybody." He squatted and, with all his weight, pushed on the door. With a loud clap it fell inward in one piece. Musty, stale air came from the opening, but enough light was cast by the overhead lamps to make clear a vacant, dry, dirt floor.

"Well, I'll be," mused Gus again. "I've worked here since this place was built, but I never knew any storage space existed under the stage. Sure, we can pack the bottles and glasses in crates and just push 'em in for a day. Matter of fact, it could serve as additional storage space for us from now on." Gus looked at the three Irishmen. "Come on, boys, let's get to work and pack the hooch and barware in there. After all, who ever heard of a church serving whiskey?"

(Or with an altar above a liquor storage area, thought the padre.)

Meanwhile, Patrick Shanahan was making his way down the muddy Main Street in search of the heavy J. Murphy. It was nowhere in sight. "Oh, Lord," he prayed, "please don't let that freight wagon be on the way to Last Chance Gulch."

The firehouse was closed. After all, Muddy Creek's fire department, such as it was, consisted of volunteers. Pat noticed that the fire bell had been unloaded and lay to the side of the building. No one was around. He gave it a kick, it swung and rang once, loud and clear. Pat was embarrassed; he walked quickly away. But he had also seen the heavy, eight-inch-wide wheel tracks made by the big freight wagon.

"I'll just follow 'em" he said to himself, "but not all the way to Last Chance Gulch."

The thin young man placed his hands in his pockets for warmth and, in the gloaming, started on down Main Street, which would end very shortly and, he knew, become just two tracks into the wilderness. In the big Montana sky the first stars were showing. "Please, Lord," prayed Pat, "let the teamster be spending Christmas at Muddy Creek."

About a hundred yards along the road, which by now was rising as it veered around a hill, so far out of Muddy Creek that Pat was losing hope, the wide wagon tracks made a quick turn to the right, off of the "road" and down into a shallow slough, then up into an open pasture beyond which ran Muddy Creek. There, grazing, were the oxen. On the right side of the pasture loomed the huge prairie schooner with its seven-foot-high rear wheels, its body six feet deep, its great canvas top looming into the sky like a circus tent. Next to it, nestled in a grove, was a small, one-room cabin. A latch string—really an old rope—hung from a hole in the door. To the left of the door was a square four-pane window showing a flickering, pale yellow light.

Pat walked quickly to the cabin, took a deep breath, and knocked on the door.

"Yesssssss?" a thick, gutteral voice replied.

"Merry Christmas to ye," replied Pat, hoping his voice did not waver. "May I come in?"

"Zee latchstring iss out," came the reply.

Pat pulled on the dirty old latch rope and stood still as the door squeaked on iron hinges and slowly opened. He viewed a crude table made of sawed wood upon which stood a flickering kerosene lamp, its chimney glistening from recent cleaning. Two tree stumps about two feet high and a foot in diameter served as chairs. In one corner was a bunk with a buffalo robe upon it. In the left wall was a fireplace with a small, crackling fire casting shadows on the walls and heating a kettle suspended above it. The fragrance of a nourishing stew reminded Pat that he had not eaten supper.

Sitting on one of the stumps at the table was a grizzled, bearded little man with long, graying hair. A huge meerschaum pipe hung in his mouth, from the bowl of which rose small clouds of fragrant smoke. On the table Pat observed wood shavings, for as the little man sat he was working over a piece of solid wood, carving it with a sharp knife.

Pat was struck by the teamster's face as it shone in the firelight: he sensed in it strength, sincerity, dignity, a touch of kindness, and a touch of sadness. The young Irishman estimated the teamster to be between thirty-five and forty-five years old. Pat immediately thought of a picture of an elf in a book of fairy tales he remembered from his childhood. The teamster's face could have been a model for the illustration.

The little man put down the knife and the wood he was carving, turned toward Pat, and removed the pipe from his mouth. "Vell," he said, "don't just stand there letting in ze cold. Come in and close ze door."

Pat complied, removing his hat—he knew not why. The wind whistled around the corners of the little cabin; the fire crackled and momentarily flared up.

"I…my name is Patrick Shanahan," he said hesitantly. "Sir," he continued, "I've come to ask a favor of you."

"A favor?" asked the German. "I have never zeen you before. Vat kind of favor? You hungry? You're velcome to my stew. Smell gut, eh?" He replaced the meerschaum in his mouth and motioned toward the other stump. "Pull up a stump and sit down," he said, his voice softening.

Pat complied. Nervously he took stock once again of the little cabin. What struck him immediately were the wood carvings. On the fireplace mantel was a beautiful crucifix, the suffering figure done in remarkable detail in perfect proportions; the whole was perhaps two feet high. In a dark corner on a crudely made shelf he observed the half-completed carving of a sheep. Behind it, leaning against the wall, was a shepherd and his staff. And what was the teamster carving now? The Madonna?

"You are a woodcarver," said Pat.

"Yah. I carve a bit."

"Religious carvings?"

"Yah. For vant of someting better. Vat you vant me to carve here in Montana? Rocks? Mountains?"

"The carvings are beautiful," Pat commented with sincerity, standing up and going to the mantel. "It's very appropriate that you be carving a religious ornament on Christmas Eve."

"Yah. Something to remember Christmas by, I guess." The little man paused and stared blankly at the wall. "And happier times, for sure."

Pat turned to him again. "What's your name, sir?"

"Schroeder," the little man replied, refilling his pipe. "Gunter Schroeder. I run my freight business between Last Chance Gulch and Muddy Creek and Salt Lake City. I run it out of zis little cabin."

"Where are you from?"

Gunter Schroeder rose from his stump chair and went to the fire, from whence he fetched a brand with which he relit his pipe. Sucking on it and making clouds of smoke, he returned to the stump. "Originally from Erlangen, in Bavaria," he replied, "but now I have been in Montana for t'ree years. It iss lonely, but I like it here. Some of it reminds me of home."

Pat hesitated. His charge was to enlist the aid of the German teamster into contributing his huge covered wagon and his oxen, run the wagon down to Reece's, use the wagon as a warehouse for the tables and gambling paraphernalia, drive it all back to the cabin, unhitch the oxen, only to rehitch them and return the wagon to Reece's Christmas morning, empty it, then back to the cabin, unhitch the oxen, and put them out to pasture. For nothing. Pat realized suddenly the immensity of what he was about to request.

"Now, vat iss it dat you vant of me?" asked Gunter Schroeder, briefly removing his pipe.

Pat Shanahan weighed his words carefully. He asked, "Are you a Christian, Mr. Schroeder?"

The little German puffed on his meerschaum. "Am I a Christian?" he mused, looking up at the rafters. "Am I a Christian? Hmm. Vell, I tell you. I vas raised a good Lutheran and baptized in ze faith. At one time I even planned to be a—" He paused, changing his mind about what he was about to say. "But ven I came to America, I…fell avay from ze church. And here, in Montana, there iss no Christianity. At least," he added waving his arms, "not in Muddy Creek."

"But there is," ventured Pat excitedly. "Christianity is right here in Muddy Creek! A Catholic priest came into town this afternoon, and he's holding Christmas Midnight Mass in Reece's Music Hall.

"Ahh, a Catholic priest," replied Gunter Schroeder. "I heard about him. He gave last rites to William O'Bryan, didn't he? But vat do you mean, a Christmas Mass in Reece's Music Hall? Dat is ridiculous!"

"It's the truth, Mr. Schroeder," countered Pat, once again sitting down opposite him at the table. He then explained how Jack Langford had given up his business and his profits in order to let the padre hold Mass in the Music Hall. "But," Pat added, "we have to clear it of the furniture and the gambling devices, everything except the chairs. And then we have to get everything back into the hall before ten o'clock tomorrow morning."

"Dat iss a lot of doing," muttered the teamster.

"And there is no place to store it all, Mr. Schroeder."

"Too bad."

Pat realized that Schroeder was not picking up on his line of thought—or if he was, he was not letting on.

"Here goes," thought the young man to himself. He took a deep breath while becoming aware of Schroeder looking him straight in the eyes. "One place where we could store all that is in your freight wagon." He waited for Schroeder's reaction, fearing what it would be.

Silence. Gunter Schroeder leaned back a little on his backless stump-chair and puffed so much smoke that Pat thought he was going to disappear into the blue clouds, like the elf in some fairy tale out of Germany's Black Forest.

"Ze priest iss Catholic," Schroeder finally said. "I am Lutheran. In my part of Germany, Lutherans and Catholics hate each other. Vy should I help a church dat burned my ancestors at the stake, and tortured zem and buried zem alive?"

"But Mr. Schroeder," Pat parried, "that was hundreds of years ago, in Germany! This is 1865. This is America!"

"My mother, she vould turn over in her grave if she knew I ever helped a priest of the Church of Rome," he said.

"If—if there was a Lutheran church here, would you be attending?" asked Pat.

Schroeder tilted back and forth on his backless tree stump. He nodded positively. "Yah, I tink I vould. It vould remind me of home. Something about church makes one feel—gut. Especially at Christmas."

"But Mr. Schroeder," countered Pat, "there isn't a Lutheran preacher within a thousand miles of here. The Roman Catholic Church is all there is in Muddy Creek. And anyway, all churches worship our Savior and His birth on this night. Everyone is welcome at church tonight, and I venture to say half of the worshipers will be Protestants."

Schroeder puffed and puffed and said nothing.

"Please, Mr. Schroeder, I'll help hitch up the oxen and you won't have to do any of the work. We've got a whole crew to load and unload the wagon. It would be such a… Christian thing to do."

Schroeder rose and walked slowly to the fire. He picked up two tin bowls from the mantel and, using a dipper, ladled stew into them. He fetched two spoons. "Here, *mein freund*, let us have some sustenance before ve hitch up ze oxen."

Patrick Shanahan had never enjoyed stew so much.

Meanwhile, Father de Mara, his Irish helpers, Gus Logan, and Julie Montgomery had been busy at Reece's. In short order the shelves loaded with liquor and glasses behind the bar were cleared. Boyd O'Connor, commenting that he was already dirty, made his way on hands and knees into the cavernous crawl space. He received the excelsior-filled barrels and wooden crates containing the bottles and barware and carefully deposited them in the under-the-stage storage space. At one point he was long in reappearing.

Big Mike leaned down to the opening. "Boyd, me boy," he yelled into the darkness, "I better not smell whiskey on yer breath or ye will celebrate Christmas Eve with two black eyes. Ye hear me? I know ye. I suspect ye alone in that dark cavern with all that good hooch! Show yerself, me boy, and quick!" O'Connor did reappear—fast—but there was a flush to his cheeks and a cheerfulness in his voice that raised eyebrows.

The mirrors and paintings remained. "The mirrors can stay," the padre commented, "but the paintings must go."

Teague Cosgrove observed the "art" with something of a connoisseur's eye—or was it lust? They were certainly the ultimate in barroom decorations. Spread five feet wide and three feet high on either side of the mirrors, both displayed overweight, reclining nudes with tiny wisps of gauze sweeping across certain key parts of their anatomy. At the other side of the big room were three smaller nudes. These emphasized the softness, whiteness, and symmetry of milady's behind. Teague assessed them all. "Oh, 'scuse me, Father."

Again the padre reminded himself that as a Jesuit he was to be a man among men—a man of God among men—so he refused to allow a show of any embarrassment. After all, he had grown up in northern Italy, birthplace of the Renaissance. With the embarrassed Teague, he appraised the three smaller nudes critically. "They're really quite good, you know," he commented to the surprise of those within hearing distance. "There's an affinity with the can-can painting at the entrance, which better be withdrawn, too. Why not line them up in the back hallway with the paintings behind the bar?"

Big Mike Mitchell smiled. "They should have an affinity, Father," he said. "The big nudes behind the bar were done by some unknown artist. I think you'll agree they aren't so good. But the three nudes and the can-can girl were done by a different painter. He came into town a month or so ago. Name of Titian Reynolds."

"He lives here?" inquired the padre.

"In a manner of speaking. See, Padre, when he went looking for work, everyone saw his soft hands, with no calluses, and so they wouldn't give him a job. Then the girls at Madam Dahlia's took pity on him. He agreed to paint them in exchange for room and board. So there you have it, a painter living in the liveliest whorehouse—er, *maison de joie*, Padre—in Muddy Creek. He lives in a room off from the stable and paints the…girls and sells the paintings to their clients. Many a miner's cabin is decorated with his paintings."

"You should see him work, Father," volunteered Boyd O'Connor. "He can paint a nude in two hours and a landscape in three. And as you say, we think he's a cut above the norm. Sure, he's wastin' his talents out here on the frontier, though. Has a liquor problem."

"Too bad," mused the padre. "We could use a painting of the Madonna and Child in our little church."

"Why, I wonder," began Boyd O'Connor. "I'll bet Titian Reynolds could do that for us."

"Isn't it too late?" asked the priest, looking at his silver watch. "It's six o'clock and it's dark already."

"I know Titian could do it!" Boyd O'Connor exclaimed again. "Begorra, I'm goin' up to Madam Dahlia's and ask him!"

"It's Christmas Eve, Boyd," warned Big Mike. "Ye be damned sure ye don't taint the night of the Lord's birth by—"

"I promise in front of the padre, I won't. But I'll bet I can get a pretty painting of the Madonna and Child by midnight. I'll bet you." And with that, Boyd O'Connor was gone.

All the paintings were removed as the padre had suggested.

Boyd O'Connor stepped into Muddy Creek's Main Street. A gust of wind struck him. His teeth chattered as he wrapped a dirty woolen scarf around his neck and buttoned his threadbare coat. He glanced up and down the thoroughfare. It was just after six; the street was still full of miners and shoppers. The shebangs, saloons, the barber shop, restaurants, and a few other establishments promised continued activity with their kerosene lanterns casting soft, dim light onto the boardwalk.

"Tisn't much like Waterford in the Old Country at Christmas," he thought. "Tisn't much like Christmas without Father an' Mother and Uncle Bill gettin' drunk and all the kids, cousins, and nieces and nephews runnin' circles 'round the house." He sighed. "But," he shrugged, "this will have to do."

Then it occurred to Boyd as he made his way toward the quagmire named "A" Street that ran at left angles up the hill from Main, that this could be a great Christmas because, just maybe, the Lord had heard his prayers and had brought the Jesuit priest to Muddy Creek. Just for him and his Irish friends. Had the padre not arrived, Boyd O'Connor knew, they would already be up to their cups in good cheer and would have been lucky to have woken up in their bunks. More likely they would have been kicked awake in the gutter, as had happened a time or two before.

This was their challenge, a challenge from the Lord and to the Jesuit: to create by midnight the most beautiful little church that frontier Montana had ever seen. To do it for the Christ child. Tough, unshaven day laborer that he was, Boyd's soul possessed the tenderness of a child. His pace quickened. Wouldn't it be great if he could persuade Titian Reynolds to make a religious painting? Titian could do it, Boyd knew, for he had watched the artist sit at his easel and paint a reclining nude—one specific nude with whom Boyd was rather well acquainted—from blank canvas to finished picture in two hours. Even the whore had liked it.

Another time he had come across Titian sitting at his easel on the west edge of town painting the landscape at sunset. To Boyd's undisciplined but aesthetic taste, it was a masterpiece. A visiting capitalist from Denver, investigating the mines, had seen it and offered to buy it for ten dollars. Titian had rolled up the painting, presented it to the man, and with the ten dollars headed for the nearest saloon.

That was Titian's trouble: he was drunk early and often and late. White, uncallused hands he may have had; slim, unhealthy body; sallow complexion under his prematurely graying hair (for Titian was not yet thirty); but at least Titian Reynolds could drink anyone—anyone—under the table.

Boyd turned up "A" Street, hardly a road as yet, past rustic cabins where the flickering yellow light in the little paned windows indicated habitation. In some dwellings the only light, he noticed, was from candles; the occupants did not even possess kerosene lamps. At one residence he heard children's laughter. That would be the Lancaster cabin. Lancaster was foreman at the Consolidated Hard-Rock Mines. He was a Cousin Jack, the name given Cornishmen who were brought to the American West because of their knowledge of hard-rock mining. They had learned about stopes and flues and supports and drainage as tin miners in Cornwall.

"A" Street came to an abrupt end. It ran smack into a wide, one-story-long structure of puzzling dimensions. In front of it was the hitching rail, vacant of horses, and straight ahead was the entrance. Boyd knew, of course, that behind the log walls were the rooms of Madam Dahlia's girls, all four of them. From the crude saloon-sitting room one went down a hallway either right or left to the room belonging to the girl of his choice. Boyd also knew that behind the building was a well-constructed stable, that it was in a rough, unfinished room of that structure that Titian Reynolds lived, courtesy of Madam Dahlia. Why she had taken pity on him no one understood, but she and her girls had given Titian board and room ever since he pleaded near starvation because no one in Muddy Creek appreciated fine art and no one would give him work.

Boyd entered Madam Dahlia's without knocking, although he felt a little strange because not a single horse was tethered outside. Oh, well, lots of miners, like himself, could not afford a horse and had to get around on their own two feet.

But upon entering he noticed that no clients were in sight. Madam Dahlia, overweight, overdressed, and over-perfumed, was sitting in the plushest, most ornate chair within a thousand miles of Muddy Creek. On a sofa at right angles to her were three of her girls. One was clad in a lacy chemise, torn at the hem; one wore a flowery but faded kimono; and the other was clad in a dance dress that came to her knees, but a good deal of white thigh showed as her legs were crossed.

"Well, if it isn't Boyd O'Connor," Madam Dahlia began. "Lucy's in her room but I'll call her. Lu—"

"No, no," Boyd begged, lifting his hands as a sign of rejection. "I'm not here for that. I want to see Titian Reynolds."

The Madam frowned. "What do you want to see him for?" she asked. "Don't you know it's Christmas Eve? Lucy might have something special for you."

"Ahhhhhhhh, no, Madam Dahlia," Boyd replied. "Not on the night of the Lord's birth. Never."

The Madam snorted. "You men," she retorted. "On Christmas Eve all you think of is your mothers, and we girls die of loneliness. A week later, it's New Year's, and all you think of are the pleasures of life, and we're overbooked." She blew her nose loudly into a scented handkerchief then waved with her arm. "He's out back in his room in the stable, last I knew. Probably dead drunk. But go on out and see."

Boyd O'Connor thanked her, made a friendly comment to the girls wishing them a Merry Christmas, urged them to attend Christmas Eve Mass, and darted out the back door, down a wooden walk that ended in a "Y"; one walk led to the outhouse, the other to the stable. A small window showed light inside. "At least," Boyd thought, "Titian's here and awake." He opened the stable door, stepped into the darkness, smelled the odor of two horses that moved their hooves as if nervous at the invasion, and knocked on the door to the left, the entrance to the finished room.

"Who is it?" came an angry voice from within.

"Boyd O'Connor. May I come in?"

"The door's not locked."

Boyd turned the knob, opened the door, and stepped inside. He had never been there before, and so different was it from any other bedroom he had ever seen that he stood with his mouth agape taking in the surroundings. In one corner of the small room was a single bunk covered with a couple of rumpled blankets and a pillow. At right angles was an open closet, with clothes hanging from dowels placed in the wall; a shelf above contained a dust-covered, heavily used carpetbag. Hanging on the walls wherever there was space were paintings of nudes, landscapes, buffalo, a herd of elk, cattle being rounded up by mounted horsemen, a mine entrance, placers, and one of Muddy Creek's Main Street. In one corner were two or three rolled-up canvases. At one end of the room was a little stove for cooking and heating. Titian had let the fire die down, and the room was cold.

In the center of the room was Titian's easel, a big, triangular one with blank canvas stretched over a three or four-foot frame. In front of it was a dilapidated wooden chair. To the left was a bench full of paints and brushes and a painter's palette. To the right, facing the easel, was an old cushioned chair, one that had, without doubt, once graced Madam Dahlia's parlor. In it sat, sprawled out and hunched down, Titian Reynolds. He was not looking at Boyd. He was staring blankly, almost angrily, at the vacant canvas.

"Merry Christmas to you, Mr. Reynolds."

Boyd's voice jolted Titian out of his reverie. He straightened up, looked blankly at his caller, and replied, "I guess so."

"May I sit down?"

"Go ahead. Sit on the chair in front of the easel. I sure as hell ain't using it."

Boyd turned the straight-backed, wooden chair so it faced Titian Reynolds and sat down. This was not a visit of friendship, but one of serious business. Boyd was just as nervous as his pardner Pat had felt with Gunter Schroeder.

Titian scowled at Boyd. The young Irishman gazed back upon this strange man who was wearing even now his artist's beret and a threadbare velvet cloak. Reynolds was tall, cadaverously thin, with a receding hairline, a thin, hatchet face with a sharp nose, and a Van Dyke beard.

"What do you want?" asked the artist in a high, clear voice.

"It has to do with—church," replied Boyd.

"Church? In Muddy Creek? And even if it had a church, which it hasn't, what business would that be of mine?"

"I guess you weren't downtown this afternoon," replied Boyd. "William O'Bryan, the Register of Claims, was gunned down by Jack Langford in self-defense. When O'Bryan was breathing his last, who should appear but a Jesuit priest, a Father Demetrius de Mara. And he's got Reece's Music Hall for the night. To hold Midnight Mass in."

"Very interesting," mused Titian. "In Reece's, of all places. But of what concern is that to me? I was christened a Presbyterian, although I haven't been to church in years."

"They've removed all your paintings," commented Boyd.

"And without my permission. They've got a lot of nerve." Then Titian's face showed understanding, as if he suddenly remembered the nudes. "But it figures."

"Not that they're not good," Boyd added hastily. "Father de Mara, who is from Italy, even said they were a cut above the usual barroom art." Boyd paused. "But of course, they just don't fit a religious decor."

For the first time, Boyd saw Titian smile. "I know," commented the artist. "I never could figure why mankind rejects images of the most perfect being created by the hands of God." He paused then added, "Those walls are going to look pretty barren without the paintings."

Boyd saw his opening. "That's why I'm here," he blurted out. "Mr. Reynolds, won't you paint a picture of the Madonna and Child for us? To have in time for Midnight Mass?"

"Me? Paint a picture of the Madonna and Child by midnight? For a Catholic Mass?" Abruptly Reynolds rose from his chair and went to a small cupboard in the wall to the side of the stove. From it he withdrew a bottle of whiskey. He began unstopping it. "Forget it. I've planned on getting dead drunk this Christmas Eve, and all tomorrow, so that when I come to and sober up it'll be December twenty-sixth and all the sad memories'll be over with." He continued working on the cork while sitting down.

"Everybody in Muddy Creek is lonely like you," countered Boyd. "Our parents, brothers, and sisters, wives and sweethearts are thousands of miles from here. We aren't quite in civilization, Mr. Reynolds. This is the American frontier. But some of us—" Boyd paused, raised a hand to emphasize what he was saying, "—some of us are getting some joy by converting that Music Hall for just one brief night into a place of worship for God, and the Christ child. Hell, Titian," he added, getting more personal, "I was planning on getting stone drunk myself, to drown my loneliness, but now I'm excited over accomplishing this one shining chore, doing something for others, bringing a bit of civilization and religion, and tenderness, to the people of hard-bitten Muddy Creek. Think about it."

Boyd remained seated, saying nothing. Then Titian rose and turned to him. "Get up and get out and let me get drunk in peace," he ordered, opening the door.

Boyd stood up and started out. "I guess you couldn't do a Madonna and Child in five hours anyway," he taunted. "Besides, artists are known as selfish people, thinking only of themselves. I guess they live in their own little world."

"Get out!"

Boyd paused in the doorway as cold air and the odor of horses rushed in. "But just one thing, Reynolds. You'd be a lot happier on December twenty-fifth if you'd do this one service that only you can do. To give a Christmas gift that only you can give to all the lonely people in Muddy Creek. For Christ. Aye, go on and laugh. But I'll be sober and pleased with myself tomorrow, Titian Reynolds. How will you feel?"

The young Irishman stepped outside and heard Titian slam the door behind him. Opening the stable door, he walked outside. Angry and disappointed but still determined that the "church" would be a place of beauty by midnight, he headed back to the Music Hall. He did not bother to go through Madam Dahlia's, but took the little pathway around.

And Titian Reynolds, still working the corked whiskey bottle, slumped, brooding, in his chair, then paused and stared blankly at the easel.

V

Boyd O'Connor hated returning to the Music Hall to report failure. He kept wondering how he could have presented his case better, concluding that there was no way the artist could have been persuaded. "Oh, well," he reflected, "lots of churches don't have paintings and rose windows. Why should people expect them in Muddy Creek?"

When he reached Main Street his thoughts were diverted. There, making its way slowly toward Reece's, was the big freight wagon, the patient oxen lumbering along placidly.

"Boyd," someone alongside the wagon shouted to him, and he turned to see Pat Shanahan, walking alongside the wagon, successful in his mission. Boyd related his failure with Titian Reynolds, but Pat cheered him up. "We don't have a painting," he commented, "but we're going to need more things than that for a church, like an altar, a lectern, and spruce and pine bows to decorate the walls and the stage and to improve the smell. We need all these at the very least. We can't let one defeat stop us."

"Even before that," added Boyd as they came flush with the Music Hall, "we need to put the tables and gambling equipment into this wagon and line up the chairs for the service."

Upon entering Reece's, they saw that changes had already taken place. The double-size can-can girl placard had been removed outside the entrance and the nudes had disappeared from where they had hung. The liquor and barware were gone from the bar. Big Mike, Teague, the padre, and Julie were busy segregating the chairs from the tables.

Gunter Schroeder, the teamster, entered Reece's with Pat and Boyd. "Ach," exclaimed Schroeder, removing his meerschaum and surveying the big room, "vat a change!"

"Let me introduce you to Father de Mara," said Pat, and the threesome—Pat, Boyd, and Schroeder—hailed the priest, who put down the chair he was carrying and came over to them.

"I am a Lutheran, Father," the teamster announced quickly after he had been introduced, "but I am also a Christian. And if ve can't haf a Lutheran service here on Christmas Eve, then, if you don't mind, I'll vership vith the Catholics."

Father de Mara smiled and held out his hand. "Glad to have your help, Mr. Schroeder," he said warmly. "There will be no persuasion, no condemnation here tonight. We are all Christians assembled to honor the Savior's birth."

Gunter Schroeder beamed. "Then let's get to verk," he said. "A few Irishmen and a German can get zeese tables loaded fast." He assumed the duty of foreman, guiding the men lifting the tables through the swinging doors to his huge J. Murphy. He jumped into it and, with Big Mike's help, began systematically stacking the tables at the front of the vehicle, working toward the rear, until they were all packed, and table legs poked mountains and hills in the white canvas top. Within a half hour the task was completed.

"Now," Schroeder volunteered, "I'll take ze vagon back to my cabin vere it vill be out of ze way, and tomorrow morning, if you vill promise to be here to help, ve'll return with the tables and put them right back vere zey belong." He grabbed his bullwhip and positioned himself behind the left rear team. "Lava, lava ho!" he yelled, swishing the whip in the air over the beasts' heads. The oxen responded and Schroeder, walking just in front of the huge letters "J. Murphy" printed on the side, manipulated a perfect U-turn of oxen and wagon on Main Street and clattered slowly down the street and back to his cabin.

The Irishmen and the padre watched the wagon for a few minutes and then walked back into Reece's. There was Julie, the young taxi dancer. She had changed into work clothes—a drab, long dress and dirty old shoes—and with a mop and bucket was on her knees, getting started on the floor. She looked up as they entered, brushing a few blond strands of hair from her eyes. "The pail contains some kind of essence of pine that I found in the broom closet," she said. "Maybe it will take some of the stale beer and whiskey and tobacco smells out of this place." She wrinkled her nose. "Chewing tobacco," she said disgustedly, scrubbing at a lump on the floor. "Of all the despicable habits of men, chewing tobacco has to be the worst."

Just then, Jesse Tinsley, Muddy Creek's only furniture dealer-undertaker, appeared at the swinging doors. "Holy mackerel," he exclaimed, looking around. "Am I in the right place? This *is* Reece's Music Hall, isn't it?"

"Of course," Big Mike replied. "You haven't heard? This here's Father de Mara. He's a Catholic priest."

"I heard there was a Catholic priest here," Tinsley interrupted. "Just the man I want to see." He faced Father de Mara. "I've got Mr. O'Bryan laid out nice and neat in a casket, Father, and the boys dug the grave while the thaw's on and the ground is soft. How 'bout mornin' of the twenty-sixth for the last rites?"

Father de Mara hated being reminded of the terrible happenings of a few hours ago, but he was fully aware of his obligations. "Of course," he replied.

Big Mike showed resentment at Tinsley's interruption. "The padre's goin' to celebrate Midnight Mass here. Jack Langford gave us the Music Hall to use as a church."

"Jack Langford did that?" Jessie Tinsley exclaimed, the matter of O'Bryan's burial settled. "My, my. Miracles do happen, don't they?"

Among the men in the big room, the word "ordinary" probably best described Jesse Tinsley. He was about thirty-five years old, with brownish hair and a clipped beard. He stood five feet eight inches tall, had a body in proportion with a sagging belly, the result of too much time in a store and too little physical labor. He had removed a strong smelling cigar from his mouth in order to speak; now he clamped it between his yellowish but even teeth. "I swear. Jack Langford's the last man in the world I'd expect to give up a night's profit for the Lord."

"I think he feels guilty for gunnin' down William O'Bryan this afternoon. It was clear that O'Bryan fired first after swearing at Langford, and Langford was exonerated, rightly, I think. But still, I'm sure it bothers him," Boyd volunteered, frowning. "I'm mighty sure it would bother me to kill a man on Christmas Eve, no matter what the circumstances. Or even not on Christmas Eve," he added thoughtfully.

Pat Shanahan appeared. "You're coming to Midnight Mass, aren't you, Mr. Tinsley? Even if you're not a Catholic you're invited, you know."

Jesse did not reply. He puffed on his cigar and began making a tour of the room, gazing at the blank walls, the empty stage, noticing the chairs gathered in a corner, not yet set in rows. He had planned on drinking more than usual tonight. Christmas Eve. He deserved to be lonely, he reflected, having made a total mess of his life. But, now that there was something else to keep him busy, getting drunk could wait a while. "Hey, Padre," he asked, "what you goin' to do for an altar?"

Father de Mara, who had been analyzing the stage, trying to comprehend how to make an altar and a lectern there, replied, "I really hadn't thought about it until now. I have the linens and my chalice, some wafers and sacramental wine, and a portable tabernacle packed on Lucifer—that's my pack mule. But that is a question: what do I do for an altar and a lectern?"

Jesse chewed on his cigar, then removed it. "I've got a narrow rectangular table that could do in a pinch as an altar," he said. "It's a lot more formal than one of the round ones the boys drink and play poker on. Ain't quite that tainted with sin neither." He replaced the cigar in his mouth, chewed on it a few moments, and added, "I've got a couple of long candlesticks that you'll need."

"That would be fine," ventured the padre.

"And what you doin' for a lectern?" the furniture dealer-mortician asked.

"I hadn't thought of that either," replied Father de Mara, at the same time realizing that he hadn't prepared a homily.

"I have a lectern I can loan you," Jessie said matter-of-factly, as if every furniture dealer-mortician had one, even on the frontier.

"Jesse," asked Boyd O'Connor, "what would you be doin' with a lectern here in Muddy Creek? Not much market for them here, I wager."

Tinsley laughed. "My Irish friend," he said, "you forget that I am not just a furniture dealer. I sell coffins and prepare bodies. I'm a mortician. And it occurred to me that since there were no clergy in these parts—until now, anyway—I might have to do the obsequies. True, so far I've buried a batch of the deceased, but for some reason, no one's yet asked me to deliver a funeral sermon."

On a few occasions Boyd O'Connor had sat at a table drinking with, among others, Jesse Tinsley, and he was not at all surprised that no one had asked Jesse to speak for the deceased. For Jessie Tinsley was Muddy Creek's prime dullard—a nice enough person, but...dull. Even when he had something of interest to tell, his style of presentation produced yawns. Boyd O'Connor surmised that Jesse Tinsley had always been what he was now: a dull bourgeois businessman.

The padre had approved of the loan of the lectern, and Jessie had nodded acceptance of his offer. "Tell you what," he announced. "I'm going over to Robinson's café for some vittles, after which I'll hitch up my horse and wagon and bring over the table and lectern." He sauntered out.

Jesse Tinsley walked across the street and down a few storefronts to Robinson's. The restaurant was jammed with miners, businessmen, and a few families having a Christmas Eve dinner. He found a small, two-chair table in a corner and ordered a steak, probably from beef sold to Robinson's by the Flathead Indians. Someone in eastern Idaho had given up prospecting, returned to farming, and discovered that potatoes flourished in the local soil. So Jessie ordered a baked potato. And a side order of beans, for want of anything else. The furniture dealer-undertaker then sat quietly, oblivious to the commotion around him. He puffed on his cigar while awaiting his food, and lived over his life.

Muddy Creek! Of all places for him to be on Christmas Eve! How, he asked himself as he had a thousand times recently, had he ended up running a furniture store in Muddy Creek, Montana Territory?

Quickly Jesse ran through his past. He was born of a middle-class furniture dealer in the small town of Splendid Glen, Ohio. His early years had been typical of the nineteenth-century small town boyhood experienced by thousands of others. As he had grown into his early teens, Jesse had been just one of the gang. As far as anyone could tell, not one outstanding trait did he possess to separate him from the crowd.

But the Tinsley kid did have one secret that set him apart, in his own mind, at least, from the other boys. That was his fantasizing. Jesse had nourished his childhood fantasies so that they were flourishing full-blown by the time he was in his late teens. He may have been the most ordinary kid on the block, but in his fantasies he was the Superior One, the Leader. In his reveries he seduced the prettiest girls (plural) in town, slayed hundreds of Mexicans during the Mexican War, saved maidens from fates worse than death from Indians, and discovered fabulous gold mines in California. He became president of the United States. In sum, nothing was too fantastic for the daydreams of that ordinary Tinsley boy. Only occasionally, as he grew to maturity, did the contrast between the real Jessie and the creature of his imagination strike home to him and put him into the depths of depression. But it was never for long.

It was partly to close the gap between reality and fantasy that Jessie succumbed to Molly Stratton's mild flirtations. Molly was a standout among the local belles because she was proportionately larger than the other girls. In her budding maturity at age eighteen, she was a lot of young woman in the right places: large, well-formed breasts, a narrow waist, and a caboose that caused more discussion among the young bucks than any of her other parts. Obviously Molly attracted the boys—for one or two dates. Then her swains always lost interest.

She was friendly, cheerful, conversed well, and was not against hugs and kisses. But Molly was a pusher, a decision maker. She gave orders. And that was the trouble. "She's not for me," a temporary beau said. "She insists on wearing the pants." In fact, there was general agreement among the young blades about that.

Jesse either had not heard, or was not bothered, by such tales. Molly Stratton was by far the prettiest girl he had ever had the privilege of courting. As for her pushiness, he rather let her lead.

When he subtly let the fellows know that he and Molly had tarried amidst some trees off a remote lane, Jesse reveled in his notoriety. In his mind, it elevated him among the fellows.

He did not hear their private conversations. "I wonder which one was on top?"

"Whichever she wanted," was the consensus.

Jesse refused to face the reality that it was Molly who had quietly grabbed the reins and guided Dobbin off the lane into the trees; that it was Molly who had stepped out of the buggy first; that it was she who had grabbed the buffalo robe and spread it on the ground. Nor did Jesse ever consider who determined the position. What he did know was that their mutual joy brought Jesse and Molly to a justice of the peace in a neighboring county. Married at eighteen, Jesse was a father at nineteen, and at twenty-one, and again at twenty-three. And how did he earn his living? He was his father's partner in the furniture business, of course.

Jesse was a good husband, a loving father, a dutiful son, and a pretty good businessman. He worked hard, taking time off now and then to indulge his first loves, hunting and fishing. And he really was an excellent marksman. But deep within his soul the fantasies remained. The dreams of adventure by now had transferred to the Pike's Peak mines. Only when he dwelt upon the futility of his fantasies was Jessie an unhappy man. But it did not happen often.

The depression of 1857 hurt Tinsley's Furniture Store, and competition from a second furniture store in town hurt still more. When his father died in 1858, Molly, who did things rather than fantasize them, suggested one day: "Jesse, why don't we sell out, take the money, go west and start anew? Why not go to Kansas? They say it's the garden spot of the West."

And so it came to be. Dear wife Molly, more adventurous in reality than he, had provided the spunk necessary for the move. They sold the store and their home, netting them a nice nest egg. With their three little girls in hand they took the train to St. Louis. There Jesse purchased a freight wagon and a load of furniture at wholesale and, at the pace of an ox-drawn vehicle, they made their way across Missouri and into Kansas. At a place called Lawrence they stopped, built their furniture store, and prospered. Many of their neighbors were New Englanders, or people from Ohio, Indiana, and Illinois.

Many were abolitionists, and there was the problem. Jesse had never bothered much with the question of slavery versus abolition, although he had heard fiery preachers ranting about the evils of slavery and even advocating war on the South. Jessie was a rather quiet man, not caring either way. But in Lawrence, he soon discovered, abolition was the principal subject of conversation. As the years went on and the Civil War came, violence in eastern Kansas, including Lawrence, became an accepted part of life.

Jesse wanted none of it. His fantasies did not include freeing slaves or slaying pro-slavers. Instead, he dreamed of prospecting in the Rockies, of hunting grizzly bears and living from the hunt with his companions. He dreamed of being relieved of purchases and sales and waybills and overdue bills and prices and, sometimes, of being free of his headstrong wife and the little girls, whom he loved dearly but who still demanded so much of his time. When he was not fantasizing he just desired that people, especially young people with a few dollars saved for a table or a bed, would come to his furniture store and give him business.

Possibly, even in so volatile a place and at such a terrible time, Jesse Tinsley could have been left in peace, had it not been for his dear wife, Molly. She, the one who had suggested emigrating to Kansas, soon showed her stripes as an ardent abolitionist. She attended meetings. She fed strangers who rode up stealthily through the grove of trees behind their house, knocked quietly at the back door, were served a meal, and sometimes were welcomed to sleep in the stable with the horses. Jesse, though busy at the furniture store, soon learned that the Tinsley house had become a friendly house—known today as a safe house—to abolitionists who were working to checkmate the activities of the Missouri Ruffians and other pro-slavers in the Territory.

Jesse's reaction was what one would have expected of a man of his temperament. He played dumb. He pretended that he knew nothing of what was going on. And Molly never asked him to take up arms, go on a raid, carry messages, or otherwise participate. He was pleased about that, because although Jesse loved to hunt and was a good shot, Molly knew that he had no stomach for violence among humans.

Tensions increased. Jesse was aware that merely being a resident of Lawrence constituted prima facie evidence of his abolitionism. The time came when Molly and Jesse were witnesses to violence, once watching horrified as two men whom they knew well were gunned down in cold blood on Lawrence's main street. The ruffians quickly galloped away. They were never caught.

The Civil War was on. If only the war would end, they thought, then peace would come to Lawrence. The girls were in their late teens and would soon have beaus.

Mr. and Mrs. Jesse Tinsley hoped the violence would end before their daughters' lives were affected.

Their hopes were in vain. Missouri ruffians of the 1850s became Confederate guerrillas during the Civil War. As irregulars, they took few orders and obeyed no mandates about the rules of warfare. Some of their leaders were psychotic killers, men who in peacetime would have been, and indeed later became, train and bank robbers. Their acts of cruelty spread throughout western Missouri, eastern Kansas, northwest Arkansas, and into Indian Territory (later Oklahoma). Severing the heads and placing them on fence posts, tying others to wagon wheels and torturing them prior to killing were practices not unknown to these brigands. The best known of their leaders was William Clarke Quantrill.

One day in the fall of 1862, Jesse was alone, hunting deer in a grove of cottonwoods a few miles out of Lawrence. Through thick brush and trees he got a bead on a buck and shot it, or thought he had shot it, from a hundred and fifty yards. He presumed the deer had fallen; he did not hear it running or see bushes move. Quietly he made his way to the spot. In a small, grassy opening lay the deer, shot through the heart. Jesse laid his rifle against a log and kneeled down. He was reaching for his knife in its sheath when he heard a click. Surprised, he looked up to see a shabbily dressed, bearded young man not ten paces from him. He was holding a rifle aimed at Jesse's head.

"Why, howdy," said Jesse, showing surprise. "Didn't know anyone else was around."

"I always hunt this grove," hissed the man, "and I don't take to others claimin' my game."

Jesse looked first at the deer, then at the man. "Hey, wait a minute, stranger," he replied. "Look where the deer's been shot. Came from where I was. You're on t'other side from where the bullet struck. Nor did I hear your shot."

"If my name is James Harte, I shot that deer," the man said, not moving an inch, not moving his rifle. "Now, git goin' afore I jest might take me some other game of the human variety."

Jesse stood up. He saw brutality and evil in the man's face. He was aware of the proximity of his own rifle. "I don't know you, stranger, but in these parts we don't look favorably on the likes of you."

The man sneered. "What are you, one of those abolitionists from Lawrence?" He moved the rifle just slightly, indicating a predilection to kill. "Get goin', mister. Fast! Leave your rifle where 'tis."

Jesse backed up slowly to the edge of the woods and close to where his rifle rested against a log. "Git!" repeated the gunman. Jesse, weighing his chances, leaned over as fast as he could, grabbed his rifle, and plunged into the forest. Twice the gunman fired at him; Jesse heard the bullets whistling through the branches above him. Soon, however, he was deep among the trees and he felt safe.

But, quiet man that he was, Jesse Tinsley did not run far. His anger exceeded his fear. He circled the clearing wherein lay the deer until he was behind the culprit who, he quickly perceived, was busy cutting up the game. Jesse took aim, not at the man but at his rifle, which lay propped upon the same log where Jesse's rifle had been. Jesse was a good rifleman—had even won some shooting awards—but what he accomplished this time was extraordinary, even for him.

He fired. The bullet hit the rifle, knocking it to the ground. When the man, who was taken by surprise, reached for the gun, which was farther from him than before, Jesse's voice rang out clear and strong: "Grab that rifle and you die."

Later Jesse, amazed as his own courage, allowed as how he was so angered he would have pulled the trigger had the gunman reached, and in later years Jesse regretted that he had not killed James Harte then and there. For, after the stranger had fled without his rifle or his knife, and Jesse, with supreme confidence, had cut up the deer and taken the good parts home, he made a frightening discovery. The man he had encountered, James Harte, was the man pictured in a pen and ink sketch he had seen as the horse thief, murderer, and border ruffian William Clarke Quantrill!

The knowledge that Quantrill headed a band of over four hundred guerrilla fighters who were active in the region did not make Jesse feel any better. The pro-slavers knew of Molly's activities; surely they knew that the Tinsley residence was a place for food and a night's sleep in the barn for active abolitionists. Jesse never divulged to Molly his episode with James Harte/William Clarke Quantrill, but he suffered privately with the knowledge and, fantasist that he was, his fear of retribution almost overwhelmed him. He heard a rumor that the brigand leader had a score to settle with a Lawrence businessman, and, Jesse figured, that tradesman had to be him.

In the summer of 1863, Jesse became more nervous than ever. Lawrence had become the seat of Kansas abolitionism. Quantrill's raids were getting bolder and more vicious. Not only were men being captured, tortured, and killed, but women were also victims, being kidnapped, raped, and murdered. With a wife and three daughters beyond puberty, Jesse decided the time had come to get them out of Kansas. In July, the months of Gettysburg and Vicksburg, he sent Molly and the girls back to Ohio, there to stay with Molly's parents until such time as Jesse deemed it safe for them to return. Even headstrong Molly concurred in the decision.

On August 21, at dawn, the attack came, worse than Jesse had ever dreamed it could be. William Clarke Quantrill and his four hundred-plus raiders rode into Lawrence and sacked and burned it to the ground. One of the first businesses to be torched was Tinsley's Furniture Store. After sacking the business buildings the marauders began torching homes. The first one Quantrill rode up to was the Tinsley residence. The guerrilla leader booted open the front door and ran through the house with orders to "search out that sonofabitch Tinsley and if he ain't there, grab his wife and daughters."

Of course, the wife and daughters were in Ohio. And Jesse? Fantasy had served him well. He had imagined the scenario and prepared for it. According to plan, he ran out the rear entrance to a cluster of stately old trees, which in August were still in full leaf. He had already made a trial run, grabbing a low-lying branch of one, hoisting himself up, and making his way so deeply into its leafy recesses that only sheer luck would give him away to horsemen below.

It was from there that Jesse Tinsley witnessed the sacking of Lawrence. He watched the town go up in flames, heard screams and shots, and later discovered the human destruction: one hundred eighty men, women, and children killed.

"Quantrill was specifically looking for you," a survivor told him. "He kept shouting, 'git the one who owns the furniture store!' Jesse, you're lucky to be alive."

Indeed, Jesse Tinsley did consider himself lucky to be alive, lucky to have had the judgment to send his family back to Ohio, lucky to have deposited savings in a St. Louis bank and in a hole covered by turf and leaves in the grove of trees where he had hidden.

But now what should he do? No one knew the whereabouts of Quantrill. Between Lawrence and safety to the east were several hundred miles of guerrilla-infested, sparsely-settled, pro-slave Missouri terrain. Jesse knew he was a marked man. So when he heard of a well-armed wagon train heading for Denver and the Pike's Peak mines, Jesse dug up the gold coins he had buried, placed them carefully in a bag inside his trouser waist, shouldered his Winchester, and headed west. He did not write his wife for fear the letter would be intercepted. Quantrill might track him down or send someone to kill him.

Denver had some appeal, but the furniture business was saturated there. For a time Jesse clerked in such a store and learned the rudiments of a new profession, embalming, which the owner practiced along with retailing furniture and caskets. Still, Jesse failed to write Molly, even though he could have sent the letter via Julesburg and Nebraska Territory, so that Quantrill would not have intercepted it.

Then the opportunity arose for Jesse to fulfill his fantasy about gold prospecting. He joined a party of prospectors headed for the San Juan Mountains of southwestern Colorado. For nearly six months he was out of contact with a post office. That, he rationalized, was why he did not write Molly. Others struck it rich; Jesse didn't. Someone told him about the Idaho-Montana diggings, and especially of a place called Muddy Creek, just opening up. The strike had been made in April and already the camp had a couple thousand inhabitants. Hard-rock mining was beginning, which meant that Muddy Creek would probably become a permanent community.

Back to Denver went Jesse. As soon as he received his funds from the St. Louis bank, he purchased a freight wagon, filled it with furniture, and, just as he had done years before in St. Louis, headed out from Denver. He joined a well-armed party headed up to the Oregon Trail, then west via South Pass, and then north to the Idaho-Montana mines. In late August 1864, just a little more than a year after the sacking of Lawrence, Jesse Tinsley and his wagon reached Muddy Creek. He purchased a half-completed wooden business building, completed it, and opened Muddy Creek's one and only furniture store/mortuary. His initial stock, including caskets, was hardly on the floor before it was sold. This very afternoon of December 24, Gunter Schroeder had unloaded a wagon full of new merchandise that Jesse had ordered. It included caskets, for his last one had been used for poor William O'Bryan. Jesse was doing well.

But he had not written Molly.

It bothered him. This Christmas Eve he was lonely—very lonely. Molly and the girls: he thought of them, and he, a grown man, almost sobbed right in Robinson's café. Why, he asked himself as he awaited his meal, had he failed to write his wife? For all she knew, he was by now a buried, charred corpse found in the ashes of Tinsley's Furniture

Store or in what was left of his home in Lawrence. He rationalized that his failure to write was due to his fear that Quantrill might intercept a letter and track him down; that Indians were pillaging the mails; that there had been no post office in the San Juans.

Jesse rubbed his brow. Were those the reasons, the real reasons? Or was it that, no matter how much he loved Molly and the girls, he had enjoyed the single life on the rampaging frontier, enjoyed sewing his wild oats, living some of his fantasies? He loved hunting, and in Colorado and now Montana he had pursued the hobby to the limit. To rise on a frosty autumn morning in Muddy Creek, ride his horse out into the hills, hear the whistle of the bull elk, dismount, tether the horse, and stalk the game until he could draw a bead on it—that was the life! To come and go as one wished, dining at the local restaurant if he was not inclined to cook his own meal in his tiny apartment in the back of the store—that was the life. To amble to the saloons and imbibe and have long talks about his hunting prowess and narrow escapes—that was the life he enjoyed.

Or did he? Was he tiring of the realities of his fantasized life come true?

The waiter brought the meal. Jesse had lost some of his appetite. All of a sudden he yearned for Molly, yearned to be once more a respectable town father attending Baptist church with wife and daughters, to be a deacon, a member of the chamber of commerce. Tonight, more than any time since his wife and daughters departed from Lawrence, Jesse Tinsley missed them.

He sighed. "Have I burned my bridges?" he asked himself, rising from the table. "Maybe Molly has remarried. On, my God. What have I done with my life?"

The furniture dealer paid for his meal, left Robinson's café, and started for his darkened store. He would load the narrow table to be used as an altar, and the lectern, and hitch up Nellie to the wagon and transport the pieces of furniture down the street to Reece's Music Hall.

"Better think about it," he concluded. "Of course I'm lonely tonight. It's Christmas Eve. But there is just one Christmas Eve a year."

VI

Barry Millard realized that he had been too long in the tub. The water was getting unpleasantly cool. He stepped out, dried himself—being very careful to just pat the places where the whip had burned his skin—shaved, dressed in clean clothes, and contemplated what to do next. He had brooded in the tub for nearly an hour over Julie, the little taxi dancer. He knew he had not ended their relationship entirely. If his memory was correct (and he had to admit that things had gone awfully fast out there in the muddy street), he had told Julie that he would "think about it." That meant, he assured himself, that if she could talk with him, they could work out a reconciliation. But is that what he wanted?

He knew what he should do: leave her. Put her out of his mind. It had to be infatuation. He was young and robust and normal, and few females were around western Montana. As soon as he was back in civilization, in Chicago, New York, Boston, he would forget her. So—forget her, now!

He shook his head. The rationale, he knew, was right. But he also knew the old adage, love is blind. All the logic in the world could not rub out of his mind Julie's soft blond hair, blue eyes, pert nose, white teeth, and well-shaped mouth; neither could he erase the memory of her breasts, flat tummy, and perfectly shaped legs, for indeed, on walks in the forest they had observed more of nature than chipmunks going about their business, even though she had never given in completely.

What to do? The young man brushed his blond hair, slapped his geologist's felt hat on his head, and sauntered down the stairs of the hotel. When he stepped outside the lobby onto the boardwalk he was caught by the brisk wind. He looked up at the sky. The clouds had almost disappeared and stars were appearing. As he closed and opened his fists, undecided about what he should do, he rather absent-mindedly tramped across the street to Reece's. He was surprised to find few loungers outside and the absence of sounds, especially of the "orchestra." The twice life-size can-can girl was missing too. He entered.

And stopped. "What in the pluperfect hell—" he began, surveying the big room devoid of tables, gambling paraphernalia, paintings, and people; chairs had been lined up in rows with a center aisle leading toward the stage.

"Howdy, Barry. Merry Christmas to ye," said Big Mike. "Surprised, ain't ye?"

Julie saw Barry, caught her breath, and quickly turned her back to him, busying herself with a dust cloth.

"What's this all about?" asked Barry.

"Jack Langford gave it to us for Midnight Mass," Teague Cosgrove volunteered. "We've stored the tables and gaming devices in Gunter Schroeder's freight wagon and now the chairs are in place. We've got an altar and a lectern on the way, and by midnight we should be ready."

Barry removed his watch from the watch pocket in his trousers. "It's almost eight o'clock," he commented.

"I know," replied Big Mike. "There must be something we can do to make it look better. More like a church," he said, looking around the big room. He sniffed. "And make it smell better."

Just then another person came in through the swinging doors. He was nattily dressed with his coat open, displaying a gold watch chain with a Masonic symbol attached. He was smoking a freshly lighted cigar. It was Jack Langford. He stopped and looked around the room, removed his cigar and tapped it so lightly that some ashes fell to the floor. Julie glared at him but said nothing. She had just scrubbed the floor clean. "You sure cleared it out," Langford commented, "but don't you need some decorations?"

"Sure, but what?" asked Father de Mara, walking up to him.

"Boughs. Spruce boughs, pine boughs, juniper boughs," replied Langford with the confident tone of a successful businessman.

"But it is dark, and we'll be holding services in less than four hours," said the padre.

"Why, Padre, I've got all the fresh boughs you need. They're down at my sawmill."

"And where is that?"

"Just a mile or so out of town. Down by the creek. We could take a wagon down there and fill it with boughs and be back here within—oh, an hour and a half, I reckon. I have a wagon in the stable behind this building. We can have the horses hitched up and be on our way in just a few minutes."

Barry Millard, who had noticed how Julie had turned her back to him, saw in Langford's suggestion an opportunity to postpone his talk with her. "Let's go," he announced. "Anyone else?"

Just then a low voice from the entrance asked of no one, "What's going on here? I had a poker game scheduled for tonight. Don't take too lightly to forced changes in my plans."

All turned toward the speaker. He was a slim, swarthy figure wearing a cream-colored, checkered vest exposed by his Prince Albert coat, which was open. He was smoking a long, crooked cheroot. All knew him as Charlton Edwards, though most suspected that it was not his real name. As he awaited comment from someone, he reached into a deep side pocket and came up with a deck of cards. "I thought someone would like to win some Christmas cheer this holy evening."

Jack Langford's eyes narrowed. He removed the cigar from his mouth with his left hand. "You don't own Reece's Music Hall, Edwards, even if you did kill my partner. And I don't take orders from you. I suggest you take your smelly cheroot and your cards and your flamboyant clothes to one of the other saloons for your Christmas Eve cheating."

Edwards' hand reached toward his waist where, as the coat was pushed back, all observed a pearl-handled Derringer. "No one," he announced, all pleasantness gone from his face, "accuses me of cheating."

"Everyone accuses you of cheating," Langford replied in a stern voice. He was standing squarely in front of Edwards, closest to him of all present. Even as he spoke, everyone heard a click. Barry noticed that Langford's right hand had slipped into a coat pocket, and the pocket now had form. Something inside was pointed at Edwards.

The two men glared at one another. Then Edwards relaxed and laughed. "Oh, what the hell. It's Christmas Eve. Let bygones be bygones. I'm not all that bad." Nervously he turned to the padre. "I may attend services," he said as he whirled on his toes and strode out the door.

Langford placed the cigar back in his mouth and removed his right hand from his coat pocket. "He better," he muttered, "because it may be his last chance before meeting his maker."

The padre relaxed. Everyone relaxed. For a few moments the padre had been afraid that the sanctity of this temporary chapel would be tainted by spilled blood. He concluded that Charlton Edwards was the gambler who had approached Robert Sungren, the Gilmer and Salisbury Stage clerk. The priest frowned. That was another problem he must deal with before he left Muddy Creek. It occurred to him that he had been in town less than eight hours and he already had enough obligations to keep a parish priest busy for a month.

Langford strode the length of the room, hearing how the liquor and barware had been stored, the tables and gambling equipment packed in the big freight wagon, and the paintings removed and placed along the hall wall leading to the back door. To that door he headed. "Anyone wants to come along, just follow me," he announced. "We'll have this room looking like a Black Forest chapel, with spruce and pine and juniper bows covering the stage and walls." He paused and glanced around. "We can do a lot for you, Father de Mara." He opened the back door and Barry, Teague Cosgrove, and Patrick Shanahan followed him.

In jig time the horses were hitched to the wagon, and with Barry and Langford on the seat and the two Irishmen sitting in back, they clattered down Main Street, whose surface was beginning to freeze and was therefore easier, though rougher, to traverse. In no time they were out of town and in the blackness of a winter's night. Now they turned off the main road while Langford gave the horses free rein to find the two tracks leading through the woods. Soon the gurgling of a mountain stream underneath the ice drowned out the sound of a breeze whispering through the conifers. Looming up in the darkness were the grotesque outlines of the sawmill.

"Whoaaa," commanded Langford as he pulled on the reins. When the horses stopped, the crew jumped down and followed him a short distance to a yard of sawdust, fresh-hewn lumber, and a huge pile of boughs.

"Help yourself, boys," said Langford, fetching the first spruce bough himself. "Take only the fresh, aromatic ones. Be choosy. We don't want the church to look as if we just threw it together." As they all went to work, Langford grabbed Barry Millard's arm. "Come over here, Barry. I want to talk to you," he said.

Barry walked to the side of the brush pile opposite the other men. He was puzzled. What could this hard-nosed entrepreneur who had gunned down a man just hours before want of him?

"I heard about your fight today," Langford said, glancing at the men picking up boughs. "That fellow had it coming."

Barry was embarrassed. "I'm sorry I made a scene at the Music Hall," he began. "I guess I wasn't thinking. I just sort of blew up and acted."

"Got warm feelings toward Julie Montgomery, haven't you?"

One thing about Jack Langford. He didn't beat around the bush.

"Yes, I do. I keep telling myself it's just infatuation. Been so long since I've been around cultured women that I've lost my sense of values, I guess. Julie's the closest approach to such women I've come across out West."

Langford pulled from a pocket a fresh cigar and, with a penknife, began clipping one end. Barry could barely make out his face in the darkness. The breeze pulled at their coats, and Barry shivered. The two Irishmen were busy loading the wagon, making light of the task, laughing.

"Barry, you sure are an aristocrat, aren't you?" commented Langford.

"What?"

"Julie Montgomery is a poor little lost waif doing her best to stay on the straight and narrow," Langford went on. "She was worth that fight, Barry, although there's no question that she's learned a thing or two about the real world since becoming a taxi dancer. Most likely that fellow would have ended up at the bottom of the stairway, result of a well-placed kick. But maybe not, and if not, she was going to be raped. She was trying to avoid making trouble, trying to avoid making a scene. No doubt about it, she was in a jam. Let's assume you saved her."

"I'd like to think so," Barry replied quietly.

"Remember that she's a taxi dancer, Barry. She came here with three other girls and a man and woman to manage them. The deal they made with me was that the girls could live upstairs and keep half of everything they made. That means they keep half of the dime they charge for a dance and half the cost of drinks. The girls' drinks are just colored water, of course. Their managers collect a fixed sum of money from me. If you've wondered where the others are, the managers and one of the girls have returned to Salt Lake to recruit more girls, two others have run off with men, and that leaves Julie here alone."

"So they aren't prostitutes?"

Langford stuck the cigar in his mouth. "No," he replied then paused. "Now, of course, Barry, we're dealing with the real world here. These women are no angels. Some slip into prostitution, a lot of them marry, some go on as taxi dancers and I don't know what happens to them. Human nature has its way. A girl likes a man and he propositions her, she looks around, sees that no one is watching, they arrange a tryst, that sort of thing. But anyway, out West the taxi dancer is recognized as being a cut above a whore.

"And this Julie—she is good," he emphasized, searching for a match. "As owner of Reece's I'm afraid I made a pass at her. She let me know in short order that I could fire her and throw her out of the Music Hall, but she was not about to bed down with me." He paused. "Matter of fact, as a result of that, I've become a bit father-like to her. I don't want her to sink below her present level."

There followed a moment of silence. Barry did not know how to receive the news. His first reaction was to punch Langford in the nose for making a pass at Julie. His second was to thank the man for being so frank, and for defending her. "I'm glad to hear that, Jack," Barry finally replied.

"I've also told Gus Logan to keep an eye on her," Langford added. "He's told me that he's never known Julie to allow a man in her room upstairs. From her demeanor here in Muddy Creek, the little gal could even be a virgin."

By the look on Barry's face, lighted briefly by the flame of Langford's match, he could see that the young man appreciated that bit of intelligence. Then he added with a smile: "Of course, we know you and Julie have taken walks into the woods."

Barry blushed. "True, Jack. But we've not gone all the way. Honest."

Langford puffed on his cigar. "Well, now," he added, "I'm not just telling you all this to make conversation. I'm telling you that she's a nice girl. And Barry, she's crazy about you. I've watched her when you enter Reece's. Whatever she's doing, she loses interest, gets rid of her partner if she has one at the moment, rises from the table, and places herself where you'll see her. Believe me, son, you could do a lot worse than Julie Montgomery." He replaced the cigar, puffed on it a few times, and removed it again. "She's educated, as I'm sure you know. So, don't think you're too aristocratic to be interested in her." He replaced the cigar, puffed on it, and again removed it. "Barry, something tragic has happened in her life. Has to have happened, otherwise she wouldn't be here." Langford looked the young geologist straight in his eyes. "I have no idea what it was. Do you?"

Barry shook his head. "I agree there's something tragic in her past," he replied, "but Julie just clams up when I begin prying."

"Well," said Langford, "as I say, you could do a lot worse, even in New York or Boston, than Julie Montgomery. Think about it." Then he turned to look at the fragrant, fresh boughs piled high on the wagon. "Looks like our job's about finished here," he commented. "Let's get on the wagon and head back to town."

While Jack Langford, Barry Millard, and the two Irishmen were obtaining boughs from the sawmill, Jesse Tinsley arrived in front of Reece's with his wagon, upon which was painted in crude white letters: TINSLEY'S FURNITURE AND UNDERTAKING, and in smaller letters, "Chairs, Tables, Beds, Stoves, Caskets." He alone had lifted onto the wagon the heavy, narrow rectangular table that would serve as the altar; the lectern had been no problem.

"Can somebody help me?" he yelled. Big Mike Mitchell and Boyd O'Connor came to his aid immediately. Soon the table/altar was placed on center stage and the lectern at its left (from the front of the room) just as in a real church. The three surveyed the scene. Big Mike volunteered that the boys should be back shortly with the boughs.

"That'll help soften the looks of the place," Jesse commented, "but it's Christmas Eve. Something is missing. Something more is needed."

"Most churches have a nativity scene," volunteered Julie.

"That's it!" exclaimed Jesse. "We need a nativity scene."

"But where could we get a manger?" asked Big Mike.

Jesse thought for a moment and then said excitedly, "I've got it. A big roll-top desk came in today packed in a huge wooden box. I don't know why, but instead of breaking up the box I kept it intact, just opening one side. We could bring it here, cover it with boughs, put in some hay, and lo and behold! We'd have a manger!"

"Wonderful," the girl replied, clapping her hands.

"Come with me," urged Jesse. "We'll fetch the box and be right back."

Hardly had the three left before Langford, Millard, Cosgrove, and Shanahan showed up with the boughs. "Miss Julie," said Pat as he opened the back door for them, "we've got enough boughs to hide every ugly thing in the Music Hall. Smells nice, too. We'll make it look like God's own room." And Barry, who was acutely aware of how Julie kept her distance and avoided eye contact with him, helped the Irishmen pile the boughs just inside the door while Langford drove the horse-drawn wagon back to the stable, saying that he would be back.

Julie took upon herself the task of decorating the stage. She was terribly aware of Barry's presence, but it was Teague and Pat who brought the boughs to the stage, while Barry busied himself along the wall behind the bar. Carefully Julie placed the fragrant boughs along the edge of the stage; she piled them in front of the altar table so that the legs were hidden; and she placed them in such a way around the lectern that it seemed to have grown out of the brush. Someone had fetched a hammer and some nails, with which the men were pounding the boughs into the wood behind the bar.

"I hope Langford doesn't mind this," said Barry. "I know he prizes the bar here, but not even the mirrors fit the decor of a church." He covered them with boughs. In time the task was finished, with a few boughs left over. Certainly they added a festive look to the room. More important, perhaps, Reece's Music Hall finally exuded a fragrance that overcame, or nearly did so, the smell of stale beer, whiskey, tobacco, and unwashed humanity.

Then Big Mike, Boyd O'Connor, and Jesse Tinsley returned. Into the room they manipulated to the left of the altar, and below the stage, a wooden box five feet long and four feet high. On the open side, which faced the congregation, they set to work creating a manger scene. On the way from Tinsley's they had stopped at a livery stable and fetched several armfuls of loose hay plus three extra bales. The task was quickly accomplished.

"There," announced Jesse, standing back from the box. "Now to cover the wood on the outside with boughs and, voila, we have a nativity scene."

"Too bad we can't have the animals and the Wise Men and the Christ child and Mary and Joseph," commented Julie.

Patrick Shanahan snapped his fingers. "I wonder," he said thoughtfully, "if Gunter Schroeder, the teamster, would loan us his wood carvings? They're of religious subjects, and they're beautiful."

"Why should he have such things?" asked Barry, joining the group but ignoring Julie.

"When I called on him for his freight wagon, he was sitting at his table carving a piece of wood. He has assorted wood carvings around his cabin, and he told me that under a buffalo robe in the corner is a whole stack of them. He has a beautiful crucifix on his mantel. It must be two feet high."

"No problem in asking," said Jesse. His words were hardly out before Pat started slipping on his greatcoat and scarf and heading for the entrance. "Begorra, it's worth a try," he said. "I'll be back soon, with or without the images." He started down Main Street toward Gunter Schroeder's cabin.

Schroeder, having parked his huge J. Murphy close by the cabin, unhitched the oxen and put them to pasture, then entered his one-room cabin and replenished the fire. From a cupboard he fetched a gallon whiskey jug and set it on the table. He removed his coat, sat down on his stump chair, and went to work with his knife on the same block of wood that he had been busy carving when Pat Shanahan had knocked on the door two hours before. He paused, gazed at the half-completed carving of a Madonna's face and reached for his tobacco pouch. He filled his meerschaum, stood up, fetched a flaming twig from the fire, and lit it. Then he sat down again, removed the pipe, uncorked the jug, lifted it adroitly to his shoulder, then to his lips, and took a big swig. He wiped his bearded face, set down the jug and corked it, replaced the pipe between his lips, and picked up the knife. But he just stared at the carving. Finally he laid the knife on the table. The spirit was lacking.

Wind whistled around the little cabin. Coyotes were howling outside in the wilderness. He surveyed his cozy domicile, placed his elbows on the table, and smoked. "How," he asked himself, "did I get here? From Erlangen in Bavaria to Muddy Creek, Montana Territory, in America? What am I doing here?"

His memory drew him back to the year 1848 when he had been a twenty-one-year-old student at the University of Erlangen. The son of a boot and shoe merchant, Gunter had entered the university with his eyes upon a calling: the Lutheran ministry. From his earliest boyhood, friends had turned to him for advice. He was, his parents told him, a born minister. And Gunter had agreed with his parents. In 1848 he was in his senior year, expecting to graduate with honors and enter a Lutheran seminary.

One day as he walked across the campus he was confronted by a group of young liberals—radicals was perhaps a better description—who handed him their socialist tract which advocated unification of the Germanys into a single nation with a democratic form of government. Often in the years that followed, Gunter wished that he had not followed their will-o-the-wisp radical politics. He became a leader; he found that he could rouse a crowd with his strong voice and logical arguments. So when news of the Revolutions of 1848 in Paris reached the Germanys, Gunter was in the vanguard of those who took action. Subsequently, when the Revolution failed, he became a wanted man. Were he to be apprehended, a long prison sentence or even the hangman's noose awaited him.

As the wind whistled around his cabin, the coyotes howled, and the fire crackled, Gunter recalled being guided by a sort of "underground railroad" to Bremen, where he took steerage for America. He had a small sum of money slipped to him by his parents by way of a fellow socialist. His mind, however, drew a complete blank as to what to do when he arrived in the United States.

He pulled the whiskey jug toward him, uncorked it, and took another swig. It was warming his belly, flushing his face. All of that had happened in the autumn of 1848. This was Christmas Eve, 1865. What had he done in those sixteen years?

"Ach," he grunted, then burped, breathed deeply, and stared at the table. "What have I done?"

His mind wandered back to January 1849 and his landing at New Orleans; how he had walked the gangplank into the strangest, most exotic city he had ever seen. Black stevedores sang rhythmic, lonesome songs in a patois of English, French, Spanish, and the language of their native Africa. Hardly was he on terra firma before street walkers accosted him; they ranged in color from ebony to Nordic white. Even in January he felt the humidity of the place, for a tropical depression was blowing in, bringing with it sheets of rain. How it could rain!

Gunter quickly decided that he did not want to remain in New Orleans. The humidity as well as the city's character hardly attracted a hard working, energetic, religious young German. He contacted a German society that made arrangements for him to board a Mississippi River steamboat for St. Louis. He still did not know what he was going to do, but he was by now very low on cash, so he knew he must find some kind of work, and soon.

It was while leaning on a railing, watching the ever-changing scene of humanity and nature along the Father of Waters, that one of those fortuitous incidents occurred that set the stage for Gunter Schroeder's next years. A well-dressed man who knew some German struck up a conversation with Gunter. After having ascertained where the young man was from, he asked him what he was planning on doing in St. Louis.

Gunter shrugged and his face conveyed a blank expression. "Ach, I don't know," he blurted out in broken English.

"You're small, but thin and wiry," commented the stranger. "Ever been sick?"

Gunter, who was blessed with excellent health, replied in the negative.

The stranger looked off at the changing shoreline. "How'd you like to be a bullwhacker?"

"A—bull—?"

"Yep. An ox skinner or a mule skinner. A fellow who drives a freight wagon across the Great Plains. We call them bullwhackers."

Gunter frowned.

"Yep. You'd get a chance to go to New Mexico and see Santa Fe. Or you might go to Fort Laramie and Salt Lake City. Good work for a healthy young man not yet tied down with a wife and kids."

Gunter understood, and was suddenly excited. Germans were fascinated by the American frontier, its Indians, its promise of adventure, its exciting gold and silver rushes. As a youngster growing up in Bavaria he had read everything he could get his hands on about the American West. Now he had an opportunity to see it all. He seized it. The stranger turned out to be an official of the frontier freighting firm of Russell and Waddell (later Russell, Majors, and Waddell). At the firm's expense, Gunter accompanied his new acquaintance from St. Louis up the Missouri to Westport (today's Kansas City), and north up the river to Leavenworth, headquarters of the big freighting firm.

The years that followed were years that Gunter would always consider among the happiest of his life. He acquired frontier English rapidly, although he never lost his German accent. He got along well with the other men, rough-cut Missourians and Southerners with their drawls and racist attitudes, hard-working Yankees from New England and the upper Middle West, foreigners new to the country like himself. And he took to managing oxen very quickly.

Gunter had a way with the beasts. He was also fascinated by the frontier society he observed. At Leavenworth, he was a part of the hundreds of warehousemen, shipping clerks, wheelwrights, carpenters, blacksmiths, wranglers, trail bosses, mule skinners, and bullwhackers who made up the polyglot society. When he went into town he found blue-attired soldiers from nearby Fort Leavenworth. Gunter tasted the wild life, such as it was, of the frontier community. He learned to drink with the best of them, although he did not become a drunkard; a time or two he visited the girls on "maiden lane," but again, he did not become a whoremonger. Although he was strong and lithe and healthy, a man who got along, he still kept to himself much of the time.

As the days progressed toward April, when the greening of the grass ensured nutrition for the oxen, activities at Russell and Waddell's facilities accelerated. Every day a train of twenty-six wagons headed out from Leavenworth. One would be bound for Salt Lake City with stops at Forts Laramie and Bridger; another for Bent's Fort on the Arkansas and on down to Santa Fe and even points south and west. By the time his assignment came along, Gunter had earned the confidence of the firm's personnel manager (although such a phrase was not then known). Gunter would start as a bullwhacker with promise of elevation to assistant wagon master and, if his work was satisfactory, wagon master in charge of a train. Gunter Schroeder, revolutionist once with a price on his head, could look out upon the greening Kansas prairie with considerable hope for the future, as well as the promise of adventure.

The day came. Already he had practiced, but the actual experience of rounding up his oxen, yoking first the wheelers, then the pointers, then the swing teams and the leaders, turned out to be more chaotic than he had imagined. From a grazing herd of three hundred, Gunter and the other bullwhackers had to sort out their twelve oxen, herd them to the wagon, and hitch them up. The first two or three days on the trail, he wondered if they would ever be ready in time to make the ten or twelve miles a day the train was expected to travel. Within a week, however, order had come out of chaos. All the men, all the oxen, seemed to know what was to be done. While breakfast of fried pork and coffee was being prepared by the cooks (one for every five men), the bullwhackers were singling out their oxen and hitching them up. Then breakfast.

All too soon the wagon master yelled "lave, lave ho!" To the sounds of creaking wagons and the crackling of twenty-foot bullwhips with the dollar-sized leather popper at the end, and plenty of curses, the slow-moving Great Plains freight train began its day of travel.

Gunter, with the others, walked, not rode, along the left side of the wagon or next to the left rear animal. He kept the oxen moving with shouts and the swing of his whip, with which he soon became a recognized expert even among the whackers. He learned to be on the lookout for rattlesnakes, which were incredibly numerous on the plains. The flat Great Plains, the region dubbed by Major Stephen H. Long as the Great American Desert, proved to be anything but flat and barren. It was plentiful with birds, jack rabbits, prairie dogs, coyotes, wolves, buffalo, and occasional bears, even a grizzly, lizards that the men called horned frogs, and insects including centipedes and scorpions.

Gunter loved the life, the crystal clear air, the continual change of scene (it only seemed the same, he discovered, as miles upon miles of prairie were crossed), and the camaraderie of the men. Even though he tended to keep to himself, it was soon obvious that the men looked to the young man for advice, to settle quarrels, or to just talk. There was something about Gunter: he was respected.

Yet many a time he did desire to be alone, to meditate, to consider the Great Questions. It was the part of his personality that had led him to plan a career in the Lutheran ministry. He would fetch his knife, find a likely hunk of wood, and begin carving. In time he became known as Gunter the Woodcarver. He didn't mind. He carved oxen and buffalo and Indians and wagons and prairie dogs. He even fashioned some rattlesnakes on the verge of striking. And one night, with a million stars overhead and the fires low and the men asleep, he began thinking of Bavaria and his parents, of the warm, loving home in which he had been raised. Most of all, he recalled his initial calling, and it agitated him. Before he entirely understood what he had done, he had carved a delicate crucifix replete with the suffering Christ. It was about two feet high. This he hid, but as time went on, Gunter's nascent religious feeling strengthened, and almost before he knew it, he had a collection of all sorts of religious carvings.

Once, his carving abilities served the wagon train in an unusual way. A Missouri bullwhacker named Lem Thomas was pulling his rifle out of its holster muzzle first when it discharged. It shattered the bone of his left arm just below the elbow. Gritting his teeth to help stand the pain, the frontiersman insisted that it would heal. "Just bandage it and put it in a sling and let me ride in the wagon for a few days," he pleaded.

But it was soon clear that it would not heal. When the bandage was changed, the nauseous tell-tale odor of gangrene permeated the wagon, and gangrenous spots appeared above the wound. The bullwhacker lost some of his courage; he was feverish and becoming disoriented. In such condition, it did not take much persuasion on the part of his companions to convince him that unless the arm was severed just above the wound, he was going to die.

"You can carve a sheep's nostrils in a two-inch sheep's head," said the wagon master to Gunter. "Come on over to Lem Thomas' wagon and help us sever that left arm."

Gunter tried to beg out, but it was clear that he was expected to do his part of a procedure no one wanted to perform. Everyone thought Lem was going to die anyway.

He found the wounded man lying on the ground by his wagon, a hot fire blazing not far from him, and a small saw nearby. In the fire was a white-hot, four-inch-long bolt. The saw interested Gunter: the men had considered the teeth too big for cutting bone, so they had cut smaller teeth on the smooth top and would use that as a saw. Gunter grasped the uses of both the saw and the bolt, but he swallowed hard at the thought that he was going to be a participant in the operation.

He had heard the saying "bite the bullet"; now he learned its meaning. Fortunately, Lem was so feverish that the consensus was that he would fall unconscious at the pain, but to help him prior to that, he was given a Colt six-shooter bullet. "Put this between your teeth, Lem. Bite it hard. This ain't goin' to take long. First thing you know, you'll be good as ever."

The feverish man, pale beneath his whiskers, perspiration bathing his forehead, bit the bullet as strong hands took over his left arm, laying it on a clean piece of canvas. The wagon master nodded to Gunter. "Quickly, with your knife, encircle the flesh all the way to the bone," he ordered. "Do it fast."

The woodcarver knelt on both knees and leaned over close to the arm. The stench, as well as the sight of diseased flesh, slivers of bone, and blood repelled him, but Gunter overcame his repulsion and concentrated on his task. The flesh cut like butter. As soon as he sensed its consistency he applied the proper pressure, the proper cutting rhythm, and circled the arm, which was lifted—as Lem groaned— so that Gunter could cut the underside.

"Fine," announced the wagon master when Gunter had finished. "Now for the saw." Gunter was handed the upside-down saw, its fine teeth sharp and new. Steadily he applied it to the top of the exposed bone and began quick back and forth movements. As with the rotted flesh, Gunter soon sensed the consistency of the bone and adjusted the pressure and the rhythm to serve it best. Gunter was surprised at how little bone there was, and how quickly it was severed.

"Now, quick, the bolt," ordered the wagon master, noting that Len had slipped into unconsciousness while blood spurted from the exposed arteries. The man was sick enough without being further weakened by loss of blood.

With a big clamp used in repairing wagon wheels Gunter grasped the white-hot bolt from the fire. Carefully he laid it flat against the remaining stump of the left arm, moving it slowly to cover the wound. It sizzled. The acrid odor of burning, diseased flesh filled the air.

After a short time the wagon master said, "That ought'a do it." The cauterized stump lay on the canvas.

"You think he wants this as a souvenir?" someone asked, holding up the severed hand and forearm with his thumb and forefinger.

That broke the tension. Everyone laughed. Even Lem, tough frontiersman that he was, responded by regaining consciousness. "We've done it, Lem. You were one brave hombre," said the wagon master. "We'll put you in your wagon and let you sleep. If you want a few swigs of whiskey, you can have 'em."

A few days later, Lem was learning to do the things one had to do without the use of a left arm. Before the train reached Santa Fe, he was a well man.

Again, as the wind whistled around his cabin, Gunter Schroeder took a drink. He reminisced how he had advanced steadily from bullwhacker to wagon master, or bull boss, as that position was also known. More times than he wanted to recall, he had experienced episodes with Indians, especially the Kiowa and Comanche in the Southwest and Sioux and Cheyenne on the high plains, and with the Bannock in northern Utah and Idaho. He had survived, he reflected, with his scalp intact. He drew a hand through his graying hair. By 1858 he was an experienced frontiersman. In that year he had been bound for Salt Lake City with supplies for the United States Army. War was threatening between the Mormons in the Salt Lake Valley and the United States government.

It was also the year that witnessed the virtual end of the freighting firm of Russell, Majors, and Waddell. The company suffered a cash-flow problem when the Army was unable to pay it promptly; it also suffered severe losses in the Wyoming winter, with Mormons raiding its freight trains, burning them, and running off the stock. When he returned to Leavenworth, it was clear to Gunter that the firm was headed for bankruptcy. It had inaugurated the Pony Express and was losing money every day of the operation. He wanted nothing to do with the Pony Express; he was a freighter.

With money banked safely at Leavenworth and his future questionable, Gunter began looking for something new to do. Once he had led a wagon train to the Fort Hall Indian Reservation in Idaho. He had been intrigued by the country. It was farther north than St. Louis and the forested, mountainous terrain reminded him of Bavaria. He decided to become an independent freighter serving the Idaho-Montana mines. He purchased the huge J. Murphy wagon, built to his own specifications, and chose twelve of the finest oxen available. Thus he began his career as an independent freighter.

Thoughtfully, like Jessie Tinsley had done with furniture, Gunter had filled his wagon with liquors, picks and shovels, and washing pans and other miner's needs. He made money even as he made his way to the mines. Now it was Christmas of 1865. He was doing well, not yet forty years old, in good health, and well liked by all who knew him. And, he thought, getting misty eyed (possibly from the whiskey, although he was far from drunk), he was lonely. Could he change his life? Could he return to St. Louis and enter the Lutheran seminary and still become a Lutheran minister?

There was a knock on the door.

VII

When Boyd O'Connor slammed the door of Titian Reynolds' single room in the stable behind Madam Dahlia's fancy house, he left alone a tormented soul. Titian still had not succeeded in uncorking the whiskey bottle. The slamming of the door caused him to pause in his task. He sat in the tattered easy chair, facing the easel with the blank canvas mounted upon it, subconsciously noting the small side-table cluttered with paints, brushes, and a palette. Still holding the bottle, he stared at the easel. Titian was oblivious to the dying fire in the little stove. He was unaware of the shadows from its flames as they danced on the walls, or of his own lanky shadow. He did not hear the whistling wind or the coyotes howling.

Slowly he placed the bottle, not yet uncorked, on the floor beside the chair and leaned forward, elbows on bony knees, chin cupped in hands. His facial expression changed from one of anger to pensiveness. He bit his lower lip; his eyes misted. "How," he asked himself for the ten thousandth time, "did I, Titian Reynolds, promising artist, son of prominent Philadelphia artists, end up in a stable room behind a busy bordello in, of all places, Muddy Creek?"

Although photography was making inroads on the number of commissions portrait painters could command, Titian's father, Thomas Reynolds, had continued to keep busy in Philadelphia. He was welcomed in the city's finest homes; he had, in fact, done paintings of dozens of Philadelphia's elite. Titian's mother was well known too.

She was a sculptress. Her bric-a-brac portrayals of farmers working the fields, their horses and wagons nearby, and, very recently, of Union soldiers, had gained her national renown. In Philadelphia, as the decade of the 1860s progressed, it was known also that the Reynolds had a talented son named Titian who, it was predicted, would carry on the family traditions. Indeed, it was a tradition: the Reynolds family and its artistic talent traced back to England, from whence Titian's father, while still in his teens, had sailed for Philadelphia.

Titian had asserted his artistic merits early. As a small boy he mastered watercolors and began painting everything from dogs and cats, vases and bowls of fruit, to buildings and landscapes. Indeed, his catholicity in painting anything and everything was considered a problem.

"Titian," his parents were telling him when he was still in his teens, "you must concentrate on one form of painting. And the real money is in portraits." Titian complied, or tried to, although his desire to paint all kinds of things, not just the faces of rich but not always handsome Philadelphians, left the young man bored. And yet, at age twenty-four, the city knew of Titian Reynolds as a talented portrait painter following in the steps of his illustrious parents. He had improved his gift with a two-year sojourn in Europe, working with oils as well as watercolors.

One day in 1862, a prominent, wealthy Quaker businessman knocked on Titian's studio door. When the young artist opened it he saw not just the Quaker scion, but with him, dressed modestly but stylishly, his eighteen-year-old daughter. When the two, painter and maiden, first glanced at each other their eyes set as if entrapped.

Titian gazed upon the girl until her Quaker father cleared his throat. "Ahumm, Mr. Reynolds,"—and the spell was broken. Titian escorted the father and daughter into his studio and sat them down.

"I am Nelson Morris," began the father, handing Titian his card, "and this is my daughter, Cecilia. She is starting at Swarthmore College next year, and before she leaves our home, Mrs. Morris and I would like her portrait. We know how busy thou be, sir, but dost thee think thee could work her in?" He gestured toward his daughter.

Truth was, Titian's commissions filled his appointment calendar, but he did not stop to think; he nodded his affirmation before he spoke. "Yes, of course," he said simply. He knew he could rearrange previously scheduled sittings.

"When can thee begin?" asked Cecilia's father.

"Right away," Titian replied.

If Mr. Morris noticed in Titian rather more interest than was usual in a purely business transaction, he did not reveal it. "Very well. I will drop off Cecilia tomorrow afternoon at, say, three o'clock. How long will the sitting last?"

"Not more than two hours," replied Titian absentmindedly, looking at the girl, not at her father. "The number of sittings will depend upon our progress."

Cecilia's smile of approval was unusually beauteous, revealing teeth even and white, unusual in an age of poor diet and primitive dentistry. Titian gazed at her luxurious dark hair enclosed in a huge bun at the back; her fine, even features; her smooth, creamy complexion without a blemish. He thought her eyes were the prettiest blue he had ever seen. Already he was envisioning the cameo-like portrait he would paint of this lovely Quaker maiden. It would be his best ever.

Just as he said he would, Nelson Morris dropped off Cecelia the very next afternoon punctually at three o'clock. All business, Titian posed her close to the easel. He worked diligently to get just the right light on her face, stepped to her sitting figure and lightly placed his hands to her shoulders to position them just so. Gently he tilted her chin. "I won't ask you to maintain this pose for too long, Miss Morris," he said in his most professional voice, "but try and remember the position, especially the angle of your pretty head, so that after we have tea and return to work, we will not have to waste time re-posing you."

She smiled prettily. "I'll do my best," she said.

Thus began the sittings. When she protested that her pose was tiring her, Titian put down his palette and invited her to sit at a little table and have tea with him. That is how they became acquainted. His initial attraction to the girl strengthened. As with so many Quaker daughters, Cecelia's education had been equal to men's—no common thing in nineteenth-century America. Her schooling had commenced early and continued steadily. While many a genteel girl mastered sewing, knitting, how to paint china, and quilting, Titian discovered in Cecelia Morris a blossoming young lady who knew some Latin and Greek, history, literature, something about art, and even a bit of science.

It was during the second sitting, while he was posing her, that Titian made a psychological slip. "Your throat is beautiful," he said. "It leads so gracefully toward your—your—bosom," he said. He blushed. "Excuse me, Miss Morris. As an artist, I have to visualize the whole form."

Her reaction surprised him. "Too bad they just want my face, isn't it? There's really much more to me than that." Then Cecelia blushed. "You know, Titian," (it was the first time she had called him by his first name) "I've been taught some art. I'm aware of all the naked women painted by the great artists of the Renaissance."

"Oh?" he responded. "You know, Cecelia," (and it was the first time he had called her by her first name) "I have several art books full of paintings of the Great Masters. Would you like to see them?"

"Oh, I'd love to," replied the girl.

When they took their next break Titian led his model to a coffee table where lay several large books. Nervously, he opened them and in no time, nudes, albeit in black and white, were exposed to their analysis. The girl savored the wickedness of her behavior. She pointed to one voluptuous nude. "She's too fat," she said flatly. "Why should a painter choose her for a model?" At another, she observed, "Her bosom isn't perfect. Mine is better." She lowered her eyes and blushed as Titian looked at her. At a third painting emphasizing the naked derriere of a reclining female, she added with mock seriousness: "She's positioned awkwardly. This painting should be titled 'Nude with a Broken Neck'."

They laughed.

But Titian was also perspiring. He was not even breathing regularly.

The girl looked at him, a mischievous gleam in her eyes. "Have you ever painted naked women?" she asked.

"I—well, yes, when I was in Italy I experimented. But I didn't have a model. I had to paint from my—my—imagination and the memory of nude paintings I had seen," he lied.

"Hmmmmm. I think you can paint as well as any of the Old Masters," she said. "If you had a live model."

Titian blushed. He perspired. Could this be? Surely this was fantasy! Here was this lovely girl whom he looked forward more and more to seeing at every sitting, volunteering—was she?—to pose for him in the nude! While he grasped for something to say she added, "Titian, next sitting you spend one hour on the portrait and the second hour I'll pose nude for you."

It was settled, for of course Titian approved. After the girl had left, he sat bathed in perspiration, breathing deeply, sexually aroused, overjoyed at the prospects.

The day came.

Both were nervous. He kept telling himself to be professional, to concentrate, that indeed, this was the opportunity of a lifetime to do a wonderful nude. He had always fantasized such a project. And now he had a beautiful model and a great opportunity. (Of course, he had to admit that in Victorian America there was no market for such works of art, not even a gallery that would display such a subject.)

Was he being honest with himself? Did he really give a tinker's dam about the painting? In his heart, didn't Titian Reynolds know that he was in love with this beautiful young Quaker lass, Cecelia Morris? Didn't he know that he really wanted not just to pose her in the nude, but to possess her physically? Titian Reynolds never admitted having carnal desires toward Cecelia, either at the time of the event or in the years to come. At that moment in time (he was convinced) he had been determined to overcome his passion and concentrate on painting a masterpiece of this beautiful girl, even if it would not be shown publicly until a less prudish generation came along.

As for Cecelia, at eighteen she was fully molded, fully feminine, and curious about the male world about her. It may have been, and indeed was, an overdressed, prudish age. But it was also a time in which animals furnished motive power for the vehicles that passed up and down the streets. No one grew up without being aware of the procreation methods of animals. They begged comparison to the human condition. Besides such knowledge, Cecelia had been to a Quaker girls' school. When teenage girls got together, they talked about—boys.

It was not wrong to suggest that neither the thin, lanky twenty-four-year-old painter, who after all had been to Europe and indeed had experienced sex and once or twice painted nudes of live models, nor his lovely young Quaker virgin model, quite understood the intensity of those primitive powers that were playing within them that afternoon.

The portrait was nearly finished but so enamored was Titian with Cecelia that he puttered and fussed over it just to extend the sittings. Nervously, on this exciting day, he again worked on the portrait for the hour allotted. Then he placed the palette on a table. "Now, Cecelia, I'll start painting the rest of you," he announced, "that is, if you are still willing. You do not have to do this."

"Oh, I'm still willing," Cecelia replied excitedly.

Titian removed the portrait and replaced it with a fresh canvas. Upon it he had already made a stick drawing of how he would pose her. She was to be sitting on a sofa examining her face in a mirror which she held at arm's length. Her left hand was lightly laid across her lap, and her nude legs were to be demurely together, with feet on the floor. What amused Cecelia when she saw the outline was her head, for already Titian had painted it. She was too modest to say so, but she knew it was beautifully done.

"Why is my head already painted?" she asked.

"That's all I've seen of you so far," he answered, and they both laughed.

She looked around the room. "And that," she added, pointing to the couch they had sat on at teas, which Titian had already positioned close to the easel, "is the sofa?"

"Yes, Cecilia."

There was a moment's silence. Then she asked, "Where should I disrobe?"

He pointed to a movable screen.

"Fine," she replied. "I'll be out in a minute, Titian. Go ahead with your preparations."

Titian was perspiring; he continued to tell himself that this was going to be a magnificent work of art that he was about to bring into being; that he would feast his eyes on this lovely girl but not touch her; that somehow perhaps he could obtain her father's permission to marriage. Yes, he was already thinking about that.

"I'm ready," the girl announced from behind the screen.

"So am I, Cecelia," he replied.

He watched as she modestly, yet with firm steps—no hesitation—stepped from behind the partition. Titian gasped. The girl had undone her bun so that her soft black hair fell like a rippling waterfall down her back. She held both hands folded in front of her loins while her perfectly shaped breasts, her flat tummy, her navel, her slim legs and thighs were all exposed. She possessed, Titian thought, the most marvelously perfect female body he had ever seen, including European models or any nudes he had studied in art galleries.

"Tell me if I assume the right pose," said the girl, sitting demurely as close to the figure in the stick drawing as possible.

"Perfect," Titian whispered. He was aware of the swelling in his trousers, and he hoped she did not notice. He turned to the easel and the palette and mixed the paints. He knew he must turn to her, to begin the painting, but sex was far more powerful right now than art, and he was flustered. His hands shook.

Finally he turned to her, appraising the beautiful girl and contemplating where to start. She smiled at him, but what was worse, her eyes, bright as stars, a wild look in them, were focused on his loins. She was aware of his excitement.

Titian tried to act professional. He started to paint, but realized he was incapable of it. He paused.

"What's the matter, Titian?" asked Cecile,

"I–I–Oh, Cecelia, you are too beautiful. I cannot concentrate," he blurted out, staring not at her but at the canvas.

He heard movement, and turned. "Neither can I, dear," whispered the girl as she took two steps and threw her arms around him.

Minutes later they were not just artist and model, but lovers.

Twice more she came to Titian's studio to pose, and twice more they made love. Her father, Nelson Morris, was inquiring about progress, and the time came when Titian felt that they would have to announce the portrait's completion. He decided to use the occasion to ask Mr. Morris for permission to court Cecelia, explain that they were attracted to each other, and suggest that quite possibly, after a reasonable courtship, they would be married.

The Morrises, mother and father, were delighted with the portrait but they were less pleased with Titian. First, they had their hearts set on their daughter attending Swarthmore College, due to open its doors in 1864. They anticipated Cecelia being in the first graduating class. They were, Titian readily observed, terribly possessive, Cecelia being their only child. And they were very wealthy. It was made clear from the first that Nelson Morris did not consider an artist a suitable mate for his lovely daughter.

"We'll see, Mr. Reynolds," he announced. "For the time being, however, let us say three months, I would prefer that thee and Cecelia not see each other. We are going to our summer home in the Poconos in a couple of weeks. When we return in August—we'll see." Could they write? "No. Let us make sure this isn't just an infatuation. Cecelia is very young, Mr. Reynolds. Thee and she must be separated completely for three months. Then we'll see."

It was clear, Titian could tell, that the Morrises' ardent desire was that Cecelia forget him. She in turn gazed at him with moist eyes, trying to tell him, without her parents noticing, how sorry she was. Her parents paid Titian generously for the portrait—it really was a painting of lasting merit—and then they, including his beloved Cecelia, were gone.

Titian sat on the sofa where the lovely girl had not only posed for him, but where they had made love. He had many worries. They had tried to be careful, but young love was incredibly demanding of its full satiation. He hoped Cecelia was not pregnant, although if she was, he reflected, why, after much embarrassment, she would be his wife, and that would be wonderful. Could he see her somehow? He knew no one in the Poconos. He looked blankly at the easel. He was lonely, discouraged, and at his wit's end.

Suddenly he thought of the unfinished nude, rolled up in a corner with other unfinished paintings. He walked to the corner, unrolled it, and appraised it. He had Cecelia's face nicely painted, but the rest of her body remained half flesh and half stick drawing. He had hardly got a breast or a nipple or a kneecap painted before desire had overcome them both—and thus had ended the painting for that day.

For a few days after Cecelia and her parents left Philadelphia, Titian drifted, spending more time than he should have at a saloon frequented by artists. It was there that he was invited on a tour of the Hudson River Valley with several other young artists. They would sketch and do landscapes during the summer. It would get them out of hot Philadelphia, where commissions were rare in summertime. And the trip had another advantage. The Union Army was conscripting young men, and the trip would get them out of the city where any or all of them might be caught up by recruiters and sent off to war. And so Titian, lonely and heartsick, went along.

He did not have his mind on it, but the Hudson Valley was beautiful. He understood why the Hudson River School of painting had established its reputation for generations to come, and occasionally he lost himself in his work.

Then one afternoon as he was returning to the inn he met one of his fellow artists. "I've been looking for you, Titian," he said. "Your father's here. He's up in your room right now."

Titian was frightened. Had something happened to his mother? Had yellow fever broken out in Philadelphia? He rushed to his room and opened the door. There stood his father, thumbs in vest pockets, legs outspread, a serious look on his sensitive face.

Titian began, "Father, what brings you here?"

"Sit down, Titian," the older man ordered, waving a hand toward the single chair in the room.

Titian sat down. His father looked down upon him, frowning. Then he raised an accusatory finger. "Titian," he began, "how could you?"

"How could I what?" he asked.

His father rocked back and forth on his heels, both thumbs once again in his vest pockets. "Your reputation as a respected artist. Your parents' reputations. And the moral upbringing we gave you."

Titian still expressed bewilderment. He raised his hands in a gesture of curiosity, of ignorance, of wrongdoing. "What have I done, Father?"

"Just this," said Mr. Reynolds gravely. "Three days ago Nelson Morris came to me demanding five thousand dollars."

"What?"

"To pay expenses for taking their daughter Cecelia to Boston, where she will secretly give birth to a baby, Titian. Your baby."

Titian wilted then buried his face in his hands. "Oh, my God, Father. It can't be."

"Do you deny that you are the father, Titian? Look at me!"

"No," replied the young artist, sobbing. "I love her, Father. I still love her. It's an old cliché, but—it just got the best of us."

"Titian! Cecelia is a child of eighteen. You are twenty-four. You've been to Europe. It is the man's duty to control not just his passions but also the cravings of an overly-excited young maiden." Mr. Reynolds paused. "And also, artists are supposed to be above this sort of thing! When an artist takes a commission, he is supposed to keep as emotionally uninvolved as physicians are toward their patients."

"I know, Father," sobbed Titian. "But I want to marry her. I want to marry her," he repeated.

Mr. Reynolds was quiet. He rocked back and forth on his heels, thumbs still in his vest pockets. Thoughtfully, he said, "It is out of the question with the Morrises, Titian. Cecelia is their only child and they're planning to manage her life until they die. They have it all planned. The baby will be put up for adoption, then a trip to Europe for Cecelia and her parents. In a year or so they will return to Philadelphia and its society with a bright young daughter who will have absorbed Europe's culture. You are not in the picture."

"But I love her, father. Can't you understand?"

"You have no choice but to forget her, Titian. And there is more."

Titian looked at his father, stifling a sob, knowing that men did not cry but nevertheless shaking with emotion.

"You are to leave Philadelphia for a minimum of three years, Titian. The Morrises don't want you around, either to be seen by Cecelia or to spread stories."

Titian contemplated his father's words. Probably best, he thought, to get Cecelia out of his mind. "Where should I go?" he asked.

"That is your business, of course. Naturally, you are not to travel to Europe or go searching for the Morrises. Why don't you go west and do landscapes of the Rocky Mountains?"

"Go west?"" Titian mused. He had often thought of going west, as had Albert Bierstadt and Alfred Jacob Miller and George Catlin. He could do landscapes and paint Indians, tepees, buffalo, and such events as hunts and Indian ceremonies.

That, Titian Reynolds recalled as he sat in the cold chair in the room off of Madam Dahlia's stable, was what ultimately brought him to Muddy Creek. A loud crack of firewood roused him from his reverie, but just momentarily. He got up, opened the stove door, and threw on some more wood. The wind whistled around the structure, in the stables a horse neighed, and somewhere outside coyotes howled. Titian paid no attention.

Although he had been tormented by guilt, by remorse for the shame to his family, and of sadness for poor Cecelia and the child she would bear but he would never see, by his loss of what he thought was the only girl he would ever love, Titian had made progress toward restoring his stability. His first stop west was St. Louis. There he advertised as a noted portrait artist from Philadelphia and had enough commissions to live quite well. He was beginning to forget Cecelia when, about eight months after his arrival, he received a letter from his father. It contained an enclosure, a letter from Nelson Morris in Boston, Massachusetts. It read in part:

> Our treasured daughter Cecelia died December 12, 1863, in Boston, of childbed fever. The baby did not survive.

When he read this, all life ended for Titian Reynolds. He turned to drink and lost his commissions. Eventually he sobered up long enough to be contracted to an English traveler-hunter going up the Missouri River; Titian was to paint and sketch for him along the way. On some days whiskey was not available and Titian, sobered, fulfilled his commission to the Englishman's satisfaction. But when the riverboat docked at Fort Union at the mouth of the Yellowstone, Titian was able to drink constantly, so constantly that one day when he sobered up and went in search of his patron, he discovered that the party had departed two days before down the Missouri, leaving Titian—"that drunken artist"—to make his way as he could.

From Fort Union Titian had drifted westward, first to Fort Benton, then to Last Chance Gulch, then over the mountains to Oro Fino and Coeur d'Alene. Finally, one autumn day in 1865, he arrived at Muddy Creek. At the saloons he offered to paint profiles, sketch mines and placers, do anything as an artist in exchange for a small cash fee. He even tried to give up painting for physical labor but no one would give him work at the mines because his hands were soft and un-callused, and he was tall and thin, obviously not a robust person for work in the mines.

Finally, a young prostitute from Madam Dahlia's took him to her lodgings. Madam Dahlia liked the emaciated young man. She gave him the room in the stable, encouraged him to paint her girls, dressed, undressed, and in between, and helped him sell some of the paintings to local saloons where they were displayed, as at Reece's Music Hall. Titian's drinking had continued, however, and Madam Dahlia was having second thoughts about her artist boarder. She was contemplating having some toughs drag him out, rough him up, and throw him out of town. But for the present, Christmas Eve, 1865, Titian Reynolds was safe.

Now, as far removed from genteel Philadelphia as one could be, and a year after the tragic news of Cecelia's death, tears still welled in Titian's eyes as he contemplated the lovely girl. Through the mists, the blank canvas on the easel loomed before him. Suddenly his visage changed, his mouth opened. He rushed to a corner wherein were stored his art supplies, rummaged through several rolls of canvas, and finally came to a particular one. He unrolled it: there was Cecelia's beautiful face and the stick drawing of the proposed nude. "So help me God," he exclaimed out loud, "I will!"

So rapidly did he return to the easel that he kicked over the bottle. Titian picked it up and threw it in a vacant corner, where it smashed, filling the room with the scent of bourbon whiskey. He threw off the vacant canvas and replaced it with the half-completed painting. He examined Cecelia's head, her intelligent, refined, angelic face, her lovely black hair. Then he studied the stick drawing, contemplating how to proceed. He sat down on the chair and reached for his palette. "I haven't much time," he said to himself.

Then he began painting.

VIII

Father Demetrius de Mara looked at his silver watch. It was 9:15. Standing behind the makeshift altar he surveyed the room. The chairs were in place and an aisle ran down the center. Space had been left between the stage and the front row so that those taking communion would have room to kneel. The lectern stood at his right. Jesse Tinsley's rectangular packing box had been delivered and now stood on the floor in front of the lectern, below the stage. Pine and spruce boughs hid the bare wood. People had heard the news of the impending Midnight Mass and were dropping in, partly curious to see how Reece's would look as a church, and perhaps to offer help.

One of Muddy Creek's few respectable housewives, Mrs. Lancaster, wife of the manager of the Consolidated Hard-Rock Mines, dropped by while doing last minute shopping. "You need some swaddling clothes for the nativity scene," she said. "I have some baby blankets that will do. We can wrap them so they look like they're protecting a baby." Then she frowned. "I don't have a doll the right size for the Christ child," she added sorrowfully.

Father de Mara beamed. "Oh, that is all right, Mrs.... Lancaster, is your name? Some baby blankets will add a bit of realism. We will appreciate it." True to her word, the Cornishman's Methodist wife subsequently delivered the blankets and placed them, rolled as if swaddling an infant, in the manger.

Closer by, Father de Mara surveyed with satisfaction the makeshift altar. It was now covered with not quite white linen. He had fetched it, as well as his chalice, a packet of wafers, a bottle of sacrificial wine, and the portable tabernacle, from one of the packs on either side of Lucifer, his balky pack mule.

The pretty taxi dancer, Julie Montgomery, was busying herself behind the bar, at the sink, cleaning the huge kerosene lamps that illuminated Reece's. One by one she had lowered each counterweighted nickel and glass fixture, disengaged it from the hook, taken it behind the bar, and set about trimming the wick and cleaning the glass chimney and the base. "Father," she said disgustedly, "wouldn't you think the men who pull these down every morning to fill them with kerosene, light them, and raise them back toward the ceiling, and then at the end of the day lower them to snuff out the flames—wouldn't you think they would clean the chimneys and polish the bases and clip the wicks once in a while?"

Father de Mara smiled at the girl, who smiled back wanly. He had already pieced together the story of the lover's quarrel, had noticed Barry Millard's agitated demeanor. For the present, however, he was at a loss of what to do, how to settle a lover's quarrel. Be kind, take your time, he thought. Possibly he might work out something to bring them together again.

He noticed approvingly the spruce, pine, and juniper boughs that had been nailed to the walls, covering on the one side the mirrors and shelves of the bar and the bare walls where paintings of nudes had been hanging. On the other side they simply added a festive touch to the otherwise blank wall.

The good padre sighed. It was not much, but it would have to do. He stifled a yawn. It was not every day that he performed extreme unction for a man killed in a shootout, obtained a saloon and was challenged to transform it into a chapel, heard about vigilantes and a threat to a quiet clerk's life, and celebrated Midnight Mass. Bedtime for him had been the coming of darkness; staying alert until well after midnight he was not used to, and it was going to be difficult.

Robert Sungren, the Gilmer and Salisbury Stage clerk, looked in at the goings-on. He bore a frightened look, not at all like the cheerful countenances reflected in the faces of most of those dropping by. He edged up to Father de Mara who was in conversation with others. The padre turned to him. "Glad to see you again, Mr. Sungren."

The thin, tubercular clerk glanced around and was relieved that the gambler Charlton Edwards was not to be seen.

"Have you figured out what I can do?" he asked.

Father de Mara lifted his hand. "Calm down, Mr. Sungren. There's nothing to worry about at the present. We'll find time to resolve the problem. I've already met the alcalde and Jack Langford and, well, let us for now place our fate in the hands of God."

Sungren relaxed—a little. He surveyed the transformed Music Hall. "It sure looks nice, Padre. I wish I could do something to help. But all I am is a tubercular voice instructor eking out a living by keeping invoices and selling tickets for the stage company."

"You don't sing anymore?"

"No, Padre," replied Robert Sungren. "I haven't since I left Denver."

"Why not? Didn't you say that your cough is gone, that you've started gaining weight, that you think you may be cured of TB?"

"Yes, but—"

"Then why haven't you begun singing again?"

"I—well—I'll think about it," replied the young man. "Got to go now," he added abruptly and started for the door.

"Wait," the padre said. "If you won't sing, it would help if you could enlist Reece's piano player and the cornetist to furnish accompaniment to the old Christmas carols. This masculine congregation will sound a lot better if it has some help from a piano and a cornet."

"I think I know where they are," Robert Sungren replied enthusiastically. "I'll try to get them, Padre." And he was out the swinging doors.

Again Father de Mara surveyed the temporary church. He wished there was a cross hanging back of the altar, or some sort of religious symbol, but again, spruce and pine and juniper boughs were better than nothing. He shrugged his shoulders. "This is, after all, the American frontier," he mused. "Be glad to have a place with a roof over it to celebrate the Lord's birth."

Now, briefly, only the three Irishmen were present (for Pat Shanahan had headed out for Gunter Schroeder's cabin), plus Julie, who was working on the lamps. Barry had said something about getting a bite at Robinson's café. Jack Langford had left, as had Luke Bassett, the pudgy alcalde who had dropped by to observe the changes at Reece's.

Of the four Irishmen, only Big Mike seemed unhappy and ill at ease. Something was on his mind, something was troubling him. Big Mike considered himself a good Catholic, and good Catholics didn't partake of holy communion until they had been to confession. Big Mike wanted to confess, but so far the padre had been mute about having confessions.

Finally he stomped over to Father de Mara. "Damnit it, Padre," he blurted out, "we need a confessional. I can't take holy communion on Christmas Eve without having confessed my sins."

The padre surveyed the room. The broom closet was full of cleaning supplies and was much too small. A confessional was a specific piece of church furniture, and he could envision no satisfactory substitute at Reece's.

"We can't have everything on a moment's notice in a frontier town," the padre replied.

Big Mike surveyed the big room. His eyes spotted the side door on the right side. He knew that it led onto a platform about five feet square, followed by a path leading to the substantial outhouse. Suddenly he snapped his fingers. "You need me for anything else, Padre?"

Father de Mara scanned the room again. "No. I think we are about finished."

"I'll be goin', then," Big Mike announced, "but I'll be back. Maybe with a confessional."

"What?" asked the padre. "I don't understand."

"You will," replied Big Mike. "You will, Padre," and he was out the door.

Wrapping his shoddy greatcoat around him, Mike paused, cast quick glances up and down the street, and then headed east on Main. The wind had subsided, the sky was clear, and it was cold. He passed the closed newspaper office, the Gilmer and Salisbury Stage office, the firehouse with the new bell lying on the ground next to the big doors. At "B" Street Mike paused, then turned down the narrow, two-tracked roadway. Somewhere in the darkness, punctuated by the dimly lit four-partitioned square windows of miners' cabins, was Ebenezer Cotton's.

Ebenezer was the town's Yankee carpenter. Mike had passed his cabin a few days ago, and had been amused at what Ebenezer was making in the big shed near his cabin. Mike had noticed several newly constructed structures, the wood still light and fresh, the crescent of a moon in their doors.

"Hey, Eb," Mike had yelled to him, just to make conversation, "what in tarnation are those?"

And the bearded Yankee had replied, "Outhouses, ye derned fool. What else would be shaped like that?"

"Outhouses?"

"Of course. Outhouses. This town's growin', Mike," Eb added. "People can't find private places in the woods no more. Besides, the woods can be a bit dark and scary on a snowy night. Little awkward tryin' to balance yer rear across a snowy branch, too." Eb's face changed; he saw in Mike a potential customer. "Sell you one for ten dollars delivered on my stone boat."

Walking along briskly now, Big Mike chuckled as he recalled Eb's reply when he had refused his offer. Now he was approaching Eb again, and Big Mike knew that what he was about to ask was, to say the least, unusual. He knew this was a long shot, but it was worth a try.

As he strode along, the crisp air clearing his mind from the stuffiness of Reece's Music Hall, Big Mike thought of his past. He recalled Christmas Eve in his home town of Buffalo, New York. His parents had immigrated from County Cork and his father had been recruited at dockside to work on the Erie Canal, then under construction. Mitchell Sr., something of a leader, was soon a foreman. The couple did quite well for immigrant Irish, and Michael Jr. was soon on the way. When the Erie was completed in 1825, the Mitchells settled in Buffalo. Mitchell Sr. continued to work on the canal, maintaining several locks on the Buffalo end of the water artery.

Mike was blessed from the beginning with a fine physique and excellent health. He was also a scrappy youngster who was into minor troubles from age four on. His mother insisted that he attend Catholic school, which he hated, but he did get through the sixth grade. He could read, write, and cipher and, in fact, he continued to use these abilities, especially his reading.

Besides mastering the three "R's" in Catholic school, his devout parents made sure that he learned his catechism and attended church every Sunday. As soon as he was confirmed, he was expected to go to confession at least once a month. Even when he rebelled against school and left home at age twelve to work as a "hoggee," or driver, along the Erie, his Catholic faith and training demanded that he attend services every Sunday, if at all possible, and go to confession frequently. His conscience, he discovered, bothered him no end if he didn't.

But it did not bother him about much else. He developed an early taste for whiskey, which temperance advocates noted was the bane of Erie Canal employees. For a fip—six and one-fourth cents—a young hoggee could purchase a quart of rot-gut whiskey and get royally drunk. Along with the drinking, for Mike, went carousing. Truth was, he liked nothing so much as a good brawl. Hardly had he reached puberty before he also had sex—and enjoyed it. Whiskey, sex, and fighting constituted a volatile combination, and Big Mike (as he came to be known) was a participant in many a barroom fracas.

Fortunately, Big Mike was one of those individuals who did not become so obsessed with sex that his womanizing destroyed him through disease; in fact, he remained a free floater, and sex never dominated his thoughts for long. The same went for whiskey; he would work hard for several weeks, sober as could be, then decide he needed a break from the toil along the towpaths. Come a Saturday night, Big Mike was at it with whiskey, sex, and, quite likely, a bloody brawl. Even with his fighting he was selective. He did not get into just any brawl. There was always a reason. And he survived when others got hurt. (His nose had been broken and would never be straight again, but then, as he reflected, it was a small Irish nose anyway.)

Perhaps his faith saved him from harm. No matter how badly he was hung over on a Sunday morning, he went to Mass. No matter what temptations he had succumbed to, he tried hard to get to confession at least one Saturday each month. Once, the refusal to go drinking on a Saturday night because he had to go to confession may have even saved his life. The saloon where he would otherwise have been, caught fire and ten people, including the men who had invited him, were trapped inside and burned to death. The incident made an impact on Big Mike, and his religion became more than ever his one anchor in an otherwise wild and aimless life.

Time went on. For Big Mike Mitchell, after six years along the Erie, new worlds beckoned. The winter of his eighteenth year came. The lakes were about to freeze over, and Big Mike felt an itch to see more of the world rather than returning to Buffalo to take any kind of day laborer's job available. He bought steerage on a Great Lakes freighter and made his way down Lake Erie, into Lake Huron, through the Straits of Mackinac, and down Lake Michigan to Chicago. There he found work in a brewery. From 1843 until 1850 Big Mike lived in the windy city. He almost married a Yankee girl whose father was a clerk at the brewery, but she would not give up her Congregationalism for his Catholicism and, for Big Mike, that ended the relationship.

In 1850 he read of the chartering of the first land grant railroad, the Illinois Central. Initially it was to build south through Illinois to Cairo, at the southern end of the state. Still a young man at twenty-five, free of obligations, Big Mike applied and was soon employed as foreman for a work crew along the main line. Construction was rapid; with completion, Big Mike simply transferred from construction to brakeman. It was while working in the yards at Cairo that Mike committed the only real crime of his life—if it really was a crime. It happened this way:

The yard foreman, the man charged with getting the cars strung together and ready for the engine and tender to back up, couple up, and steam away, was a mean, gruff, heartless bulldozer who would admit of no excuses. Big Mike's friend, Kyle Webster, came up sick one morning.

"Don't make him work today. I'm afraid he may have typhoid fever," Big Mike told the foreman.

"You run back to the boarding house and tell Webster that if he isn't here in fifteen minutes, he's fired," the yard foreman ordered, and Big Mike complied. When he faced Webster, still in bed, his face flushed and clearly feverish, Big Mike said, "Never mind, Kyle. I'll just tell the yard foreman that you really are sick."

"No. Don't bother. I'm all right," replied the sick man, getting unsteadily out of bed. "Go back and tell him I'll be on duty in fifteen minutes. Go on, now."

Big Mike always regretted that he had let Kyle Webster come to work. He returned and informed the foreman, who replied with an oath about damned goldbrickers. And the task of coupling freight cars got under way.

In the 1850s it was dangerous work. The brakeman coupled and uncoupled the cars. He stood on one end of the car and waited, holding a link and pin, for the next car to approach. He had to measure its speed and at the proper instant guide the link into the socket and, at an even more precise instant, drop in the pin. If the moments chosen for these acts were wrong, then the pin would have to be pounded into the link and the initial failure warranted a dressing down from the foreman.

But there was a worse possible result. If the brakeman had not concentrated on his task, fingers, a hand, or even an arm could be caught in the hardware of the couplers resulting in severed or crushed fingers, a mangled hand, or a broken and shattered arm. The pain was so great that often the poor fellow lost his footing, fell beneath the wheels, and was decapitated.

That is what happened to sick Kyle Webster that day in 1859. Big Mike always thought it was the simplest of distractions: two dogs running rapidly toward the moving cars. One quick glance, one moment's diversion—but the sick man was in no condition to be where he was, doing what he was supposed to do. The freight car rolled down the track to where Kyle was waiting, pinning his entire right arm between the couplers. Kyle screamed in agony, screamed so loud that Big Mike looked up from where he was standing at a switch and watched, in motion so slow it registered permanently on his mind, as Kyle Webster fell between the two moving cars and was cut in half at the hips. When others reached him, he was already dead.

The foreman came running up to where the dead man lay. "Damned fool," he said. "He knew he should be concentrating on his work." There was a pause. "Hey, Gus. Get on my horse and go fetch an ambulance. The rest of you guys, get back to work. This freight is supposed to be out of the yards by two p.m."

"Wait a minute," said Big Mike, facing the foreman. "You sonofabitch! I told you this morning that Webster was sick and you made him come to work. This is your fault, you bastard, and I'm goin' to beat you to a pulp. I'm goin' to teach you a lesson ye'll never forget."

A crowd of men formed a circle. The corpse of poor Kyle Webster was forgotten. The foreman replied, "We'll just see who's goin' to be taught a lesson, you Irish bastard. You've been askin' for this for a long time." He was every bit as tall and muscular as Big Mike.

The two circled each other twice then Big Mike struck at his face with all the power in his right arm. The foreman gasped and fell, paused with his hand over his mouth, then quickly reached for Big Mike's ankles, pulling him down. In an instant he was on top of Big Mike, pummeling him with all the strength in his body. But Big Mike forced the two to roll over and at one point wrenched himself free, jumped up, and stood far enough away so his adversary could not grab his ankles again.

"Get up! Get up!" taunted Big Mike.

The foreman squatted then threw dirt in Big Mike's face, at the same time jumping the Irishman. He grabbed Big Mike around the neck and pressed a thumb into his jugular. Big Mike reacted by striking the foreman's chest, but he could not break the grip. Finally he hurled both to the ground and the grip was broken. Again they rolled over and over, by now close to the tracks. At one time the foreman had Big Mike against a tie and was knocking his head again and again against the wood and a spike that stuck out of it.

The crowd sensed the bloody fury of the fight. "Come on, Big Mike!" some yelled. "Hit the bastard!" others shouted.

Big Mike rolled again, broke away, and again jumped to his feet, blood streaming from the back of his head. They faced off once again. The foreman had grabbed a loose tie spike, a piece of black iron about six inches long. He held it like a dagger. Suddenly the foreman took the offensive, striking with the spike. It slashed across Big Mike's chest, tearing his shirt and bringing blood. And it hurt. Big Mike knew now that he was fighting for his very life, and consequences about anything he might do to save himself never entered his mind.

Mike stayed his distance. Like gladiators, the two stalked one another in a circle. Then Big Mike made a grab for the foreman's arm, catching it just as the spike was headed for Mike's head. Before the arm was deflected, the spike had scraped his scalp, bringing blood flowing down over Mike's forehead, into his eyebrows, entering and dimming his eyes.

But Big Mike had a few tricks too. He tripped his adversary and the two fell, this time across the tracks. Suddenly Big Mike was on top of the foreman and without realizing his actions, was slamming the man's head against a steel rail. Wham, wham, wham! Through his bloodied eyes he could see that his opponent was no longer fighting. Next thing he knew, the crowd was silent and strong hands were pulling him off the foreman. Dripping blood, Big Mike stood looking down on the prostrate form.

One of the men in the crowd leaned over the foreman, who lay with his head on a rail, and took his pulse. Then he inserted his hand inside his shirt. "He's dead," he said simply.

Big Mike was wiping blood from his forehead, trying to clear his eyes. He could feel blood dripping down his back, feel the blood from his chest saturating his shirt. Dimly he witnessed the arrival of a horse-drawn hearse. Suddenly he felt sick. As he watched his friend Kyle Webster, in two pieces, lifted onto a piece of canvas, he began retching. He turned away from the crowd and the activity and the voices, and vomited onto the grass. When he turned his face again to the crowd, he saw the foreman likewise loaded into the black hearse, heard the mortician "kick-kick" his horses and drive away.

And Big Mike started running. He did not know where he was going, but he wanted to get out of sight of the terrible events of which he had been a part. At first he ran just to run, but as his head cleared he began thinking of what he had done—killed a man—and the probability of incarceration or even the hangman's noose. It was just mid-morning, and he was sure to be seen with his torn and bloody clothes, his bruised and lacerated face, his matted hair. He found a vacant warehouse along the tracks south of town, and there he hid until night.

Although he knew the Pinkertons would be searching for him, he nevertheless hopped a freight train headed west, jumping off before it entered railroad yards where searches would be made. He remained free. Within two days he was in St. Louis. There he obtained work as a stevedore on a Missouri River riverboat headed for Westport. His aim all along had been to get beyond the railroads, beyond the reach of railroad detectives. From Westport he hitched on with a wagon train headed for the Pike's Peak mines. That was how he got into the mining business. He learned placers and how to build cradles then took employment with a hard-rock mining company that was sinking a shaft.

Big Mike Mitchell became an experienced miner. But he was restless. He drifted from one mining camp to another. In time he arrived at Muddy Creek, where he took employment at Jack Langford's Sunnyside Mine. He batched in a snug cabin with three young Irishmen from the Old Country who also worked at the mine. And that brought him to Christmas Eve, 1865.

Big Mike's reminiscences halted abruptly as a dog barked wildly and another little frame of yellow light showed him that he had arrived at Ebenezer Cotton's cabin. In the darkness he could make out the shed and, very faintly, the forms of the outhouses the carpenter was building. The dog, some kind of shaggy cur, barked and showed its fangs so malevolently that Big Mike decided not to try making it to the door. Instead he yelled, "Ebenezer Cotton! It's Big Mike Mitchell! Can I talk with ye a minute? On business."

The door opened. Eb's form appeared. "What in tarnation do ye want of me on Christmas Eve?" he asked.

"I want to borrow one of yer new outhouses," replied Big Mike.

"You what?" replied Eb Cotton. "Mike, are you drunk? Go use the woods. My outhouses aren't for rent." He paused then added, "Come on in and let's talk this over. Caesar, shut up!" He held the dog by the scruff of its neck as Big Mike entered the single-room cabin.

"Sit down, Mike," the Yankee carpenter said as he closed the door. A fire blazed in the fireplace. "I've just started to eat. You hungry? I've got a pot of pork and beans and some sourdough biscuits, and some coffee."

"Thanks," replied Big Mike, loosening his coat. "But, Eb, I haven't much time."

Ebenezer Cotton sat down and continued eating his meal. "Now," he began between mouthfuls, "what's this about you wantin' one of these here outhouses of mine?"

"Not to buy," said Big Mike.

"Well, that's what I build 'em for," grumbled Eb. "Ain't too much work for a carpenter in the cold of winter, so I put together outhouses when I'm not workin' elsewhere. Muddy Creek's gettin' civilized and sophisticated, you know. People don't like goin' into the woods to squat. I've sold five of 'em already, at ten dollars each. It's keepin' me in grub." He wiped his narrow, craggy face with a hand then wiped the hand on his pants. "Now, what's this you want?"

"I'm wonderin' if you've got an unfinished outhouse we could use as a confessional at the Catholic church," Big Mike blurted out, looking as dead serious as he could.

"What Catholic church? There ain't no Catholic church in Muddy Creek. Ain't no church at all, last I heard."

"A Jesuit priest came into town this afternoon and got Reece's Music Hall for Midnight Mass," explained Big Mike. "And in making the hall into a church, we need a confessional."

Suddenly Ebenezer Cotton saw the light. He was from Maine, where French Canadians—devout Catholics—were prevalent. Slowly he began to nod his head. "I think I see," he said. "You ain't planning on putting one of my outhouses just outside the side exit, are you? Fer a confessional?"

Big Mike's face lit up. "Exactly," he said. "You ain't a Catholic, so let me tell you, Eb, we good Catholics don't go to communion on Christmas Eve without first purging our sins by goin' to confession."

Ebenezer Cotton roared. He slapped a hand on his leg. "Well, I'll be! One of my outhouses used as a confessional. Ain't that a story?"

The two, and the dog, stepped outside and walked toward a unit that was larger than the others. "This here's been bought by one of the saloons," Eb said. "It's a three-holer. Just right for your needs." He looked it over. "No problem installin' a couple of kneelers." Eb headed for a pile of lumber. He grabbed a saw. "And I can easily make a two- or three-inch by six-inch scrolled opening for you sinners to speak through. And a seat for the padre is no problem at all."

"How soon?" Big Mike asked apprehensively.

"With your help," Eb replied, "in a half hour."

"And—er—how much?"

The Yankee carpenter waved a hand. "Nothin'," he replied. "My Christmas present to ye." Ebenezer paused and pulled on his beard. "Maybe," he mused, "if the padre stays here, he'd like to buy this here confessional we're about to make. And—er—would your padre mind if an old Yankee Puritan attends your services?"

Big Mike assured him that indeed a thin-nosed, hatchet-faced Yankee Congregationalist was more than welcome at midnight services.

Ebenezer Cotton sawed and pounded and measured and fitted. Within a half hour he and Big Mike stood off and appraised their creation. "Me manufacturin' confessionals," guffawed Ebenezer, "on Christmas Eve." He roared again and slapped his leg.

"Now we've got to get it to church," said Big Mike. "Simple," explained the carpenter, heading for the little barn close by from which Big Mike had heard whinnies. "We'll just hitch up old dobbin to the stone boat and have her haul the outhouse—er—confessional to the saloon—er—church."

And that is how it came to pass that, a little after 10:00 p.m., Christmas Eve, 1865, in Muddy Creek, Montana Territory, sojourners observed an outhouse-cum-confessional mounted on a Yankee stone boat pulled by a work horse moving up the frozen Main Street toward Reece's Music Hall. Leaning on the building was Big Mike Mitchell, exchanging ribald comments with the onlookers. Willing hands hoisted it onto the platform outside the side entrance. People long after remembered the young Jesuit priest, who had just donned his vestments, stepping outside and, observing the structure, looking heavenward—for approval? For strength? For thanks? Then laughing with them all, and then taking his place in the center, ready to hear confessions.

IX

Big Mike started to enter the niche to the padre's right, but a bearded, overweight miner with a thick brogue tried to shove him aside. "Me first," he announced as a line formed along the wall inside Reece's.

"Oh, no ye don't," Big Mike bellowed threateningly. "I had the idee and, begorra, I'm the sinner what needs the most savin'."

Big Mike won. With great dignity he removed his floppy old felt hat, entered the tiny compartment, knelt awkwardly facing the padre through the little partition, and slammed the door on those waiting outside. It was dark inside, and cold. For long moments Big Mike contemplated all he must confess. He shivered.

Finally, he breathed deeply. His persona adjusted from the tough, authoritative, aggressive Big Mike Mitchell to meek sinner, full of contrition. In spite of the cold, he was perspiring. Inadvertently he reached inside his coat for the whiskey bottle someone had tossed him as he rode up the street on the stone boat. With a thuck he uncorked it and took a big swig.

"Yes, my son," said the padre finally, realizing that it was well past ten o'clock and there were quite a few more good Catholics waiting to confess their sins before Midnight Mass.

Big Mike lowered his eyes. He frowned and breathed heavily. "Forgive me, Father," he began, speaking just above a whisper, "for I have sinned." He paused. "Jeeesus Ceehrist, have I sinned!"

"Oh, my goodness," came from the other side of the partition. "Do not take the Lord's name in vain, my son."

"I ain't," replied Big Mike meekly. The padre heard another thuck and a gurgle; he realized his sinner was taking another swig. Then, without thinking, Big Mike held the bottle to the scrolled opening. "Here, Padre, open the scroll and take a swig or two. Yer gonna need it 'fore I'm through confessin' all I've done." Big Mike sobbed. "It's been—my God—it's been years since I was at confession, Padre."

Father de Mara refused the swig of whiskey. "No need for that," he said, voicing irritation. "I am a priest empowered to forgive. Now let's get started. Others are waiting."

"Sure are, and it's cold out here," came a voice from the niche on the other side.

Fifteen minutes later Big Mike Mitchell opened the confessional door and then the door to the hall. His face was childlike, as if he were a grown innocent.

"What took so long?" asked an exasperated Catholic. "You think the rest of us have been livin' in a monastery these last few years? We got sins to ask fergiveness for too, you know."

"Sorry, boys," replied Big Mike. "But I doubt if any of you have my list of sins. Here, take a swig of this afore ye go in. It'll loosen yer tongues." He tossed the whiskey bottle to one of the men standing in line and walked away.

While Big Mike Mitchell was fetching the confessional and, one might say, breaking it in, Pat Shanahan was making his way once again to Gunter Schroeder's cabin.

As Pat contemplated how to approach him, he wondered what the good-hearted teamster had been doing in the brief interval that had elapsed since bringing the loaded wagon back to his cabin. What was his mood going to be? It could make a difference in how Pat approached him.

After he had contributed his wagon, oxen, and himself to store the Music Hall furnishings, Schroeder had sat down at the table to carve, but the spirit was lacking. Then he had fetched a German language Bible, put on his reading glasses, and turned to the Christmas story as related by Matthew, Mark, Luke, and John. Memories of happier days, plus the whiskey, led Gunter to pause from his reading and evaluate his life: where he had once been, how he came to be at Muddy Creek, and what of his future. For several years he had been quite contented, but as he approached middle age, he had begun to contemplate his future. No longer was he happy with his place in life.

When he had worked for Russell, Majors, and Waddell, he had had plenty of friends. Although they had respected his privacy, they had looked to him for counsel when they had troubles. Becoming an independent freighter had perforce cut out his social life; he had become a loner. He missed the conviviality of the wagon train, the men around the campfires at night, the communal cooperation that was necessary if a wagon train was to reach its destination safely and on time. Surely those years were among the happiest of his life.

Things had changed when he became an independent freighter. The job was lucrative but lonely. Something was missing. Although he valued his privacy, he yearned for society, for being among men. He craved religious and philosophical conversation, sadly lacking on the American frontier. Sometimes, trudging along the lonely western trails, he contemplated returning to Erlangen. Seventeen years' absence, though—what would it be like there? At first he saw himself smoking his meerschaum with a stein of foaming German beer in *das Bierhaus*, talking for hours with his friends. But then he faced reality: the friends he pictured were young men in their early twenties. Now they were dead, or married, or imprisoned, or had gone elsewhere. "Ach," he would tell himself, "to go home–vat vould I find?" And he would nod his head sadly. "It vould never vork. I vould just be more depressed."

And what of Gunter Schroeder? What was to become of him? Here he was, a lone German, forty years old, no relatives in America, on the Montana frontier. A month ago he had slipped and nearly fallen under the wheels of his J. Murphy. The incident had caused him to think, as he was thinking this Christmas Eve, of the precariousness of life, of where he was going and of his fate. Was he to be a lone freighter all his life? Once he had been a bright student interested in the Lutheran clergy. Must he forever put aside those ambitions of his youth?

He had contemplated making a bold change. But it was so drastic, its success so questionable, what it could mean to the rest of his life so extreme, that months had blended into years, and he had done nothing. Now, when the knock came at his door, he was thinking about it all again, feeling "in his cups" with the warm whiskey and the crackling fire.

He knew he sounded grumpy when he answered, "Who iss it? Zee door iss unlocked." When the door opened and he saw who it was, he remained grumpy. "Vat you vant now? I've done all I'm going to do for you."

Pat stepped in. The first thing he noticed was the German Bible and the whiskey jug on the table, then Schroeder wearing glasses. A good sign, Pat thought.

"Mr. Schroeder," Pat began, shutting the door, "the padre asked me to invite you to Midnight Mass. He thanks you for the loan of your wagon."

"Ach. Forget it. And he has already thanked me for the wagon and invited me. Remember. I am a Lutheran."

"I know, Mr. Schroeder," said Pat awkwardly, "but where is the Lutheran service in Muddy Creek?"

The German raised his hands. "You know ze answer. There isn't any man of ze cloth here but ze priest. Ok. Just don't ask me to become a Catholic."

"No one is asking you to become a Catholic."

"Ach. Ze Jesuit. He vould."

"No, he would not," Pat replied firmly. "Jesuits don't work that way. Especially not this one. He will welcome you and a whole lot of other non-Catholics, because all of us believe in Jesus Christ and celebrate His birth on this night the same way, with praise and joy."

"Hmphh."

"Really, sir. Jesse Tinsley will probably be there. I'm sure Jack Langford will attend. I know they're not Catholics. Julie, the little taxi dancer, is helping decorate the hall. She's not a Catholic, but she'll be there. Hell, Mr. Schroeder, most of this town ain't Catholic, but I swear, most of this town is going to attend Midnight Mass."

Schroeder rose and went to the fire, lit a splinter, and with it lighted his pipe. He threw the splinter back into the fire.

"Please come, Mr. Schroeder," Pat pleaded. "Otherwise, for you, it's just another winter's night in Montana."

Schroeder stood smoking and rocking back and forth on his heels. Finally he removed his pipe from his mouth. "I'll—tink about it," he said.

Pat Shanahan smiled. "Of course," he added, "that is not why I came here."

"No?"

"I'm going to ask another favor of you, sir. See, Jesse Tinsley loaned us a big wooden packing box and we've made a manger of it. Mrs. Lancaster has lent some baby blankets but we don't have any figures—you know, sheep, maybe a donkey, the three wise men, and the camels, Mary and Joseph. And I was thinking, Mr. Schroeder—you are an expert woodcarver." Pat looked at the crucifix on the mantle, "and I wondered if, well, Mr. Schroeder, don't you have carvings of the nativity scene?"

"Ach. I am just an amateur," he replied, but his voice was softer, his pride piqued. After a moment he strode to a corner where two big burlap sacks were stored. He reached into one and withdrew from it something enveloped in a flannel rag. Returning to the table, he began unwrapping it. Pat watched in silence as the last of the cloth was removed, revealing a beautifully carved camel.

"Do you tink dis is gut enough?" asked the German as he handed it to Pat.

"Beautiful," was all Pat could say, for the camel was meticulously carved.

"Vell, I haf t'ree camels, t'ree wise men, Mary and Joseph, four sheep, and two donkeys," Schroeder said with rising pride. "Vat I don't haf is ze Christ child."

In awe Pat examined each piece as Schroeder unwound the cloth protecting it. "Never mind what you don't have," said Pat. "Mr. Schroeder, could you lend these to the church for the nativity scene? Just for tonight?"

Schroeder silently went about rewrapping, with tender loving care, his carved figures. He smoked.

"If only you would," pleaded Pat. "You could attend Mass and gather them up afterwards. I promise to help you return them to the cabin."

Schroeder puffed deeply and blew out more smoke. "Should I?" he asked himself. A thought flitted through his mind. "If I were a Lutheran minister, I would be setting up a nativity scene for my own church." Then another thought struck him: "But this is a Catholic church. My parents and grandparents and great-grandparents would be spinning in their graves!" Then he thought of what the young Irishman had said, that everyone celebrated the birth of Christ; that this was America, not Europe, not the Old Country.

He gazed at the intense young Irishman who was standing by the table, examining the carvings. "I'll need your help to bring them to ze Music Hall," he said. "Ve can each carry a bag. But ve must ve careful. Ze wood breaks easily."

"And can we borrow the crucifix too?" asked Pat, walking toward the mantel.

"Of course."

Pat Shanahan and Gunter Schroeder appeared at the swinging doors of Reece's Music Hall-cum-church on Christmas Eve, 1865, each carrying over a shoulder a big burlap bag. Gunter entered the hall behind Pat and stopped short, amazed at the transformation. His eyes fixed on the empty manger where only the swaddling clothes, rolled and arranged as if there was a baby within, lay on the hay. No sheep, donkeys, camels, wise men, or human figures were present.

"Some manger," Gunter commented. "Yah, I agree vit you. It does need some figures."

Carefully, so they would not bump the sacks and risk breaking the carvings, Pat and Gunter made their way up the center aisle to the manger. Willing hands took the beautiful crucifix from Pat's hands while others suggested a way of hanging it above the altar, a task that was shortly completed. Julie appeared, and she and Pat and a few onlookers not in line for confession watched as the German freighter carefully removed bundles from the sacks and painstakingly unwrapped each one. As he undid them people gasped with surprise. First came one, then two, finally three camels, carved scrupulously in detail down to the single hump.

"Zeese are dromedaries," commented Gunter, "single-humped camels. Dey are ze ones ze t'ree wise men rode to ze Christ child's birthplace." He handed each one to Julie, who was kneeling beside him. "You place zem in ze manger, Miss."

In time the teamster-woodcarver had unwrapped, with great care, the three wise men, four sheep, two donkeys, and Mary and Joseph.

"Isn't it fortunate," Pat commented, "that they are almost to scale with the manger?"

"Yah. Dat is very gut," Gunter agreed. "Too bad, though. I have never carved ze Christ child."

"People will think the infant Jesus is wrapped in the swaddling clothes," said Pat optimistically. "He would be asleep anyway."

"But—it just isn't right," Julie commented quietly. The placing of the figures finished, all rose and went to other parts of the room, but Julie remained, thinking.

Teague Cosgrove came up to Boyd O'Connor and Pat Shanahan. "You know what's missing?" he began. "Among other things, a church bell."

"We don't need one," replied Boyd, "everyone in Muddy Creek knows about this conversion of Reece's into a church."

"We need a church bell," repeated Teague. "What's a church without a bell?"

Just then Big Mike strolled up. "Hello, boys. Ain't ye goin' to confession? 'Tis good for the soul, ye know."

Teague Cosgrove glanced at the sinners waiting in line, then pulled his gold watch from his tattered vest (for he and others had made a quick trip to their cabins to put on their best clothes, shabby as they were). He said that the line was too long. "I'm goin' to wait," he said. "I'm hopin' the padre stays here a few days at least, and I'll get to confession before he leaves. Now as I was sayin'," he began again, "I think the church needs a bell. Boyd and Pat disagree, but I want a bell."

"Of course we need a bell," Big Mike agreed.

"And I know where there is one," said Teague. "It would do for tonight."

"The fire bell!" exclaimed Boyd O'Connor.

"Of course," Teague replied. "The four of us could fetch it and place it in front of the hall, and we could summon all of Muddy Creek to services."

No sooner was the suggestion made than the four Irishmen were out the doors and on their way up the street to the firehouse. Big Mike scanned the sky as he buttoned his coat. "Look," he commented, "the squall's blown over. The wind's died down. And the sky, boys. Did you ever see more beautiful, star-studded heavens than what's above us right now?"

"Perfect for Christmas Eve," added Pat.

As they trudged along the street, Pat thought of all the things that had happened in his young life since he, Boyd O'Connor, and Teague Cosgrove left County Mayo in June 1863. For Pat, the least robust and the youngest of the three at age twenty-one (although the oldest was just twenty-four), it had been an act of incredible courage. The young men, friends since childhood, had been talking in a pub one day about how there was so little future for them in Ireland. Not one of them liked farming, yet that was the only occupation open to them. They had all known others who had left for America and had written glowing letters about their lives in the new country.

Plans were made. Quietly they pooled their meager resources for nearly a year, and finally, hearing of the cost of steerage from Liverpool to New York City and figuring they had amassed sufficient funds—just sufficient funds—they had announced their intentions. Long had been the lamentations, and most severe had been the strain on Pat, younger by three years than Boyd and two years by Teague. His parents protested vehemently but Pat was adamant.

"If ye're goin' to go, Pat, then hold to yer faith, always be good, and stay away from whiskey," counseled his mother.

For the three of them, the journey to Muddy Creek was a lesson in growing up, a brutal introduction to the real world, and a rite of passage such as they would never have wished upon anyone. When they reached Liverpool, their queries of how to get to the wharves took them into the city's worst slums. They had been lucky keeping their precious funds intact. Finally they reached the wharf just as the *General Blount* was about the sail for New York. Steerage cost them each twenty dollars. So crowded was it with immigrants that they were wishing for voyage's end even before the great side paddle wheels began turning. Fortunately they were sailing in June, for in inclement weather the portholes were closed. Lord knows, the air was foul enough! More, people got seasick. Pat was convinced that the sour smell of vomit would never leave his nostrils. And if it did, the sickening odor of the privy would take its place. The crying babes, the irritability of husbands and wives, the complaints of older children, and the snoring of hundreds of people crowded together would forevermore in his life be there to disturb his memories.

After seventeen days, the *General Blount* sailed into New York harbor; it was July 13, 1863. Pat had picked up an itch which bothered him until he reached Montana a year later. All three felt weakened by the ordeal, but memories of the voyage would soon be crowded out by other images that quickly impressed upon their minds.

They had been warned to be careful. "You know, there's a Civil War in America. You boys watch your step when you step off the gangplank. Maybe there'll be some Yankee recruiters all set to swear you into Uncle Sam's army and march you off to war!" Another warning was to be on guard for labor recruiters. "You'll hardly get off the boat before they'll be approaching you. Free transportation to Pittsburgh to work in the iron mills. A free trip to Scranton, Pennsylvania, to work in the coal mines."

The three young immigrants listened and kept their plans to themselves. Their common dream was to go west, to the American frontier. This was what they had read about in Ireland, and this was the America they yearned to see.

As the ship docked that hot July day, the sight of New York City was marred by great clouds of black smoke arising from more than a dozen points in their view. "What is it?" the passengers asked. "Does New York always look this way?"

A newspaper boy ahead of his competition rowed out to the ship, climbed a ladder, and was selling the *New York World* to all who would pay. The headlines gave the answer: CITY IN HANDS OF MOB.

Pat, Teague, and Boyd purchased a copy and read the stories. The troubles had arisen because of a new conscription law. Orders had come to compile lists of eligible men and then, as in a lottery, choose names deposited in a huge wheel, up to the quota assigned to each ward.

To the three Irish boys this did not appear too drastic. Like most immigrants, they considered the United States of America the last best hope of the world. To Pat, Teague, and Boyd, the rebellion of the South was a threat to this last best hope, and the Union side in the Civil War was entirely justified. But they read on: Congress, in its infinite wisdom, had included a proviso: pay the government $300 and be exempt from the draft. The rich could do that, the poor could not, and this appeared to be the cause of the troubles.

The protests began in New York City's crowded slums, especially around sections known as Five Points and Mulberry Bend, where people were cramped into warrens of sin, poverty, and crime. The boys were not aware that these were also concentrations of the immigrant Irish, most of whom had come prior to 1863. How were Pat, Teague, and Boyd to know that racial tensions between the Irish and the Negroes were running high that summer? They could count the number of Negroes they had seen in their entire lives on five fingers! And after all, they knew hardly anything about New York City, except that it was enormous and full of brethren from the Emerald Isle.

The three looked to each other, searching for support. What should they do? Teague had the address of an uncle. Their plan was to find him in hopes that he could help them find temporary work. By pooling their funds and batching, they hoped to accumulate enough money within weeks to purchase their way west. Their plans had not envisioned landing in a city rent with armed mobs, lynching, and arson. Dared they disembark into such a frightening situation?

The ship docked, the gangplank was lowered. The boys hated the vessel. Perhaps that was why their better judgment left them, and they disembarked. They lifted their bags and a bundle of bedding and, looking like a million immigrants before and after them, with their sea legs making them walk like drunks, they sauntered down the gangplank.

Teague checked his uncle's address and asked a passing New Yorker for directions. The native glanced at the young men then gave directions too complex to follow. The trio nodded affirmatively then began walking in the initial direction given. After all, they could inquire again and again until they reached their destination.

For a few blocks all seemed normal. But the young men's trepidation rose as they made their way into the city. Here was a street devoid of humanity, but littered with building stones, bricks, clubs, and clots of dried blood on the cobblestones. Tramway rails had been pulled up and thrown aside. Several dead horses lay in the streets and two or three freight wagons were turned over, their contents spilled out but obviously ransacked. Houses sported broken windows; stores were closed.

What bothered Pat, Teague, and Boyd was the realization that their direction was taking them toward a big plume of smoke. Now they heard sounds, not of horses or coaches and wagons and people going about their normal activities, but a human-made rumble of unmistakable hatred, obscenities, shouts from what seemed like thousands of people. They reached an intersection and there, advancing toward them, from building wall on one side of the street to building wall on the other, was a mass of male and female humanity. Big, burly men, most of them young fellows, were leading the mob, marching, then turning to it and shouting, urging it on. Women as well as men were wielding clubs, axes, hammers, stones, bricks, pistols, and rifles. A tattered sheet held up by several mob members bore the words: NO DRAFT.

The three young Irishmen halted, not sure what to do. Their hesitation cost them. Before they could whirl around and retreat, elements of the mob had surrounded them. Suddenly they were a part of the rioters and had no choice but to be carried along with them, up a street and in a direction at right angles to where they had been heading. Their possessions were torn from their hands. As one, they realized that if they did not join in the mob's enthusiasm, then their own lives were in jeopardy. NO DRAFT, tramp, tramp, tramp, NO DRAFT, tramp, tramp, tramp, NO DRAFT, the mob shouted. When it reached a construction site, the marchers halted while leaders yelled at the workers, demanding that they join. Almost always the workers dropped their tools and mingled with the rioters. Once or twice a foreman protested, only to be threatened, even beaten into submission.

Pat, Teague, and Boyd were in a state of shock. They had lost their worldly possessions and were in the midst of a rampaging mob several thousand strong, being pulled, pushed, and at times almost carried on the crest of a human wave. Looking around him, Pat observed disheveled women, some young, some middle-aged, and some even old, some holding tightly to babes in arms, some with dresses torn and breasts exposed, shouting like demons, waving their arms in defiance: NO DRAFT.

"Lock arms so we don't get separated," Boyd ordered early on. The three did just that, and were forever thankful. The crowd turned down another street and soon appeared before a nondescript building that, it turned out, was the Broadway draft office. The crowd was soon massed before the front doors. They were protected by perhaps a dozen helmeted, blue-clad policemen brandishing night sticks. The brawny man leading the mob—they were members of a voluntary fire unit dubbed the Black Joke—quickly dispensed with them, although the policemen fought valiantly and laid low more than a few of the toughs before they were overwhelmed.

Soon the entrance was broken down and the mob swarmed inside. It sought out the draft wheel and destroyed it, pursued the building's occupants out a back door, and then set fire to the premises. Pat and his two compatriots headed for the rear entrance and, once outside, noticing that the mob had spread out, ran as fast as their legs could carry them to get away from the mayhem. When they paused on an empty street and glanced back, they saw black smoke pouring from the building. They later learned that the entire city block had been set ablaze and when firemen arrived, the rioters had refused to let them battle the flames.

"Blimey. So this is America," exclaimed Boyd.

"Our belongings—they're all gone!" mourned Pat.

"I know," said Teague. "We are alone in a strange city that's in a state of anarchy."

Again they heard the sounds of the mob. Again they were swept along with it. This time the destination was the Seventh Avenue Armory. A repetition of the events at the draft office took place: the police defense crumbled and the armory was entered.

"We don't want to go in there," Boyd yelled to Pat and Teague. "Let's ease to the edge of the mob."

Which, with considerable courage and lots of curses from the mob, they succeeded in doing. As they edged toward a side street they saw flames licking out of the armory windows. An unmistakable sickening change took place in the sounds coming from the shouting rioters. Hysterical shrieks replaced vengeful obscenities. The boys grabbed a last view of the burning building. They witnessed rioters jumping to their deaths from third-story windows because the fire had spread through the first two floors and smoke was engulfing the third. There was a loud, sickening WHOOM. Before their eyes the third story and its outer walls simply disappeared into the first two stories. The young immigrants heard screams of agony and pain, shouts of "Oh, my God!" as they realized that scores, possibly fifty or a hundred or even several hundred rioters had occupied the third floor; now they were being burned, asphyxiated, and crushed to death.

"Let's get out of here!" the three said in unison. They darted down the side street amidst running rioters, rounded a corner and—out of an alleyway flowed another mob. This one was more bedraggled than the others; if possible, it was meaner, dirtier, more vicious.

"Get the niggers," these rioters chanted over and over again.

The three young immigrants, once more caught up in the mass, exchanged glances. What about the draft? For it was clear that this mob was not thinking about the draft. It was a racist mob after Negroes. Down into a cheaper, seamier part of the city streamed the rabble, gathering strength and partisans as it went. It flowed like a deluge into an impoverished neighborhood of broken-down wooden shacks. The leaders, one of them a huge, one-armed brute brandishing a club that a prehistoric man would have had difficulty wielding—but which this thug handled with dexterity—spotted a black man. Others ran to catch him as he fled into a small, dilapidated house and slammed the door. The mob halted, the man with the club marched forward, and with one violent kick, burst open the door. Leaders of the mob swept inside and in seconds dragged out a protesting Negro. Just as they got him centered in front of the mob, Pat watched, horrified, as the one-armed leader swung his club directly on top of the fellow's head. Pat thought he heard a sickening crunch of breaking bone. The man collapsed like a jumping jack.

They were not through with their dead victim. Leaders tied a rope around the corpse's neck. Before the rope was swung over a tree, women—if they could be called that— ripped off his clothes and took turns stabbing the corpse with knives. Someone appeared with a kerosene can and doused the corpse. Then, just as it was lifted into the air, it was set afire.

Horrified, Pat, Teague, and Boyd turned away and began again working toward the edge of the mob. Finally they were free, dashing down a side street. At one point they had a view of the New York skyline. In every direction were clouds of black smoke. In rising and falling waves they heard the shouts of angry voices. New York City was in the hands of the rioters.

Eventually they found their way back to the wharves, and on a quiet side street they sat down at the curb. All the stores were closed. "Let's forget about your uncle and just get out of here," Teague suggested.

A well-dressed man appeared as if from nowhere and eyed them perceptively. "You fellow don't look like rioters," he said.

The three looked up at the middle-aged, well-dressed man with gray hair showing below a somewhat rumpled hat, and a clipped mustache setting off a cherubic face.

"Begorra, we don't want anything to do with it," replied Teague. "We're just off the ship. Lost everything. Some reception we got."

"What are your plans?" asked the stranger.

"We just want to get out of here," replied Boyd.

"You boys looking for work?"

"Yes, sir," they all replied.

"How'd you like to take employment in the anthracite mines of the beautiful Wyoming Valley of Pennsylvania?" he asked.

The three exchanged glances. Coal mining had not been their aim, and in fact they had been warned to avoid being recruited for such work. After all, their aim was to go west. But how? They were destitute except for what was on their backs. In mutual agreement, Boyd acted as their spokesman and said, "We'd like it. Anything to get us out of New York."

"OK, boys," said the man. "Follow me and I'll have you out of New York City and on a train bound for Scranton, Pennsylvania, before nightfall."

After the horrors they had witnessed, the subsequent events of the day were always hazy to the young men from the Emerald Isle. Pat recalled riding a carriage to a river bank, a trip across the river into New Jersey, a railroad coach in which, in the hot July weather, cinders from the engine poured onto them, irritating their eyes and dirtying their hair and clothing. He recalled their being met late at night at a railroad station by an authoritarian figure who took them in a rickety coach into a town of drab, identical houses.

The vehicle drew up to one of them and the coachman announced that this was to be their home. "Report for work at the tipple at four o'clock," he said, checking his watch. "That's just two hours from now."

Thus, within two days after landing in New York City, Pat, Boyd, and Teague were workers in the anthracite mines of Pennsylvania's Wyoming Valley. They learned quickly, partly because they were young and intelligent, partly because they had to.

There they remained through the rest of 1863 and into the winter and early spring of 1864. But they hated it. The work was hard, twelve full hours a day in the pits, and often they had to work on Sundays. Worse still, they were not paid in American currency but in company script. This they used to pay their rent on the hovel the company called housing; it also was the currency used to purchase groceries, clothing, and anything else they wanted at the company store. Pat, the slimmest and youngest of the three, developed a nagging cough, and even though he was given a job on the outside running the hoist, his two companions fretted about his health.

"I promised his parents we'd take good care of him," Teague told Boyd. "I think we better get out of here before he really gets sick."

"Before we all get sick," added Boyd.

Moreover, it was clear to the young men that they were being mercilessly exploited. Hardly a day passed without some kind of accident in the mines where safety was secondary to production. Employees who were hurt were escorted off the premises and told not to return—no workmen's compensation, no two week's notice, nothing. Other employees were aware of it too; in fact, it was clear to the three that in time there was going to be violence in the coal fields.

"We've got to get out of here," stressed Boyd. "I really mean it. We've *got* to get out of here!"

"We're broke," replied Teague. "We're just paid in company script. Once we get off the premises, we're paupers."

"Thing to do," said Pat, "is to stock up some groceries and catch a freight train some night. By morning when the company whistle blows, we'll be gone."

"But it's a long way to the frontier," countered Boyd.

"We can make it. It's spring. We're all farm boys. And there's a war on. They need farm labor. We should stay as far north as possible to avoid being conscripted, and work our way west," added Boyd.

And so they did. They saved crackers, flour, bacon (already rancid when they bought it with script), and apples. One dark night in April 1864, they crawled under a fence (for the compound was guarded like a prison), ran to the railroad tracks, and caught a west-bound freight. They had timed their escape just right.

From Pennsylvania the three worked their way through Ohio, Indiana, Illinois, and into Iowa. Mostly they worked as agricultural laborers, and they thrived on the outside work in the clear air. Pat felt much better. Twice they narrowly escaped being drafted into the Union Army. And one day in June they found themselves at Council Bluffs, overlooking the mighty Missouri River.

They soon discovered that it was not easy finding employment aboard a Missouri River steamboat headed upriver, so they worked at odd jobs and soon had sufficient funds to purchase deck passage upstream aboard the steamboat *Marias*. By mid-July they were at Fort Benton. There they hitched on as bullwhackers with a wagon train headed for the gold diggings at Last Chance Gulch, today's Helena. Once they arrived there, they met other men from the Emerald Isle and tried their luck at prospecting. Once they almost lost their scalps when a party of Blackfeet rode past them. They hid in a dry gulch below the Indians' path. Then, one night in a saloon, they met Big Mike Mitchell, who was purchasing supplies at the shebang. He told them of the new diggings at Muddy Creek and urged the three to come down with him and try their luck.

They did. Big Mike, it turned out, was the foreman at the Sunnyside Mine. He immediately offered jobs to his three new friends. More, he invited them to move into his cabin where the four could pool their resources and batch.

And, Pat thought as they approached the firehouse, this brought their story nearly a year and a half later to Christmas Eve, 1865, and their requisitioning the fire bell to announce Midnight Mass.

With Big Mike supervising and carrying more than his share of the burden, the bell was quietly hoisted onto the shoulders of four dedicated Irishmen and carried to the front of Reece's Music Hall-cum-church.

"There," said Big Mike finally, slapping his hands together. "When the padre says it's time for church, this town will know."

The four reentered Reece's. It was about 11:00 p.m.

X

In the Music Hall/church, activity was escalating. Father de Mara had dispensed with the good Catholics desiring confession, pushing some of them through hurriedly, for the midnight service was imminent.

Meanwhile, Gunter Schroeder had purchased the biggest candles in stock at a shebang to be fitted into Jesse Tinsley's appropriate candlesticks. The two, Tinsley and Schroeder, were busy working the candles into the holders. When they were firmly in place, they placed them against the wall near the entrance. Acolytes would light them and carry them down the aisle to the altar, where a bucket of sand on either side awaited their placement.

The padre snapped his fingers. Acolytes! He must find some acolytes! Meanwhile, he surveyed the transformed Music Hall and was moderately satisfied. If only there was a religious statue or painting to further decorate the other side of the altar from the nativity scene. And it was sad, noticing that the manger had the camels and wise men and sheep and donkeys and Mary and Joseph, but no Christ child. What a testament it was to the irreligious masculinity of the West, the young priest mused, that in all Muddy Creek a doll was not available to serve as the infant Jesus.

As details flashed through his mind, he wondered if Robert Sungren would succeed in fetching the piano player and the cornetist. He wondered if Mr. Sungren might contribute his voice in leading the mostly masculine congregation in carols. Father de Mara hoped so. Music was necessary at Christmas Mass.

He glanced at his silver watch: 11:15. Mass would start in about a half hour. Already worshipers were straggling in, filling the seats. While most were people he had never seen before, he already recognized a few. He noticed, entering through the swinging doors, Alcalde Luke Bassett and Gus Logan, the bartender temporarily unemployed, both dressed in their best frontier apparel.

Father de Mara advanced quickly to meet them. "I need acolytes," he said. "Do you have any suggestions? Protestants are welcome to attend, but I need Catholic acolytes for the processional: two to carry the candles, another to bear the crucifix, and still another to carry the Bible. One of them might also serve as an altar boy. I'm sorry that I have no vestments for them to wear."

Luke shrugged his shoulders. "Sorry, Padre. I'm a Presbyterian. But Gus—Gus, ain't you a Catholic?"

Gus lowered his head sheepishly. "I reckon," he muttered softly, "but I ain't been to Mass for years and years. I'm goin' to attend, Padre. And maybe I'll become a good Catholic again. But please don't ask me to do anything tonight. You notice, I didn't even go to confession."

Father de Mara understood. Quickly he scanned the room for other candidates. There was Big Mike Mitchell, the man who had killed the yard foreman. The padre's face lighted up. "Mike," he called across the room, "come here a minute."

Quickly Big Mike, his face red with a little too much Christmas cheer, was at the padre's side. "I want you to carry the Bible in the procession."

Big Mike's face turned from concern to joy. "Me, Padre? Begorra, ye don't want me. After all I confessed?"

"Yes, Mike, you," and without awaiting an answer, the padre continued. "Can you suggest three other good Catholics to be acolytes, two to carry the candles up the aisle to the altar, one the crucifix, and suggest one of them to be my altar boy?"

"Easy," Mike replied. "Hey Pat, Boyd, and Teague. Come over here. The padre needs acolytes." He turned to Father de Mara. "They'll do, Father. I know each of 'em. They're good boys. Boyd and Teague are about the same size, so they should carry the candles, and Pat can carry the crucifix and be your altar boy."

"I was an altar boy at St. Patrick's in County Mayo," commented Pat.

So now Father de Mara had his aides for the Mass. As for the four Irishmen, their cups ranneth over. All four thought of home, and how proud their parents would be. As for the priest, he couldn't believe his good fortune at the big fellow carrying the Bible, the two young men of nearly equal physical proportions carrying the candles, and the youngest, Pat, the crucifix. He was so slim and boyish that no one would question his performing the altar boy's tasks.

Meanwhile, down the street near the edge of town at Sang Lee's Chinese Laundry, a pig-tailed son of the Celestial Kingdom gazed out the window into the darkness in the direction of Reece's Music Hall. He had watched the goings-on for several hours. He had heard of the Jesuit's arrival, the shoot-out, and Jack Langford's release of Reece's for Midnight Mass. Sang Lee was pleased. And troubled.

Nervously he tapped his fingers. Should he or shouldn't he? And then he made his decision.

He hurried into the dark back room where he lived and strode directly to a wooden chest with Chinese characters scrolled upon it. He had ordered it months before from San Francisco along with its contents. He lifted the top as hinges squeaked and smelled the aroma of sandalwood. He reached in and came forth with clothing—Chinese clothing. Hastily he disrobed and donned the fresh apparel. Eventually he was dressed to his satisfaction, even including a Chinese cap. He then rushed to a chest of drawers and procured a small, heavily ornamented lacquer box. Sang Lee opened the top to make sure it contained what he wanted. Then, clasping it firmly, he strode out the front entrance and headed down the frozen street toward Reece's Music Hall/church.

Sang Lee breathed deeply of the fresh air. He observed that the squall had blown over, and the sky was star-studded and clear. Often he had stood on the porch in front of his laundry-home and watched the magnificent multicolored beams of the Aurora Borealis wave across the northern sky. He pulled himself up straight as a ramrod and took deliberate, masculine steps. An alien in a foreign land, he still possessed dignity. Muddy Creek was not much like Canton, but at least he was alive in this alien world, making a living, eating well. Sometimes he even contemplated buying a bride in San Francisco and bringing her to Muddy Creek.

As the crystal clear, cold air sharpened his mind, Sang Lee found himself reminiscing and philosophizing about life and the world, and what had brought him to Muddy

Creek. How had he, son of a modest businessman in a little suburb of Canton in China's Pearl River Delta, come to be living in a mining camp in Montana Territory, U.S.A.? It was halfway around the world from his ancestral home. It was populated by foreign devils.

As he advanced toward Reece's, memories flashed through his mind. He saw himself once again as a child in southern China, toddling along a dirt road filled with people, lots of people, his mother holding his hand tightly as they made their way to a tiny structure above which was mounted a cross. This was where a Jesuit missionary, Father Guiseppe Carenci, dispensed the Catholic faith to a small congregation of Chinese converts. Sang Lee was all dressed up; before he and his mother left the tiny church, the little boy had been christened a Catholic.

He grew up, therefore, in a different faith from most of his playmates. Sometimes they teased him for being a disciple of the white man's savior, but in general Sang Lee experienced a happy childhood. Then, as childhood turned to youth and youth projected into young manhood, times turned bad. His father died suddenly, and Sang Lee had to work to help support his mother and younger siblings. More, his extended family looked to him for additional support. Unskilled labor came cheap; Sang Lee was not doing well. One day a family patriarch suggested to him that, with so much filial responsibility, why didn't he do as many other young men did: sign on with what was called the credit-ticket system for employment in lands away from south China? It was a widely practiced procedure. The laborer signed a contract with an entrepreneur who paid his way to the place of work—Malaysia, the Dutch East

Indies, Borneo, the Philippines—and the laborer worked off his passage after which, in theory, he kept his pay, much of which he sent back to his family in China. Eventually the expatriate hoped to return home.

This did not appeal to Sang Lee. He knew people who had signed on, left to work on the rubber and tea plantations, had sent money home, but who, if they returned at all, returned sickly and worn out. They carried home stories of virtual slavery. Some arrived in a different way, their polished bones carefully packed in boxes to be buried in Chinese soil.

But Sang Lee had heard stories of another place, and those stories were far more encouraging. It was about a land thousands of miles to the east, a land called Mei Kwok (Beautiful Land) or Gum San (Land of the Golden Mountains). A few Chinese had returned from there, and they told stories of a moderate climate and good wages. To Sang Lee, this sounded much better than cutting rubber trees in Malaysia. And so, at age eighteen, Sang Lee signed on, the usual credit-ticket system being the financial arrangement. By the time he and the other Chinese with him arrived in San Francisco they were each in debt to a Chinese businessman to the sum of $200.

He recalled the beauty of the Golden Gate and San Francisco as they sailed into the bay one spring morning after a two-month voyage. The air smelled fresh, of green things and moist earth; the temperature was invigorating. Never had he been so optimistic of his future as when he walked awkwardly down the gangplank onto American soil.

But his exhilaration did not last long. For the first several months, Sang Lee saw little of white man's America. As soon as he and his companions debarked they were marched to a dormitory owned by a Chinese entrepreneur. There they found themselves eating Chinese food provided by the businessman; all their talk was still in Chinese. Then one day Sang Lee and a score of others were informed that their place of work had been chosen. They asked not where they were going as they were herded like sheep aboard a river steamer which sailed up the Sacramento River to the town of the same name. Always they were under the intense eyes of the businessman's agents. From Sacramento, Sang Lee and his companions carried their bedding and a basket containing everything else they had taken with them up a trail leading north and east into the Mother Lode country.

One day they were led into a gulch through which flowed a small stream. Brush arbors, tents consisting of little more than a canvas thrown over a rope strung from tree to tree, and a few crude log cabins dotted the narrow, flattish area between the stream and the bluffs. Here a Chinese overseer taught them how to shovel gravel into a long tom cradle, send water racing down its length, and then repeat the process over and over again. Every few hours, sometimes just every day or two, operations changed. The water was diverted while the overseer and trusted aides obtained gold from the cleats in the cradle. This was carefully sacked and sent on the way by a mounted courier to the nearest town.

The Chinese worked hard. They were furnished Chinese food and were allowed time out for tea in mid-morning and mid-afternoon. But after a few weeks they began to ask questions of their overseer. When, they inquired, will we have paid for our tickets to Gum San? They received evasive answers. As the days dragged on and the toilsome work continued, some of the Chinese began to lose heart.

What should they do? What *could* they do? Most of his fellow workers, Sang Lee observed, accepted their predicament. Indeed, they might still have been in China. They were fed Chinese food by their Chinese overseer, sold Chinese clothes by him, lodged by him, worked for him. They knew that if they fled back to San Francisco they would be hunted down by agents of the Chinese capitalists and punished, possibly even killed. And where else could they go?

Sang Lee became bitter. As a Christian he had learned more about the West than his fellow Celestials. He had noticed the road—if one could call two tracks through the grass and gravel a road—leading out of the placers, over a ridge, to—where? Sang Lee wondered where. He weighed his options. Dare he try to break away and earn a living in this strange land of foreign devils? Should he bring another coolie laborer or two into his plans, or should he go alone? Secretly he began saving a bit of rice and tea. (The fish was usually rancid even before they received it, so he made no effort to save any of that.)

One rainy, windy night, Sang Lee, excusing himself to heed a call of nature, left the drafty cabin where he and a dozen other Celestials were sleeping and never returned. He had opted to go alone. He knew not where he was going, but he headed up that road over the ridge and down into another gulch and then up again, and so on until after two days' travel, in which he avoided camps manned by

Chinese, he felt relatively safe. He was also hungry. And he knew hardly ten English words.

He was fortunate, however, in that several thousand Chinese had come to the Gum San under the same circumstances as had he. And some of them, just like him, were too strong-willed and independent to accept continual peonage at the hands of unscrupulous Chinese or, in some cases, American employers. On his second day he was walking above a gulch wherein placers were being worked. He had just passed the operation when from the bushes a man appeared, barring Sang Lee's passage. Whoever he was, he was another Celestial. And when he spoke, he used a dialect of the Pearl River Delta. Merely hearing the lingo from his far-off home gave heart to the depressed, hungry Sang Lee.

Chiang Wu was his name, and his story was remarkably similar to Sang Lee's. Wu was part of a coolie gang at nearby placers. As soon as Sang Lee heard this, he urged Wu to walk rapidly with him, away from the placers. Wu needed no additional urging. He picked up his basket of belongings and the two young Orientals, with their big umbrella-shaped hats flopping up and down, their black, wide-bottomed trousers and loose shirts of the same material flapping in cadence with their rapid steps, soon disappeared into a grove of trees.

It was strange how it all happened, Sang Lee often reflected. Within a week he and Chiang Wu had added another eight or ten Chinese to their group. Sang Lee found himself their leader, not because he had been the first of the group, but because they had confidence in his decisions.

One day, as their scanty supply of rice and tea was ebbing away, they came to an abandoned placer site. A straggling white prospector had told them that the placer was washed out, had been worked down to bedrock, and had been abandoned. The Chinese, however, aware of American laxness, proceeded to occupy the placers. They repaired the long tom, retrieved abandoned picks and shovels, and occupied the miners' abandoned hovels.

Sang Lee and Chiang Wu were among the six who occupied a cabin which, by its being somewhat better built than any other dwellings in the gulch, must have been occupied by the alcalde, or perhaps by the prospector(s) who had discovered the site. One quiet, sunny afternoon they were sipping tea in the cabin when Chiang Wu caught a flashing golden sparkle where a sunbeam struck the dirt floor. He knelt down, examined the source of the sparkle, and immediately began sifting the dirt. So, too, did the others. Before they were through "working" the floor, they had extracted $300 in gold dust left by the careless Americans.

In addition, the worked-out placers, succumbing to the more meticulous habits of the Chinese, produced enough gold dust to buy the food and clothing they needed. Their source for supplies was a small community nearby where the whites seemed friendly enough and were certainly glad to get the gold. The shrewd Chinese were certain, however, that they were paying double what white miners paid for the same commodities.

Gradually Sang Lee, as the Celestial's leader, acquired enough pidgin English to be designated the one to deal with the whites. The six Chinese in the cabin divided their gleanings and it was Sang Lee who, with considerable trepidation, entered the town and learned how to transfer the gold dust to equivalent American dollars and have the money sent, by way of a Sacramento bank, on to China. Thus he and the others felt that they were fulfilling their familial obligations, and there was happiness in the group.

But the placers were now giving out, and this time there was no question of their sterility. Where to go?

At this point the Chinese heard of the discoveries at Orofino and Pierce City, about twenty-five miles up the Clearwater River in a place called Idaho. The decision was made to go there. For the next several weeks they made their way slowly, on foot, along the California trail to northern Utah, then north toward the new placers.

Always they had been aware of white prejudice against them, but Sang Lee's party behaved well and avoided concentrations of whites wherever possible. When they needed supplies they empowered Sang Lee to go into town and do the buying. Even so, they were increasingly aware of prejudice. Once Sang Lee came running back into camp from a white community without the bag of supplies. As soon as he had entered the town, he told his fellow Orientals, men along the boardwalks began shouting derisively at him.

"Well, I'll be damned. A Celestial!"

"Hey, you Oriental bastard, get out of here."

Sang Lee ignored the taunts, headed for the shebang, and, a smile on his face, strode up to the counter and bowed to the white-aproned clerk. But the clerk did not return the smile.

"We don't cater to heathens here," he growled.

Sang Lee bowed again and smiled. "Just want to buy—few things—" he replied.

"Yeah. Get out and don't come back," taunted a couple of loiterers.

Sang Lee bowed again and said, "Excuse, please. I go."

As he started out the door someone tripped him and sent him sprawling onto the boardwalk. Two or three strong men were about him, lifting him up with mocking excuses; then they gave him a push into the street where he fell in the dust and some fresh horse excrement. Everyone laughed. And a still larger crowd was gathering.

Sang Lee appraised the situation quickly. Humility was a better prescription for survival than courage, he quickly concluded. He stood up and began running as fast as his legs would carry him out of town. Gradually the jeers, taunts, and obscenities faded away, and soon he felt safe enough to slow to a fast walk. It was then that he discovered that he had also been robbed of the little bag of gold dust the group had given him to make purchases.

Now they were more aware than ever, as they made their way into Idaho in the spring of 1865, that they were in constant danger simply because they had slant eyes, pigtails, and wore what was, to the whites, funny clothing. Sang Lee was puzzled at the bigotry. He did not realize that part of the discrimination was due to Chinese clannishness, so that stories of opium smoking, uncouth eating habits (such as the canard that they ate rats), and sexual deviation—all rumors emanating from ignorance—contributed to the racism. Nor did he realize that wherever the ticket-credit system prevailed, with gangs working under overseers as Sang Lee had done until he escaped, observant whites were aghast at the bad treatment. They considered the system un-American, but translated it, peculiarly, into discrimination. He did not know that the frontier business "establishment" resented the Chinese because the overseers purchased their food and clothing in San Francisco from Chinese businessmen, so that the white storekeeper made no profit from their presence. Nor did he understand that the exploited Chinese were looked upon as threats to respectable white labor. All these reasons, as well as their slant eyes, yellow skin, pigtails and apparel, contributed to their persecution. All Sang Lee and the others knew was that they were in constant danger from unruly white elements on the mining frontier.

The little group of Celestials had no alternative but to continue to the Idaho gold fields. One day they found themselves along a major tributary of the Clearwater River. They were deep inside a narrow canyon at a point where the river made a sharp right-angle bend. On the shallow side the Chinese noticed a long, wide sandbar which, they sensed instinctively, contained gold. They tried it, and it did. After a week they estimated they had removed as much as ten thousand dollars in gold dust from the bar, and they had hardly worked a fourth of it.

One morning, as they were all working diligently, one of the Chinese, without raising his head from his task, informed his fellow workers of a couple of horsemen standing still, at the brink of the canyon, looking down upon them. Gradually all were aware. A third and a fourth horseman rode up. For long minutes they watched the Chinese at work then they turned and trotted off.

The day went on and, except for an uneasy feeling about the horsemen, the Chinese continued working their cradle, and the sand bar continued to be prolific of gold.

Sang Lee later estimated that it was about eleven o'clock in the morning of the next day; everyone was working at his task and the horsemen had been forgotten. Sang Lee was around the downstream bend, climbing a bluff toward a cluster of cottonwoods which had been their principal fuel source, when he heard the sounds. Over the roar of the stream he thought he heard hoof beats approaching from upstream. Worse, he was sure he heard shots. An instant later he was certain of it. A bullet ricocheted off the opposite canyon wall and plowed into the bluff hardly two feet above his head.

Quickly the young Chinese scrambled down, but wisely remained shrouded amidst the stones and tall grass and trees. On his hands and knees he rounded the bend just in time to witness the finishing touches of a massacre. They were the same four horsemen, he was sure, who had observed them from the brink of the canyon. Still mounted, they were whirling about on their mounts shooting pistols and rifles at the helpless miners. Horrified, Sang Lee watched Chiang Wu, on his knees, pleading for his life before two armed men astride their mounts. The two shot their rifles almost simultaneously, and Chiang Wu fell in the sand. One of the men shot him twice more before galloping elsewhere. Then, suddenly, all was quiet: the Chinese were all dead.

Now the outlaws dismounted and began searching the clothes and belongings of the massacred men. One man was kicking the sand close to the bluff, finally halting, kneeling, and with a yell of "Eureka!" pulling up one tin box, then another, then another. "They've taken our lives and now they're robbing us of all our gold," thought Sang Lee.

He saw the men cluster around their find, watched as they packed the tins away in saddlebags, agonized as they remounted, whirled around a couple times for a final look, and shot a few more bullets into the already dead men. One man stood straight in his saddle. With a pointed finger he counted the corpses. Sang Lee could not hear what he said, but it was obvious: yesterday the bandit had counted twelve Chinese but there were only eleven corpses. Where was number twelve?

Sang Lee crouched lower as the four bandits scanned the bluffs. Two rode upstream in search of the twelfth man; two others guided their horses downstream toward where Sang Lee was hiding. He lowered his face behind a boulder and hoped the grass was sufficiently thick to hide his body. One of the horsemen came within twelve feet of him, but fortunately for Sang Lee, who lay in a sort of trough, the killer failed to see him. But Sang Lee had caught a glimpse of *him*. He would never forget that face. A few minutes later, the young Chinese argonaut could hear the sounds of the horsemen galloping away.

Sang Lee waited for what seemed an eternity but was really hardly a half hour, and then gathered the courage to enter the massacre scene. He had known every one of these lonely Celestials, and he sobbed at the sight of their dead bodies. Then, even though the noonday sun blazed down upon him, he grabbed a shovel, dug a crude trench as close to the bluff and away from the stream as possible, and buried them. He was well aware that coyotes and wolves would dig them up, or a freshet would wash away the gravel and carry their corpses downstream. Yet he did it out of love and respect. Then, with the sun setting behind the canyon, he gathered some rice and tea and set out. For where? He knew his life was in jeopardy if any of the murderers spied a lone Chinese walking through the region.

He could never account for where he wandered or for how long. He knew that he was in Orofino and Pierce City, where some Chinese listened to his story and, believing it, consoled him. They also urged him to put distance between the region and himself. They agreed that if the desperadoes saw him alone, they would consider him the missing Chinese and dispose of him as they would a mangy coyote. So Sang Lee continued wandering until one day in July 1865, he walked down the main street of the new bonanza town of Muddy Creek.

Not a Celestial was to be seen. To Sang Lee this was probably a sign of racial hatred, or it could mean that no Chinese had found Muddy Creek, so new was it. One thing did register: no one accosted him, no one called him a damned heathen, no one told him to get out of town. Sang Lee was hungry and willing to work, but he lacked the courage to stop at businesses and inquire about employment.

First thing he knew, he had left town and was following wagon tracks that led to the Sunnyside Mine. As he approached, he saw a stocky man in his forties, wearing a light-colored hat, a suit, and muddy boots. He was standing outside a nearby shack talking with a bald-headed white man, a miner. Sang Lee never understood what gave him the courage, but he tramped up to the twosome and, as the big miner left after eying him critically, the well-dressed individual turned to Sang Lee.

"Excuse, please," began Sang Lee, bowing.

"My goodness, a Chinaman," said Jack Langford. "What are you doing here?"

"Name is Sang Lee. Me, all alone. Come from Idaho. Looking for work."

Jack Langford pulled out a fresh cigar from a breast pocket and began clipping it with a small knife. "Sang Lee, huh? Come on into my office," he said, not unkindly.

Obediently Sang Lee followed the man into the one-story shack. Langford sat down in a chair by a crude desk and motioned Sang Lee to sit on a battered, wobbly chair close by. The mine owner eyed Sang Lee critically. "It's rare for a Chinese to arrive in a town alone," he said. "You sure there aren't some of your brethren hiding around here?"

"On, no," Sang Lee replied. And then something happened that Sang Lee, hardly twenty years old, could never explain. Probably, he thought later on, it was the nuance of kindness in the man's face; the fact that he had not ordered him off the property with curses and even a physical boot. Sang Lee sobbed, lowered his head, and sobbed and sobbed. He could not control himself.

Certainly Jack Langford had never expected this. He placed the cigar in his mouth and struck a match, with which he lighted his cigar. He leaned back in his chair, breathed out smoke, and studied Sang Lee, noting his youth.

Finally the young man gained control. "So solly. I go." He started to get up from the chair.

"Wait a minute," said Langford. Sang Lee sat down again. He saw the mine owner lean back in his chair again and finger a Masonic symbol on his gold watch chain. "Where are your friends?" Langford asked softly.

"Dead. All dead," replied Sang Lee.

"How's that?"

"Killed. All shot. By thieves."

Langford showed more interest. He leaned forward, resting his elbows on his knees. "Where?" he asked. "How long ago?"

Sang Lee continued to gain control. "I not sure," he replied. "It was a creek running into Clearwater River. Long way west of here."

"And how long ago?" Langford asked again.

"Not sure. I–I wander and wander for I know not how long."

"How come you're alive?"

Sang Lee began to explain. The young Chinese had soon told Langford the whole story.

"Those bastards," Jack Langford whispered. "Tell me, Sang Lee, how many were there?"

"Four."

"Would you recognize them?"

"One I would know, right away. The others—maybe."

"So you're just roaming?"

Sang Lee nodded. "I hungry. I want work."

Langford scowled, removed his cigar from his mouth, and eyed it absent-mindedly. "Sang Lee," he began, "I've got twenty white men working this mine. If I gave you employment you just might have an accident. You might fall down a shaft. Or maybe you wouldn't get out soon enough when they're blasting, and you'd soon be in kingdom come. That's why I can't give you a job here."

"Understand," said the pigtailed young man, rising from the chair again.

"Sit down, son," said Langford gently. He eyed Sang Lee for long moments. "Can you do anything else? Something that isn't in competition with the white man?"

Suddenly Sang Lee had an idea. In Orofino he had met a Chinese who ran a laundry. He had all the work he could handle and the miners accepted him and gave him their business. "I can do laundlee," Sang Lee blurted out.

Langford looked at him for a long moment then pounded his fist on the table. "That's it, Sang Lee. We'll set you up in the laundry business. I've got a small vacant storefront down in Muddy Creek that should do. Come with me."

And that was how Sang Lee, Chinese Roman Catholic from the Pearl River Valley in south China, came to be Muddy Creek's laundryman.

Langford set him up in business and gave him the first batch of clothes to be washed and ironed. Sang Lee was soon working from dawn to dusk and often, by kerosene lamp, well into the night. He ordered flatirons from Salt Lake City which arrived via Gunter Schroeder's freight wagon. He improvised an ironing board. Eventually he obtained a large stove upon which he heated his water. He hung clothes to dry in the back yard of the ramshackle dwelling, in the back room of which he lived. Jack Langford collected a small rent and had all his washing done promptly and free. The community had accepted having "one Chink" in town. And "that Chink" was Sang Lee.

Langford also had asked Sang Lee to be on the alert for any of the four murderers, and to let him know immediately should he see them. That autumn Sang Lee informed him that he had seen the one man he positively knew had been there: his name was Charlton Edwards, and when three horsemen who were clearly not miners came trotting into town one day, Sang Lee let Langford know that he believed they were the other three murderers. Langford thanked Sang Lee, warned him to stay out of sight, and kept his eyes on them. When they were joined by Edwards, he was sure that Sang Lee was right.

Christmas Eve. Would Muddy Creek allow Sang Lee to attend Catholic services? The young Oriental had contemplated his move for hours. Then he devised his plan, donning the gorgeous red and gold brocaded Chinese clothing he had purchased (for no good reason, he was forced to admit) from San Francisco. Then he had fetched the expensive incense that he occasionally used to get the smell of soap and laundry out of his ramshackle dwelling. It was stored in a little ornamental lacquer box.

Sang Lee now entered Reece's Music Hall/church. He realized that in the half-filled room all eyes were on him.

"Well, I'll be..." someone said slowly. "Even the heathen Chinee wants to attend services."

Father de Mara, a quizzical smile on his face, stood still as Sang Lee approached him up the left side aisle.

"Please," Sang Lee began, bowing in his splendid clothes. "I too am Catholic. I christened near Canton by Jesuit father." Then Sang Lee held out the beautiful lacquered box. "Here," he said, "gift for the church. Fine incense for Midnight Mass."

Father de Mara accepted the box, opened it, and smelled the sandalwood fragrance. "Thank you," he replied. "I have an incense burner packed on Lucifer. I'll have someone fetch it and with your incense we'll make Reece's really smell nice."

Sang Lee bowed. "May I attend Christmas Midnight Mass?" he asked hesitantly.

The priest looked upon the face of the young, lonely Celestial, and without realizing what he was doing, made the sign of the cross over him. "Of course, my son," he said. "Welcome. Sit where you wish."

XI

After a few minutes Julie had risen from the manger scene and gone upstairs to her room, off from the balcony. There she had stepped into her best dress, a demure black one covering her from neck to ankles and with long sleeves. It was stylish, but hardly cheerful. However, it fit her like a glove, revealing underneath the funereal black an exquisitely shaped young body. After changing, she had come down the stairs and sat in a chair near the front of the hall. She sat straight as a ramrod, looking ahead; only someone observing her carefully would have concluded that she was wrestling with a decision. The young geologist, Barry Millard, had seated himself on the other side of the aisle and back two or three rows from the girl. He appeared to be chatting with the alcalde, Luke Bassett. Only a discerning person would have noticed, as Luke did not, that Barry continually cast glances toward the girl sitting there, prim and alone.

Barry was absolutely undecided about her. He acknowledged that he had an enormous infatuation for her, at the very least. Or was it love? And even if it was true love, as in his heart he felt it was, could the heart surmount their differences? Could she be a true, devoted wife and helpmate, or would she be forever an embarrassment as he advanced in his professional career? What would his mother think of her?

As for Julie, she was still upset over what, in her mind, was the loss of her one opportunity to break out of the sleazy life she was leading, to marry a man she respected, and who had been convincing in his confession of love for her. Life had not been easy for Julie Montgomery. Now she clenched her fists, fought tears, and determined that she would not allow this defeat to destroy her. If it *was* a defeat. She had had worse experiences in her eighteen years of life.

But even as she fought to alleviate the pain in her heart, she was considering something else. Should she ask the padre, or shouldn't she? There was Father de Mara now, walking up the aisle toward the stage to check the sand pails, making sure they could hold the tapers. She watched as he appraised Gunter Schroeder's crucifix that hung in thin cords from the ceiling behind the altar. Now he was checking the little portable tabernacle containing the host—really hardtack— and the sacramental wine; they were situated behind the altar, to one side, on an ordinary table. Unusual for him tonight, at this moment he was alone.

"Father de Mara," she called to him, rising from the chair and stepping to the foot of the stage. "May I speak to you?"

The padre finished his examination and stepped off the stage. "Of course, Miss Julie." To the Jesuit she was like a child, with sky blue eyes, soft, honey-colored hair, clear complexion, a straight, aristocratic nose, and a delicate chin. "What a beautiful young woman," he thought to himself dispassionately. He had spoken to her several times as she scrubbed the floor and cleaned the lamps.

"I'm Julie, Father. Julie Montgomery," the girl began, "I–I'm a taxi dancer here at Reece's."

"I know," replied the padre. He was aware of the rift between the young lady and Barry Millard. What was she going to ask him? He waited.

"Father de Mara, I don't like an empty manger," she said quickly. "It lacks the Christ child."

The padre smiled, turning to the manger. "I don't like it either," he replied, "but I guess we'll just have to assume the Lord's presence. Probably no one will notice."

"Oh, but they will," Julie replied. "When they come down the aisle to take holy communion they will be looking into the manger, and they'll see that the baby Jesus is not there. Mary and Joseph are there, and the camels and the three wise men, and some sheep and donkeys, but no baby Jesus."

The padre agreed. "You are right, Miss Montgomery. But I'm afraid there are few dolls in a new mining camp like Muddy Creek."

The girl paused, looking at the manger. She paused so long it was becoming awkward. The padre could tell that she wanted to ask him something but found it hard. She had received enough blows today without the padre refusing her offer. That, she thought, would be the last straw. She might lose control and start crying. Why should he accept a gift—a temporary one—from a taxi dancer?

"Father de Mara," she began hesitantly, looking straight in his eyes. "I have a doll. It is just the right size for the manger and Gunter Schroeder's nativity figures. And Melissa was always a good doll. She'd make a wonderful baby Jesus."

The padre's face broke into an approving smile. "That would be wonderful," he said with boyish enthusiasm, "but the service will begin in less than half an hour. Can you fetch Melissa in time?"

"Oh, yes," replied the girl joyfully. "Melissa's upstairs in my room. In my trunk. I'll get her right away." And

Julie was off without another word. The padre watched her running up the stairs like a happy child, then down the balcony to her room. Quickly she opened the door and disappeared inside; the padre in a few moments noticed a yellow light gleaming from cracks in the door and knew she had lighted a lamp.

Barry Millard had also followed her every move. He was curious about what had transpired between the priest and the girl. He kept his curiosity to himself.

Julie's was a sparsely furnished bedroom. The walls were of sawn lumber covered with cheesecloth and old newspapers, which helped keep out the cold. On one side against a wall was a big china basin and stand, with a cheap, wavy mirror hanging above it. Next to it was a crude table locally made, possibly by Ebenezer Cotton, upon which was placed an old kerosene lamp. There was no closet, just a corner shelf with hooks below it upon which to hang clothes. The bedstead was of peeled logs. A rough brown blanket covered the bed, which was neatly made. Two collapsed, tattered pillows lay against the headboard.

Such was Julie's "home," save for the old trunk in another corner. She had purchased it second-hand in Salt Lake City with her last money. Into it she had deposited her few possessions. These she had transferred from the tattered carpetbag she had taken with her when she left Si Montgomery's farm in eastern Iowa; since then she had discarded it. The trunk and its contents were her only link with the past—or the future—as she had made her way with other taxi dancers from mining camp to mining camp.

The girl shivered, for there was no heat in the room save the warmth that crept through the cracks in the floor and from under the door. She rubbed her arms to increase circulation and surveyed her tawdry domain. Then she looked at the trunk. She became sad. Slowly she walked to it, unlatched the lock (the key was missing, one reason she had been able to purchase it at so low a price) and lifted the curved top.

Julie Montgomery's worldly possessions did not amount to much. All her clothing was there save the one demure dress she was wearing and a dance dress hanging below the corner shelf. Wrapped in a newspaper were two pairs of shoes, then there were cotton stockings, four pairs of freshly laundered drawers, three ordinary dresses, and a used flannel nighty. The paucity of her belongings suddenly struck the girl, and a shadow of hopelessness crossed her face. Her status in life struck home. She knew—always she knew—that unless she found a fine man, such as Barry Millard, she just might slip. She might become a hopeless prostitute drifting from one mining camp to another, abused, beaten, addicted to drugs and alcohol. And get a loathsome disease. Then there was no recourse but suicide.

Julie stifled a sob. She probably would have succeeded in dispensing with the drunken oaf who, earlier in the day, was pulling her upstairs. She'd done it before. About halfway up she simply gave a strong kick and down tumbled the assailant, usually so inebriated that he just lay asleep at the foot of the stairs. Barry, unfortunately, had just witnessed the pleading phase and had drawn a foregone conclusion.

She wiped her eyes. She moved the clothing and shoes in the trunk to one side. She paused then reached down to lift a doll from the trunk. She lifted tenderly, as if it were a live baby, an elaborately dressed doll with an angelic face.

"Melissa," she said quietly, "I haven't had a talk with you for a long time. How have you been?" She clutched the doll to her bosom and sat on the bed, sobbing quietly.

She was back in Iowa at the farm. Late one Saturday afternoon when she was eight years old, her father—at least at the time she thought he was her father—a jovial, hard-working farmer whose life was made miserable by a humorless shrew of a wife named Emma, had just returned from town. Julie had run out to the barn to meet him. There she found him unloading bags of feed and seed, placing them in appropriate places in the barn.

"Did you buy groceries, Daddy?" asked the girl, looking at the back of the wagon.

"Yep," he replied. "We'll take them up to the house in a minute," replied her father with a gleam in his eyes. "But first, Julie, I found something for my little girl at Alvin Jacobs' General Store. I shouldn't have done it, but—"

"Something for me?"

"Shhhhhhh," he said, looking around, holding a finger to his lips. "Don't tell your mother."

The little girl understood, for even at age eight it had become clear that she was the apple of her daddy's eyes, but hardly of her mother's. There were nuances between father and mother that the little girl did not understand. Her mother—she thought she was her mother—was surly, cold, and standoffish to her, yet had never struck or abused her. Anyway, if her daddy said to be quiet, she would be quiet.

From the wagon he obtained a cardboard box almost two feet long and ten inches wide, which he handed to the little girl with the blue eyes and flaxen tresses. "I hope your mother won't carry on because I bought this for you, Julie," he said quietly. "I just thought it was about time you had a—"

"A what, Daddy?"

"Open and see for yourself."

Thus did a doll named Melissa enter Julie Montgomery's life. And yet, from then on her life became more complicated and less enjoyable. Neither father nor daughter had seen the woman dressed in black and not without an attractive form round the corner of the barn. Suddenly she was there, standing before them, saying nothing while father and daughter looked at her, at a loss for words.

"Howdy, Emma," Si finally said. "I was jest unloadin' the feed 'n seeds. There's some flour and bacon and t'other things you wanted in the wagon. We was jest goin' to ride up to the house and unload them."

Icily the woman asked, "Why did you buy her that doll?"

"Oh, that," Si replied nervously, as if it was no big thing. "Oh, Emma. I saw it at Alvin Jacobs' store and—well, you know—Julie ain't ever had a doll and she's eight years old and—"

"You bought her a doll!" stormed Emma. She pointed an accusing finger at Si. "You bought this little tart who is nothing to us a doll!"

It was getting dark. Julie could barely make out Emma's face. Julie clutched the doll close to her breast.

"She is not to have the doll," Emma announced, taking a step toward Julie. "Give me the doll."

Julie gasped. Her mother had always been aloof, but never had she seen her so cross, so angry, so demanding.

"Emma, you just wait a minute," Si interceded. "This little girl deserves a doll and, by God, I've bought her one and, so help me, she keeps it."

The woman took a second step toward Julie, who clutched her doll as if it were a live infant. Si stepped between them. "No, Emma. And I mean it. This is Julie's doll and she can keep it."

Emma and Si glared at each other for long moments. Then the mother whirled on her heels and strode back toward the house.

Si and Julie watched in the gloaming until a door opened and the dim light of the kitchen showed briefly before it closed. Julie, frightened, looked to Si for an explanation. He looked down upon her compassionately. "Never you mind, Julie. That's your doll and you keep it. Might want to keep it hid, though," he added as an afterthought.

After the doll incident Emma became colder and more aloof toward the little girl. Julie had always been a bright child with a sunny disposition, but Emma seemed to do everything she could to break her spirit. She doubled Julie's household chores and found criticism with everything she did. Sometimes the impossibility of pleasing her brought Julie to tears. One night she heard her father and mother arguing in the kitchen, which was right below her bedroom. When she heard her name mentioned she crept to the heat vent in the floor and placed her ear close to it.

"She's not even ours, Si," Emma said.

"She's our daughter just is if you'd borne her," Si replied.

"I rue the day I took in those immigrants," added the woman. "Damned that the mother died in childbirth and you out of your Christian compassion offered to raise the baby."

"You showered plenty of love on her in those first few months," countered Si.

"Not half what you did, Si Montgomery. I swear, you love that child more than you love me."

"Not true," replied Si. Julie heard a chair scraping as if someone was getting up from the table. "But you never got pregnant and I admit I wanted kids."

"Get out of my sight," demanded the woman, and Si did. She heard the kitchen door slam. The little girl tiptoed back to her bed and clutched her doll. "What do they mean, I'm not theirs?" she asked her doll. "Am I adopted? Who am I?" Trying to sort out the mystery, the little girl cried herself to sleep.

After that Emma was more distant than ever, more demanding, harder to please. Sometimes she just ordered Julie to "get out of my sight."

As for her father (really her adopted father), Si Montgomery spent more and more time in the barn or going to town, or in the parlor where he read from a library of classics and occasional books purchased by mail. Therein was another mastic bringing Si and Julie together. Julie loved to read. She did not realize it, but her curiosity of the world about her, her questions, her vivid imagination, brought Si even closer to her, enriching his love for the little girl. When she reached her teens and was reading adult books, she and Si would read together and discuss what they had read. It was clear that Emma's resentment rose in direct proportion to Si's increasing attention to Julie.

Husband and wife were barely on speaking terms, and although Julie was pretty ignorant of sex, she knew that Si chose to sleep on a couch in the parlor rather than in the bedroom with Emma. And Emma brooded. Since Julie did more and more of the housework, the woman just sat, often staring blankly out the kitchen window. Long years later, Julie, looking back, realized that these had been signs of insanity.

One day Julie, in her mid-teens, worked up the courage to ask Si point blank: "Daddy, are you my real daddy? Is Mother my real mother?" They were in the barn, she collecting eggs, he pitching hay.

Si stuck the pitchfork in the hay and looked thoughtfully at the girl. Then he began pitching hay again. Then he stopped, turned, and looked at her. "No, Julie, but we love you as if you were our own."

"Then who am I?" asked Julie, her eyes flooding with tears.

"An immigrant couple on the way West stopped here one day," Si began. "The mother was in labor, so Emma and I gave her our bedroom and we got a doctor, and the couple gave birth to a beautiful baby girl—that's you—but the mother died in childbirth. We helped the father bury the mother in the Methodist cemetery. Then he moved on, promising to return when he was settled and fetch his little daughter." Si paused. "I'll show you your mother's grave some day soon, Julie. Your parents' name was Bates."

"So I do have a real father, somewhere?"

Si sat down on a bale of hay. "I'm afraid not, Julie. We later heard that he was killed by Indians on the Platte River Trail near Fort Laramie."

That night, as so often happened, the little girl sat on her bed and hugged her doll, conversing with Melissa as if she were a living close friend.

The years passed. Neighbors, rarely seen save at church, were aware of Emma's growing strangeness, of the distance between her and Si and Julie. But Si furnished Julie with the parental love Emma could not, and it was Si who encouraged the girl to attend the Methodist female seminary in the nearby town of Willow Grove. She had one year to go, and was looking forward to being a bookkeeper upon graduation, when something happened that changed everything.

Emma's brother showed up at the farm.

Emma always called him just Fred. He was a hulk of a man, a full six feet tall with proportions adequate to his height. He had an enormous black beard and a bald head. His face was dominated by a big, crooked nose. In his wide mouth were just three teeth yellowed from chewing tobacco. He smelled bad from afar, at best of whiskey and tobacco, at worst of unwashed laboring male. One eye was always half closed, the result of an altercation some years before. Fred's other eye was big as a monocle, staring wide-eyed at the world about him.

From the first time she laid eyes on him, called into the kitchen by Emma when she came home from school one late spring day, Julie was afraid of Fred. She was seventeen and blooming beautifully. It seemed to bother Emma that she had filled in so nicely, but as long as Si was around to compliment her, Julie accepted Emma's continuing hostility.

"Julie, I want you to meet my brother Fred," Emma said simply but in an unexplainably strange tone of voice. For one thing, as Julie noticed immediately, her "mother" was smiling, and that was unusual. In succeeding days Emma talked constantly with Fred, who reciprocated. They laughed together and talked of old times. It was as if Emma had been in solitary confinement for years and suddenly was released in the company of a loved one.

Well, thought Julie, a sister has a right to love a brother. But the change that had come over Emma was too pronounced to go unnoticed. As for Si, he remained outwardly cheerful, but spent more time than ever in the parlor where he read his books.

"I'll be helping ye with the harvest and chores," volunteered Fred. "Anything else ye need done around here?"

"Nope," replied Si.

A week passed. Fred took it upon himself to do some repair work on the big door into the hayloft. But Si and Fred did not work together. In fact, as Julie noticed, they avoided each other. After a few days Fred ceased working and, it seemed to Julie, hung out on the front porch or the kitchen, almost always in the company of Emma. The more he ate, the lazier he got. It didn't seem to bother Emma.

One thing about Fred bothered Julie more than the man's slovenliness, his tobacco chewing, and his dirty clothes. It was the way he watched her every move. She knew that he knew when she came downstairs to breakfast, when she walked down the path to meet the buggy that a neighbor girl drove to the female academy, picking up Julie on the way. Fred knew when she went to the barn to gather eggs. She suspected that he knew when she modestly left the kitchen to go to the outhouse. There was no key to her bedroom door, but she began propping a chair to it at night. Julie had friends. She had been raised on a farm. Without knowing the obscene words, she knew what Fred was thinking. It made her uneasy.

Should she tell anyone? Surely not Emma. Emma noticed nothing uncouth about Fred, or if she did, she never showed concern. Should Julie tell Si? She thought seriously of doing so, but she seldom saw him alone these days. She was at school, she was at home helping in the kitchen or sweeping, dusting, washing, or studying, for she was diligent at whatever she did. Si was out at the barn, in a pasture or a field, or in town. And, if they did meet in the parlor as they had always done, Julie, somehow, could not bring herself to bring up the subject.

She dreaded the end of school, for then she would be home all the time. The term ended and, as she had done in other years, Julie set about reestablishing a housework routine, doing more work than before. The days grew hotter and farm work accelerated. And Fred hung around the house. She felt his eyes feasting upon her in her gingham dress that covered but did not hide her youthful form.

Another hot day. Julie rose, slipped on drawers and dress and shoes and stockings and, after breakfast, set out to collect eggs as she always did. Julie knew where most of the nests were, and so with her basket she entered the dark recesses of the barn. She made the rounds of the stables. Then she remembered that Emma had reminded her at least twice recently to be sure and check the hayloft. She climbed the ladder. At the far side, where the morning sun's ray had not yet wiped out the dark, she suspected a prolific hen of having her nest. The girl, humming a little tune, walked across the slippery, hay-strewn floor toward the dark side of the hayloft when in front of her loomed a hulk of a moving figure.

"Hello, Julie. I thought ye'd never come," said Fred in low tones. "I been waitin' here for ye all night."

She gasped, so shocked that she dropped the basket. Before Julie could collect her thoughts Fred's right hand had grabbed a wrist and held it in a vice-like grip. His other hand clapped tightly over her mouth. He pulled her toward him.

"It ain't goin' to hurt, lassie. Fact, it'll feel good if ye just relax." He began pushing her toward the hay. "Ye lie down there," he commanded, pushing her hard as he let go of her.

The girl fell back onto the sloping hay and, terrified, looked at Fred. She was so frightened she could not scream.

"Raise yer dress and pull down yer drawers," he commanded as he unbuttoned the fly on his shabby flannel trousers.

"No," she was able to say. "No, Fred. Please—"

"Julie," came a call from below. It was Si.

She tried to reply but Fred's hand was like an iron door over her mouth. She kicked on the floor, struggling. Fred's free hand slapped her face with a stunning, stinging blow. She smelled his foul breath as he fell upon her.

Then she saw Si's form appearing above them followed by the swift, shadowy sweep of an ax handle. It hit Fred on the side of his head with a thud so hard that Julie almost felt it. The man rolled over and held up his hands as the ax handle came down upon his head again. This time Fred lay still.

"You bastard," Si hissed. "You'd destroy Julie just like you killed the Spencer girl."

Julie, sitting up and pulling down her dress, sobbing, watched as Si lifted the ax handle once more. "No, no, Daddy," she cried, casting a glance at Fred's prostrate form. "He's already unconscious."

Si paused with the ax handle in midair. "He's all right, Julie. He'll come to." He lowered the weapon. "Come on, girl. Let's get out of here. I want to talk to you. Take the basket of eggs with you."

"I was just gathering eggs—" she began.

"Hush, child," Si ordered as they descended the ladder. "I have to tell you some things. You've got to leave us, Julie. Earliest possible. Tomorrow morning," he added thoughtfully.

They walked to the milk house. Julie, wiping her eyes, looked startled for a moment and ceased walking. "Leave— here?"

"Yes, Julie. You're not safe here."

She glanced back at the barn. "You mean—him?"

Si nodded. When they reached the milk house they sat down on a couple of stools. "Julie, you're growing up fast, and I'm going to ask you to be more of an adult than you've ever been before," he began. "You see, Julie, when I married Emma I didn't know there was a strain of insanity in her family—criminal insanity. About a year after our marriage, her brother—that's Fred—was accused of capturing a sweet girl like you and doing—er—dreadful things, horrible things, to her. Then he killed her and cut up her body.

For a month, parts of her were found throughout Haines County, Ohio, where we lived."

Julie gasped, looking in the direction of the barn.

"Fred was caught and sentenced to hang but the family had political pull, and his sentence was commuted to life imprisonment. He got out in less than twenty years. First thing he did was head for our farm." Si rose and opened the door of the milk house to make sure neither Fred nor Emma was around.

He continued. "Emma, as you know, has long periods of depression when she just sits and looks out the window or sits on the porch and stares vacantly at nothing. A year or so ago she began going through change of life, Julie, and was getting more and more strange, more and more unfriendly to you and hostile to me. Then Fred arrived. All of a sudden Emma's real happy again, talking with him. But Julie, that's made her no more friendly to either you or me. I can take care of myself, Julie, although I don't like the two of 'em scheming behind my back. But I think it best for you to leave." He looked lovingly at her, for he had raised her as his own daughter. "Can you understand, Julie?"

Julie by now was getting herself under control. She sniffed, blew her nose, and nodded. "Yes, Daddy."

"Well, we've got to get back to the house now," said Si. "We've got to act as if everything is all right. Fred'll show up sometime during the day. He'll have some cock and bull story to tell Emma. We'll just go along with whatever he says, and sympathize with him. Eh, Julie?"

She agreed.

And indeed, about mid-morning Fred appeared, with two huge lumps on his head. He did not look at either Si or Julie, but related to Emma a story about a rung in a ladder giving away and his falling ten feet to the ground, where he hit his head. Emma sympathized and insisted on washing his bald head at the point where Fred was holding a dirty bandana handkerchief. Si and Julie got out of the room and tried to go about their chores as if all was normal.

Later, Julie tiptoed up the stairs to her room. She sat on the bed and grabbed her doll Melissa and hugged her and then lay on the bed crying into a pillow. She realized her probable fate if she did not leave. "If he tried once, he'll try again," she reflected. "Daddy is right. I've got to leave." But the thought of going alone into the world was almost as frightening.

There was a knock on the door. "Julie?" It was Si. She walked to the door and let him in. "Fred's out showing Emma where he fell," he said. And he sat on the bed and spoke quietly to her.

"Listen carefully," he began. "When you are free from your chores today, go to the closet off from the parlor and get my carpetbag. Take it to your room and pack it with clothing and whatever else you want to take with you. Then, if you can do it without being noticed, replace it in the parlor closet."

"Daddy. I don't want to leave. I love you and you can protect me—"

With his strong farmer's arms outstretched he held her shoulders with his hands and looked straight into her face. "Julie, the time has come for you to become a woman. You must leave, my dear child. You must!"

She sobbed quietly. "Yes, Daddy," she whispered.

"Now, Julie," he continued. "I want you to rise very early tomorrow morning. You've got to get downstairs, out the door, and down the lane to the road where Ed Ladd picks up the milk. I'll meet you there with the bag. You'll ride to Willow Grove with Ed. He'll drop you off at the railroad station. Buy a ticket to Council Bluffs. I'll give you money and a letter addressed to my brother, Rufus Montgomery, who lives there. The letter says that you're trained in bookkeeping and want to find work, and that as soon as you have a job you'll move into a boarding house." Si looked out the window. "Here come Emma and Fred. She's bandaged his head and has her arm around him. Hmmff," Si snorted. "They're a pair, Julie. I wonder if she'd treat him different if she knew the real story of how he got those lumps on his head."

Si left. That afternoon Julie got the opportunity to fetch Si's carpetbag. She packed clothing, chose the dress she would wear on her trip, put in a brush and comb and some cornstarch powder, a tooth brush, and—after hugging her and talking to her quietly—Melissa. She closed the bag and snapped the fastener. Then she waited. When she saw Emma and Fred heading for the milk house she ran downstairs with the bag and hid it in the closet as Si had instructed her to do. Then she began fixing supper. When the others entered, all was as usual, though it was hard acting that way, Fred with his bandaged head and Si and Julie knowing what had happen and was about to happen. As Si commented the next morning, considering all that had happened and was about to happen in her young life, she had put on a good act.

That night Julie slept fitfully. Her door was jammed shut with the chair propped against it. The creaks and cracks a wooden two-story farmhouse made as it cooled off during the night were sufficient to keep anyone who was distracted from getting to sleep. The girl waited for dawn, which finally arrived with a pink blush in the east before 4:00 a.m. on that early June day in 1865. Even getting out of bed (which seemed like security to her, like a stable to a horse) seemed to make too much noise. Quickly Julie put on her freshly laundered gingham dress, her newest stockings, her dull-looking go-to-church shoes. She bit her lip to stifle a sob as she surveyed the little bedroom that had been hers for as long as she could remember. Then she opened the door as quietly as possible—although it squeaked—and stepped gingerly down the hall, past her "parents'" bedroom (which Si had not used for years) and down the stairs.

She knew her way in the darkness, and was soon at the front door. It was unlocked (they rarely locked it) and in no time she was on the porch. Still treading quietly, she tiptoed across it, down the steps, and onto the path. There she began running, in her imagination seeing Fred in every shadow, wishing the day would hurry and get brighter.

The road seemed miles away, but the girl ran as fast as she could and was finally there. A figure stood in the shadows by the big twenty-five-gallon milk cans setting high on a bench so that Ed Ladd could easily manipulate them onto his big wagon.

"It's me, Julie. Did you get away without them hearing you? Seeing you?" asked Si.

She threw her arms around him and held him as tightly as she could. "I think so," she replied. "Oh, Daddy—"

"Shush, Julie. It will be all right. I'll write you at my brother's and we'll keep in touch. This is just something that has to be done. Why, Julie girl, I think it will all be settled by fall and you can return for your last year at the academy."

"Oh, I hope so," she sobbed. It was fortunate she could not see Si's face. It was glum, stern, concerned, and his eyes were watery.

"Julie," he said, "you've been endowed with a lot of common sense. You show good judgment. You are already well-educated for a young woman of this day and age. Now you've got to use your head more than ever before. You've got to weigh your every move. You've got to consider the move beyond the next move. And keep in mind the moral lessons you learned at Sunday school. I have every confidence that everything will go well with you, my child."

Down the road they heard the rising clatter of the wagon, the metallic sound of milk cans banging against one another, the clop-clop of horses' hooves, a whinny. The wagon loomed up against the rapidly brightening eastern sky.

"Whoa," spoke the teamster. Even before the wagon had stopped flush with the milk bench, Ed Ladd was saying "Mornin', Si. What's up?"

"Mind if Julie hitches a ride to Willow Grove?" Si asked. "She's goin' to visit her uncle in Council Bluffs. Needs to catch the mornin' train."

"Don't mind at all," replied Ed. "But I'm runnin' late. Could ye help me get the milk cans on the wagon, Si?

And Miss Julie, you come right up here." He held out his hand and so strong was he that she and her carpetbag were quickly elevated to the seat. She sat down and watched as Si and Ed manipulated the heavy cans onto the wagon. Then Ed was seated.

In the moments before he yelled "Giddap" Julie looked down at Si who, if not her real father, had been as good and loving as any real one could be. She knew his eyes were misting, as were hers. Si raised his head and waved, and the girl waved back. Just as the rays of the early morning sun cast long beams through the trees the wagon lurched ahead. Julie turned in her seat and waved back at Si. She waved, and he waved, until the wagon rounded a curve and Si was out of sight.

Julie heard coyotes howling in the wilderness outside of Muddy Creek. A slight breeze sent a cold draft through the cracks in the wall. She shivered and hugged Melissa harder. Was all that just six months ago? She recalled how she had arrived in Willow Grove, had purchased a ticket on the Mississippi and Missouri Railroad, had found a seat and sat alone all the way across Iowa, green and luxurious in the June warmth. She reminisced briefly how she had learned to ignore interested men, to pretend a relative or a husband was going to meet her, and how to stay amidst crowds because in crowds there was safety. But those were fleeting thoughts not germane to the memories of what had brought her to Muddy Creek as a taxi dancer.

Si had given her fifty dollars in specie that she had placed in her purse, which she clutched as if her life depended on it. In Council Bluffs she had inquired of Rufus Montgomery, only to find others inhabiting his house and to be informed that he and his family had departed for the Pike's Peak region just as the grass was greening, about a month ago. Well, thought the girl, I'll find a home where someone will give me board and room.

How to do that? She found a Methodist church and asked the minister (who may or may not have believed her story of leaving home with her parents' permission to find a job) where she could find room and board. He was a good man and saw an innocence in her face that led him to give her lodging, for a reasonable rental, in his own house. His wife was a kind, motherly sort with three small children and another on the way. Julie accepted the invitation and agreed to stay and help.

In no time at all she knew Council Bluffs. It was full of dust in dry weather and mud when it rained. She found it an exciting town, with plans underway for construction of a transcontinental railroad beginning across the Missouri on the Nebraska side. She had been in Council Bluffs about two weeks when, one day, she was reading a local newspaper. Halfway down the front page her eyes caught these headlines:

HORRIBLE DISCOVERY

Three Dead Found in Farmhouse

With typical curiosity, the girl began reading. Her heart skipped a beat at the by-line: Willow Grove, Iowa:

The Sheriff was called to the farm of Si Montgomery outside of Willow Grove when Ed Ladd, the milk collector, reported that the usual milk allotment was not awaiting him on Tuesday morning, June 18. He walked to the house and shouted, but no one answered.

When he reached town he reported to Sheriff Lorimer, who rode out to investigate. The bodies of Emma Montgomery, her husband, Si Montgomery, and a man later identified as Fred Sheeler were found dead in the kitchen.

According to Sheriff Lorimer, Sheeler had been released from the Ohio State Prison on May 1. He is believed to have been Emma Montgomery's brother.

As close as the Sheriff could determine, there had been a family quarrel. Emma Montgomery, whose body was found sprawled over the stove, was even in death holding a butcher knife with dried blood on the blade. Fred Sheeler was in a sitting position on the floor, leaning on the kitchen door as if he had fallen there after receiving a bullet in the center of his forehead. In his hand he held a small Derringer. It had been fired twice, according to the Sheriff.

Sprawled on his back on the floor, holding a Colt six-shooter, was Si Montgomery. He had slashes across his face and another across his chest, but what had killed him was the two bullets from the Derringer. Emma Montgomery had been killed with two shots from the Colt, which was also the weapon used to kill Fred Sheeler.

The Sheriff is looking for the Montgomery's daughter, Julie, who is reported to have left a few weeks past for Council Bluffs. It is believed that she can shed light upon the cause of the tragedy.

The girl's horror almost equaled her feelings when Fred had attacked her. Daddy dead? He was the only person who had really cared for her. Emma and Fred? They had done it. But why? Julie felt that she was responsible, although she had been gone several weeks. Then she thought: They're looking for me. I don't want to have to tell about Fred and what happened in the hayloft. Almost without thinking, Julie determined to leave Council Bluffs. She did not want a sheriff bringing her back to Willow Grove.

Her way out of Council Bluffs materialized at the parsonage. The Danforths, a California-bound family, had pulled their big, ox-drawn covered wagon into the parsonage yard and requested of the minister of their faith a couple days to rest. The mother, like the parson's wife, was burdened with children down to a suckling babe. Julie had made their acquaintance and recognized in the bearded man of thirty-five years a competent, moral head of the family. He was a farmer of obvious competence who reminded her of Si. She showed great interest in their outfit and their plans. It was no great surprise to Julie when the mother invited her to accompany them. She could certainly use a young girl's help in looking after five youngsters under age ten, a husband, six oxen, and some chickens in a coop hanging from the wagon's tailgate. When the emigrants pulled out of the parsonage yard, Julie was with them.

She remembered with pleasure the journey with the Danforths to Salt Lake City. They were as she had judged them, an intelligent, educated couple from Indiana, and their children were obedient and healthy. Julie enjoyed the clear air as the wagon, part of a caravan numbering more than a dozen, wended its way west first along the Platte River, then along the North Platte.

At Fort Laramie she sought out the details of the Indian massacre that had taken the life of her real father. Then it was up and through South Pass, down to Fort Bridger, and on to Salt Lake City, where they arrived in late August. At this point the Danforths took the advice of experienced pioneers and decided to lay over for the winter. They encouraged Julie to stay with them, but Julie sensed in their invitation a nuance of half-hearted urging. She set out to find work as a bookkeeper and a place to stay.

Because she was not a Mormon, she found most doors closed to her. Truth was, there were too many eligible, single Mormon women around willing to work; their presence denied a gentile girl a fair chance. She met two or three Mormon girls and felt sorry for them because they were ordered to marry men who came into town from lonely farms, seeking healthy young wives. It was not slavery, but neither was it quite freedom to consent or refuse. She was approached by Mormon men who had matrimony on their minds, but Julie, tutored in Methodist theology, refused to accept their tenets. Things got difficult when a particular Mormon farmer kept after her. She was afraid he might peremptorily kidnap her some night and take her to his lonely farm, there to bear a dozen Mormon children and pay homage to a Mormon husband she did not love. No thanks.

One day in September 1865, she was walking down Temple Street, contemplating her future, when she came to a theater. Yes, a theater, for the Mormons did not object to theatrical entertainment. But something was happening at this playhouse. Her curiosity aroused, she came closer and overheard some of the conversation. A troupe that had been playing there was moving on. Two very official looking men, obviously Mormons, stood by, watching the process. Trunks came out the doors, then big placards advertising the group. Julie's eyes opened wider as she glimpsed the placards—of young, curvaceous women in tights! And the sides of the wagon being loaded said it all: Professor de Lattier's Theater of Dancing, Singing, and Magic Arts, and lurid paintings of can-can girls, their derrieres covered with lace, legs in black stockings—quite a come-on for lonely men. Small wonder, thought the girl, that the good Mormons were sending them on their way.

A matronly woman was fussing with the movers, occasionally getting in a snide remark about the two Mormons. Then her husband joined her—Julie thought it must be her husband—and was heard to say, "Now, now, dear. We'll be on our way to the mines before sunset. Don't alienate these gentlemen."

"Hmmph," grunted the woman, suddenly eyeing Julie. "I don't mind being kicked out of town, but I don't like it when they convert one of my girls and persuade her to stay here." Then she began walking toward Julie.

"Camille, what are you doing?" asked her husband.

And half to her husband and half to Julie, she said, "Hello, dearie. Want to join our troupe?"

"I—no—I mean, what is it?"

"Well," she began, placing her hands on her hips and turning toward the wagon with its lurid pictures, "it says we're a theatrical troupe. Really, dearie, we dance and sing a few songs and my husband does magic tricks. And the girls are also taxi dancers. We do saloons and music halls and the girls get paid for dancing with the patrons. It's all legitimate."

Julie arched her eyebrows. She had learned much since leaving Willow Grove. She knew of prostitution.

Camille saw Julie's skepticism. "Taxi dancers, dear. No whores. Not at all. Any girl in our troupe caught whoring is kicked out, fast."

Now Camille de Lattiere became more serious. "We charge men to dance with us," she explained. "I take half of everything the girls get, and the girls keep the rest. With drinks, the saloon gets half. In a busy mining camp, it can run into real money fast." As she talked, Camille practically undressed the girl standing before her. "Hmm," she said, "dearie, I swear, you'd do so well you could retire in a year." She looked at Julie's innocent face and frowned. "But I suppose you're a good Mormon girl, or you're married to a Mormon, or you're goin' to be married to a—"

"No," Julie cut in. "I'm not. I'm here, and I'm out of a job. I—just—might—"

In her cold room above Reece's big barroom, Julie held Melissa tightly. Quickly she reminisced how this couple had hired her, trained her to dance the can-can, taught her to sing, and clued her on tips beyond the charge on the one hand, and how to dispense with overzealous suitors on the other. The troupe had started north, stopping at one mining camp after another. By the time Professor de Lattier's Theater of Dancing, Singing, and Magic Arts reached Muddy Creek, Julie had worked at least a dozen mining camps and still more saloons, for often they went from one saloon to another in the same camp.

At first she had found the life exhilarating. It was a free and, to Methodist Julie, a raucous life in which, although she saw much, she did little that was beyond the precepts of the Bible. The other girls—oh, my goodness, she thought—each one's life was already a little book. The other girls were not as well-educated, nor as pretty, nor as moral as Julie. Still, their affairs were usually with one man, and not for money, though a couple of the girls seemed to latch onto a specific man at each saloon.

At Muddy Creek, two of the four girls ran off with men. The professor and his overweight, heavily painted wife, Camille, took Rose, one of the two remaining, to Salt Lake City with them to recruit more girls, leaving Julie alone at Reece's in Muddy Creek. Her earnings were excellent, and during their absence she did not have to share them with Camille and the professor; drinks, of course, were fifty-fifty with Reece's.

But recently she had tired of the routine. Dancing with unwashed men, fending off advances, doing the can-can in front of leering miners, singing popular songs to half-drunken men who were indulging in gambling, all began to be old hat. She was eighteen now. She knew she was beautiful. But when she was alone, when she and Melissa had talks, she thought of Si and his encouragement. "You are bright, Julie. You have good judgment. You've got to use it. You'll do all right." If Si could see her now, would he think she was doing all right? Would he approve? She knew he would not.

She sobbed. She knew she had let him down.

Julie hugged Melissa. She heard commotion in the big room downstairs. The service, she realized, was due to start in a few minutes. Quickly Julie stood up, looked in the wavy mirror, patted her hair, and rubbed her face, trying to obliterate signs of crying. Then she picked up Melissa and tenderly, as if she were a real infant, opened the door and started downstairs.

XII

While Julie pondered her fate in the bare, rustic boudoir, preparations continued in the big room. Father Demetrius de Mara was checking his silver watch, noting the time: eleven-thirty, fifteen minutes to go, when he heard sounds of a wagon backing up to the entrance. A teamster's harsh commands were followed by voices of strong-hearted men saying, "Here, let us help you with that," and "Where'd you get it?" and "That's great."

Curious, the padre strode to the entrance just as the swinging doors opened and were held that way by a couple of spruced-up strangers. "Slowly, boys," he heard, "easy does it." Soon an instrument of dark wood, about four feet high and three feet wide, entered the room in the hands of three strong men.

"An Esty organ!" someone exclaimed.

And indeed it was. Robert Sungren, dressed in a black suit, white shirt, and string tie, entered behind it. "Padre, look what we've got for the service!" he announced. "I thought, 'whoever heard of a Christmas service without organ music?' and I went to Will Benson's saloon and asked if we could borrow it, and blimey, he said yes!" Sungren turned to the men carrying it. "Shove the piano out of the way, boys," he ordered. "To play Christmas carols on a tinny out-of-tune instrument would be an act of heresy. We're going to have organ music!"

"But who's going to work the organ?" someone asked.

"I am," replied the piano player, a sop who had shaved for the first time in two weeks and had even found a clean shirt. "I know how to pump this here machine with my feet while makin' music with the keys. Ye jest you wait and see. I had a mother, you know. She taught me."

"And if it's ok with you, Padre, I'll announce the procession with my silver cornet," added one of the tallest, slimmest men in Muddy Creek. "Don't worry. I ain't drunk, leastwise, not that drunk. It'll sound real good."

Father de Mara was so busy thanking people that he could hardly keep up. Big Mike appeared. "Father de Mara, when can we ring the bell? Gotta let people know they should be at church, ya know."

"In just a few minutes," replied the priest. "I'll give you a sign."

Again there was a flurry outside. The priest heard a woman's shrill voice. "We're comin' in. You ain't stoppin' us."

"No, you ain't, Madam Dahlia. Ye and yer gals ain't invited."

"The hell we ain't!"

"What's wrong?" asked Father de Mara as he stepped briskly to the entrance. There he beheld a sight his superiors had never witnessed, nor envisioned, nor instructed novices how to handle. A fringe-topped surrey stood in front of Reece's. Just now dismounting was the last of five women, sedately dressed with feathered hats and faces strangely devoid of make-up. Obviously they were trying to be prim and correct. Standing at the entrance was a portly woman, body straight and head erect, as dignified as a wealthy matron. This, of course, was Madam Dahlia. And the other four were her—girls. Someone else, and something else, was still getting out of the surrey, but Father de Mara did not have time to take stock of everything.

"Padre," protested a stocky miner, cap in hand, "ye don't want these—these—women to attend yer services. They're—they're—"

"I know," replied the priest, holding up his hand. "But didn't you ever hear of Mary Magdalene? Are you without sin? Have you never heard the saying, 'Let he who is without sin cast the first stone?'"

The protester looked around at the people silenced by the discussion and faded back into the crowd. Madam Dahlia and her girls entered, albeit with an undertone of resentment.

"Titian Reynolds!" Boyd O'Connor shouted at the male figure just stepping from the surrey. "You didn't let us down after all." He ran to the vehicle to help Titian manage an artist's tripod and a big, flat, rectangular object wrapped in what appeared to be a faded cotton bedspread. "Is that a painting?"

Titian, tall, almost cadaverously thin, stood with his back to the crowd, struggling with his burden. He glanced over his shoulder. "Help me with it, will you? After all, if you hadn't made that call tonight, I'd be dead drunk by now, and there wouldn't be any painting."

Quickly Boyd O'Connor was at his side. "You carry the tripod," Titian ordered, "and I'll take the painting. It may not be all dry and it must be handled ve-r-r-y carefully."

Boyd grasped the awkward device firmly and reentered the Music Hall/church with it, the people giving him room. Up the middle aisle he marched, then to the right side opposite the manger scene. There he set it up even as Titian Reynolds gingerly followed him with the covered painting. Boyd stood aside to let the artist do the honors. Titian was an artist, all right, thought Boyd: tall and slim with a mustache and a Van Dyke beard, the cape clasped at his neck, all to give some protection to his shabby black suit, white shirt, and string tie. He wore a felt hat with a narrow trim and a feather in it; the hat was jauntily set at an angle. But most noticeable about Titian Reynolds, the alcoholic local painter, was his stance. Titian stood tall, dead sober, with his chin tilted up just enough to exemplify the confidence he placed in his talent. People who had seen him only as a drunk noticed the difference immediately.

As everyone waited (and by now the chairs were filling rapidly), and no one talked, Titian advanced to the tripod, centered the big wrapped object on it, slightly adjusted the position of the tripod so that the painting could be seen by the largest number of worshipers. He cast his eyes at Father de Mara, who stood in the center aisle.

"Padre," began the artist, bowing and swishing off his hat. "A church must have a painting. It must have a Madonna and a nativity scene. And Madonnas are not common in frontier Montana and not too many babes are born in this man's society. So I have painted for your church a Madonna of the Mountains. With the nativity scene thrown in."

With a flourish befitting a Shakespearian actor, Titian Reynolds swept off the covering. People gasped. Father de Mara, hardly aware of his actions, whispered a prayer. Soon from the congregation came "oooohhhs" and "ahhhhhs." For

Titian Reyolds' hasty painting was, all agreed, a true work of art. Different, but a beautiful, appropriate painting.

The Madonna was sitting on a low barrel with black letters spelling out NAILS. Behind her were stables with a donkey, a mule, a cow and a calf, and horses standing patiently, munching hay. Beside her at an angle were two bales of hay as high as the Madonna's waist. On top of the hay was Joseph's open sheepskin coat, and lying in swaddling clothes on the warm fleece was the Christ child; the Virgin Mary was looking down at the infant. On the other side of Mary stood Joseph, also looking at the babe. He wore the clothing of a Muddy Creek miner: heavy, dirty boots; loose-fitting woolen trousers held up by wide, brown suspenders; a blue flannel shirt open at the neck; his head bare. His hair was light brown and fell to his shoulders. Joseph's face, seen in profile, was tanned from long hours working the placers, and his features were well-chiseled but not harsh. He was clean-shaven, and intelligence was written on his face. Clearly, here was a young man both proud and concerned for the well-being of his wife and new child.

An 1860s kerosene lantern hung from a crude pillar, shedding light on the scene. Facing Mary and the Christ child and Joseph were the three wise men. One was a husky miner with an Irish face and a shaggy beard, a buffalo robe coat, and rough boots. In his hands he held a two-pound can labeled ARBUCKLE'S COFFEE—popular and in demand in the mining camps. A second wise man, this one with the narrow face and pointed nose of a Yankee, held a white five-pound sack labeled SUGAR. And the third wise man—a smaller person with an olive complexion and a round face fitting the common image of a Mexican, some of whom were in the camps, held in his hands a small greasy leather pouch needing no label. Everyone knew it contained gold dust.

Behind them stood three animals: a donkey loaded with prospector's gear, a mule with a washing pan sticking from the diamond-hitched pack, and a tired looking horse with a rolled up blanket behind the saddle.

Above and to the right of Mary was a rectangular window. It was not crystal clear; instead, it had a beautiful lavender tinge, a color leaded glass of the time took on after a few years' exposure to sunlight. The terrain revealed by the window was not of desert but of mountains, recognizably the mountains overlooking Muddy Creek. The focal point of the window was a beautiful star.

But all eyes were drawn magnetically to the Madonna, incredibly beautiful with her tender, angelic face of refined features and sky-blue eyes. Her brown dress could have been of gingham or wool or linse-woolsey. Her feet were covered by rough-shod low-heeled shoes of the kind worn by thousands of American pioneer women.

After long moments, Titian spoke. "This, Father de Mara, is the Madonna of the Mountains." He paused. The congregation was still. "I have not intended to be sacrilegious. I felt this in my heart, and when one feels something in his heart, perhaps it is God talking." Then he added, "As you know, Padre, many Italian artists painted nativity scenes with Italian backgrounds. I have painted one with a western Montana background."

Father de Mara was fascinated by the painting. Finally he turned to the tall, lanky, emaciated painter standing beside his work. "God bless you," whispered the padre. Then aloud: "It is beautiful, Mr. Reynolds. I, and the entire congregation, thank you. Please allow it to remain just where it is. We will enjoy it during the Mass."

Spontaneously the congregation applauded long and hard. Titian had hardly expected that. He bowed and smiled. When the applause ended, the young artist said, in a voice loud enough for everyone to hear, "I hoped you'd like it. I had to do it rapidly, you know. Perhaps you'll want to hang it in your permanent church."

The padre started to say, "What church?" but thought better of it. "You mean we can have it?" he asked instead. "We have no money, you know."

Titian shrugged his shoulders, examining his painting. Especially did he analyze the angelic face of his lost Cecelia, whose face it was, and which he had carried all the way from Philadelphia. The remainder of the painting he had accomplished in the past few hours. No, by presenting it, without charge, to a church, Titian Reynolds had in his mind done penance for the young girl's death. He felt as if a great weight had been lifted from his chest. He felt as if he could face the world again.

"I would be honored if you were to keep it for the church that will eventually be here," he said.

"We shall treasure it," replied Father de Mara. "Won't you sit here," he invited Titian, motioning to a chair a miner had vacated for him, "and enjoy the service? You do not have to be a Catholic to be welcomed here."

Titian had not planned on remaining at church. His thoughts had ended with the presentation of the painting. "I accept," he replied almost without thinking, again making a flourish as he took off his hat. It flashed through his mind that while services were being held, he could make plans for his future.

Someone tapped the priest's back. He turned to face Big Mike Mitchell and Patrick Shanahan. "Padre," Mike whispered, "it's about twenty minutes of twelve. Hadn't we better ring the bell?"

Father de Mara checked his silver watch. "Yes, Mike, I think we should. Go out and ring it loud and clear. 'Tis for the celebration of our dear Savior's birth."

Mike disappeared out the swinging doors and thirty seconds later the congregation, by now all chairs occupied, people standing along the walls, and some spilling outside the entrance because no space was left inside, heard the loud, brassy clanging of the new fire bell. It went on—and on—rather too long. But the padre was so pleased at all that had transpired that he did not care.

Then Patrick Shanahan returned. "Father," he asked, "I see you have an incense burner. May I fill it with Sang Lee's incense and light it and swing it around? To make the altar smell nice?"

Permission was granted.

Meanwhile, among the many waiting worshipers were several men of local note sitting quietly, contemplating their religion, their lives, their futures. One was Jack Langford. He sat straight and dignified, smooth-shaven save for a clipped mustache, with pronounced, even features and black hair, nicely parted. After all, he reasoned, it was *his* music hall, and killing William O'Bryan earlier in the day bothered him. He had never killed a man before. He considered himself an Episcopalian and a man of morals and integrity. He felt obliged to attend church. Possibly it would relieve his mind of the burden of guilt. As befitted the owner of Reece's, he had seated himself in a chair just over halfway up the aisle.

Jack Langford's life had not been marred by the horrors experienced by others in the big room, at least not until today's incident, when he had killed a man in self-defense. He was a Yale graduate, son of a New England wheelwright who had supplied the stagecoach firm of Abbott and Downing, manufacturers of the famous Concord coaches. When that company began making their own wheels, the Langford business declined. By the time Jack graduated from college, his father was bankrupt and the family fortune, once considerable, had disappeared. Jack returned home to discover that he not only did not have a job waiting for him in the family business—he had no money.

No matter. He had an education second to none, enjoyed excellent health, and, if the truth were known, was almost glad his father's bankruptcy had happened. Jack was not interested in what had been the Langford business. Full of vinegar, as his father said he was, Jack set out to make his fortune. The world was his oyster, and he was determined to open it and savor its contents.

It was 1850. News of the California gold rush had become old news by then, but the wonders of California and the opportunity to make one's fortune in a new country as well as the promise of adventure were a combination too rich to pass up. Young Jack joined a company of argonauts who chartered an old whaler and set sail on the high seas for the Equator, stormy Cape Horn, and the Pacific north to San Francisco. It took all of five months, by which time the company had fallen apart. They disembarked at the wharf, each going his own way.

Jack Langford's way was to Sacramento and the northern fields of the Mother Lode. He soon grasped the reality that few fortunes were being made in gold mining per se, but his bright, entrepreneurial mind saw potentialities in a host of auxiliary operations. He and some Yankees he met along the way hit upon the idea of damming timberline lakes far to the east in the High Sierras, building aqueducts down to the mining sites, and selling the water. With barely sufficient funds, the Boston and Mother Lode Hydraulic Service Company came into existence. All fall and winter of 1850-51 they labored. By late spring they were ready to sell water to the big sluice mining operations. Their scheme succeeded, and Jack Langford emerged as a young local capitalist.

Soon he had investments in a wide area of the northern Mother Lode. He owned or had stock in several mining operations, in a shebang and, for a while, in a stagecoach line. He enjoyed the work and the challenge. But the sluices gave out and other companies had preempted other high mountain lakes and were also building aqueducts. The Boston and Mother Lode Hydraulic Service Company shut down operations. Some of Jack's investments proved profitable, but after eight years of conducting business in the Mother Lode country, he realized that he was losing ground. He decided in the spring of 1859 to cut his losses and head east, to see Boston and New England and his parents again. So, far from being broke, but not rich either, he had embarked for the East Coast via the Isthmus of

Panama, across which he could now travel in the relative comfort of a railroad car.

After visiting parents and friends and seeing old landmarks, he found himself fidgety, anxious once more to grab for the One Big Chance. One day he read in the Boston *Globe* about the discovery of oil in northwest Pennsylvania. A man named Drake had ignored the scorn of friends and neighbors, sunk a well, and come up with oil. It could be refined into kerosene, better known then as coal oil. Used as a source of fuel for heating and cooking, and for lamps, it far surpassed coal, candles, or sperm oil. "A revolution in heating, cooking, and lighting is already underway due to the discoveries at Oil City and other nearby communities," the item read.

The next day Langford was on his way to the oil boom towns. He met with almost immediate success and was soon a wealthy man. But it was apparent that while he was in an expanding industry, it was also an industry punctuated by severe surpluses—oil gluts—which brought on devastating price wars. It was not unusual for him to earn and lose as much as $30,000 in a week. He became aware that one group was eliminating competition through purchase of competitors or through underselling them by means of rebate deals with the railroads. To checkmate this, Langford joined a group to fight the company. They failed.

Again, Jack Langford cut his losses with still enough cash to invest elsewhere. The elsewhere was in the West, for he found himself more and more dreaming of the region where he had started his career. He found the social conventions of the East stultifying.

He had read about the gold discoveries at the Idaho and western Montana mines, and by the summer of 1862 was in the region. Because he already possessed considerable knowledge of placer mining, and hard-rock mining too, he almost immediately doubled and then tripled his fortune. Langford could have returned east, but he realized that he had fallen in love with life in the American West. When a boom town became too settled he was prone to leave it for a new one. That was what brought him to Muddy Creek almost as soon as it sprouted out of the gulch in early 1864. In no time he had an interest in the local shebang, owned considerable business property on Main Street, had a couple of exceedingly profitable placers, and had purchased from William O'Bryan the Sunnyside Mine. With Reece he had built Reece's Music Hall, and when Reece, without a will and with no known heirs, was killed in a shootout with Charlton Edwards, Langford had become sole owner. Around town he was respected as a tough dealer but a square shooter, and he enjoyed being the big fish even if it was in a little pond.

Sitting in the church converted temporarily from his Music Hall, Langford deeply regretted the killing that afternoon of William O'Bryan. His fingers played with the Masonic symbol on his watch chain. He wanted to do right, he told himself. That was why he was the catalyst in bringing together fellow Masons to form a vigilante group to eradicate the region of its increasingly bold criminal element. Four times that fall, the Gilmer and Salisbury Stage carrying gold had been robbed. Someone in Muddy Creek had to be informing the highwaymen of the gold shipments. Gradually the vigilantes had drawn a list of suspects. The time was coming to act. Langford hated the thought. He knew that vigilantism was a poor second to the machinery of law, but that machinery had not yet arrived at Muddy Creek. He had suggested giving fair warning first: a card shaped like a coffin showing up in a deck of cards while suspects were gambling. The smart desperadoes would get the message and leave.

As he sat fingering his Masonic symbol, staring blankly at the altar and Titian Reynolds' painting, contemplating on this Christmas Eve what events might soon transpire and how Christian would they be, his eyes fell suddenly upon a swarthy, nattily dressed character sitting in the front row on the other side of the aisle. It was Charlton Edwards, the gambler. In front and to one side of Langford sat Sang Lee. By the way the Chinese was twitching uncomfortably in his chair Langford knew he was agitated. Sang Lee was staring at Edwards even though he could just see his back. Langford frowned and also studied the back of the gambler's head.

Edwards was a peculiar gambler, thought Langford: he was a professional card shark who did not always win. That had been established about three o'clock one stormy morning when six poker players, the only occupants of Reece's at that hour, finally tallied up their winnings and losses. Langford had won big, and Charlton Edwards, the professional, had lost badly. He had, in fact, lost so much gold dust that Langford wondered where in tarnation he had got it. One thing was certain: Edwards had never earned it fair and square through hard labor at a sluice box or cradle.

Could he, thought Langford as he sat waiting for the service to begin, have stolen it from Sang Lee's miners? He stared blankly at Edwards. He knew the vigilance committee considered him a prime suspect, a member of a gang that had held up the stage and had possibly committed other crimes.

After the game broke up, Langford recalled, Edwards and a couple of the boys, including Langford, had poured themselves a nightcap and Edwards, down in his cups at his losses, began reminiscing about his life. He had been born in New Orleans' French Quarter to a beautiful octoroon and her Mississippi plantation paramour. By the time Edwards (which, Langford always thought, was not his real name) was twelve, his mother had lost her beauty and her paramour, and was a prostitute with deteriorating clientele. Edwards was left pretty much to his own resources. The boy soon learned how to survive along the riverfront, now pimping for his mother and other fallen women, again rolling drunks for their money, watches, and jewelry. He did not add, but Langford pieced together, that Edwards had also learned how to avoid the law, that he carried a hidden Derringer on his person and had used it, that he knew something about fighting with knives, and carried a scar across his left cheek, proof that he had learned the hard way.

Edwards did tell how, by the age of eighteen, he had mastered cards and was a riverboat gambler. When the Civil War ended Mississippi River transportation, he headed west. That night at Reece's he hinted that something else had happened to turn his feet west, something he did not divulge, merely saying that he had come west partly to avoid dancing in mid-air.

Could he, mused Langford, be a member of the gang? Sang Lee's agitation was clearly evident when the Chinese turned in his chair to catch Langford's eyes. When the two made eye contact, Sang Lee jerked his head in the direction of Edwards. Ever so slightly, Langford turned his face to where Edwards sat and then nodded understanding back to Sang Lee. Noticeably relieved, the Celestial promptly settled down in his chair, knowing that he had made his point. Edwards, Langford realized, must have been a member of the gang that murdered the Chinese. That was probably the source of Edwards' gold dust the night of the poker game. The gambling had taken place, Langford reflected, at just about the time Sang Lee's companions had been murdered.

Still another Protestant businessman sat quietly among the worshipers. Jesse Tinsley, after loaning the shipping box for the manger, the lectern, the narrow table for the altar, and the candlesticks, quietly sat and awaited the service. He had dressed in his one good woolen suit, carried all the way from Lawrence, and from Ohio before then. It reminded him of home. Jesse was very depressed. He thought of his family, his wife and three daughters, and was almost overcome with guilt. "Why," he kept asking himself, "why have I failed to write Molly back in Ohio? She must think I'm dead. Perhaps she has remarried." He swallowed hard. "My God," he repeated to himself, "could Molly have remarried? Are my daughters forgetting me?"

Jesse tried to understand and explain to his satisfaction the reason for his actions.

Imaginative, fantasizing Jesse had been married at eighteen before he could sow any wild oats (save those that brought on marriage and his eldest daughter). After marriage, all Jesse could do in the wild oats department, until Quantrill's raid, was fantasize. Although he loved Molly and the girls, he had daydreamed constantly about the West, of striking it rich, of swaggering into a saloon, playing poker or faro and winning, having an affair with a dance hall girl. Indeed, when the opportunity arose to break for such a life, Jessie had cast aside conscience and obligations and grabbed at the opportunity. He knew that he was not the first man to do it, nor the last.

Now he knew that he'd had enough of that freedom. He was a lousy poker player and always lost at faro and wouldn't get involved with a dance hall girl or visit Madam Dahlia's. He was not attractive to women with his too big nose, weak chin, receding hairline, and growing paunch. A furniture dealer he was, and a good one able to make a profit, and a furniture dealer he would always be. Such were his thoughts as he awaited the service. He needed a church this Christmas night—any church.

At the back of the big room, from whence he could leave unnoticed, sat the pensive German teamster, Gunter Schroeder. Gunter felt a peacefulness he had not experienced since, well, he thought, since Germany, before he became a flaming revolutionist. It was the peace of home and church in the years when he was growing up in a loving family. "Ach, why did I fall for all that radical tripe? I should haf remained a political eunuch and taken a degree in theology and today I vould be a Lutheran minister. Helping people. Being respected like dis Catholic Vater de Mara." The longer he sat and the more he admired the Jesuit priest, the less happy he became with his own place in life. Gunter's face was a picture of troubled concern.

Barry Millard was likewise engrossed in thought. He was sure he loved Julie, taxi dancer though she was. Unusual taxi dancer! She had read Darwin's *Origin of Species*! He knew she had been raised on an Iowa farm, had attended a female academy, and had searched for bookkeeper's work in Council Bluffs and Salt Lake City. Failure to find such work, so she had told him, was how she came to be a taxi dancer at Reece's Music Hall. It wasn't enough. Barry had kept plying her with questions, for something in her story was lacking, but so far she had not divulged the secret.

She was so exuberant when she was with him, her blue eyes flashing, her conversation constant and intelligent, that he could not believe she had been dishonest to him. No, it was not that. It was a gap in her story. He had figured this much: that it concerned her father and mother. When he asked about them a shadow crossed her pretty face, her eyes drooped. Something unpleasant had happened, Barry was sure. But what?

Beyond that, Barry kept pondering this: could Julie adjust to a professional scientist's life? Would she be an embarrassment? What would his mother think of her? "And what did Julie do in Muddy Creek?" he pictured his mother asking. "Oh, she was a taxi dancer at Reece's Music Hall." And Barry gasped. "Oh, my Gawd, how Mother would react to that! Quick! Get the smelling salts!"

Big Mike approached the padre at the entrance. "Padre, we beginnin' pretty soon?"

And the padre replied, "In five minutes. Why don't you and Teague lower the lamps and reduce their light by at least one-half? Then light the tapers."

Big Mike and the boys set about following his directions. Just as this activity was taking place, all heads turned to the narrow balcony where a door opened and Julie emerged. Barry caught his breath. She looked so lovely in a black, stylish dress. Her blond hair was pulled back into a bun. She walked rapidly the length of the balcony to the stairs and then began descending, slowly, for she appeared to be carrying a baby snuggled in her arms.

The congregation, already talking in hushed tones, became silent; one could have heard a pin drop. Before she was halfway down the stairs they heard the girl singing softly an old Christmas carol: "...Round yon Virgin Mother and Child," they heard her sing in a clear, pure voice, "Holy Infant so tender and mild ..." Julie sang the carol as if to a live babe. At the foot of the stairs she turned and walked slowly to the manger. Barry Millard's eyes misted as Julie ended her song and carefully wrapped the doll in the swaddling clothes that had been placed on the hay. Then she hugged the doll and kissed it on the forehead before returning it to the makeshift crib.

Julie now stood up, suddenly aware of her audience, not quite sure what to do next. First thing she knew, Barry was at her side. "Julie," he whispered, for he realized all eyes were upon them. "Julie, I have to see you. Come sit with me. The man next to me will vacate his chair for you." For Barry Millard had made his decision. Julie was a good woman and Julie must become his wife.

Her eyes fluttered as she looked up at him. Without replying she took his hand and allowed him to walk her to the chair being hastily vacated next to his; its occupant, being a gentleman, had graciously offered her his place and walked to the wall.

XIII

Jesuit Father Demetrius de Mara stood at the doorway to the Music Hall-cum-church. He was surrounded by miners dressed in their best clothes, shabby, unpressed, but for the most part clean, and a few wives. The only children present belonged to the Lancasters, who had arrived early enough to get seats for their washed, scrubbed, yawning, squirming children, including a suckling babe. Muddy Creek was at least ninety percent male.

Not a bit of wall space up to six feet or so could be seen, so packed were those standing at the sides of the "church." Crowded also was the back of the hall, near the entrance, and an overflow of humanity extended outside even beyond the boardwalk. Pine, spruce, and juniper fragrance was doing a fairly good job of obliterating the sour whiskey-unwashed male smell that had permeated the big room. The priest eyed the altar and saw that young Pat Shanahan had transferred Sang Lee's sandalwood incense to the burner, had just succeeded in lighting it, and was now waving it from side to side, the puffs of fragrant smoke emitting from the open grillwork. Father de Mara thought he caught just a whiff of the sandalwood even as he stood at the entrance, and it smelled good.

He stood at the start of the center aisle and surveyed the "church." Every seat was taken. Among the many he had not met was the carpenter, Ebenezer Cotton, standing against the wall close to the door leading to the confessional that, he proudly thought, was a result of his Christian generosity.

And up close to the altar was the alcalde. The center aisle led directly to the two steps leading to the stage. Straight ahead was Jesse Tinsley's table-cum-altar, covered with not-so-clean linen. To the left on the stage was the lectern; buckets of sand were strategically placed for the two tapers and another to hold the crucifix. Four chairs were placed against the back wall to the left of the altar; these were for the acolytes, and an armchair was strategically located a few feet to the right of the altar; this was for the priest. Hanging from the ceiling behind the altar was Gunter Schroeder's crucifix. To the left, from the worshiper's view, and against the back wall from the lectern, was an ugly table upon which was the padre's crude, portable tabernacle, containing the host.

In front of the lectern but below the stage, barely discernible from where he stood, was the manger scene. It was now complete with Jesse Tinsley's packing box, Jack Langford's spruce, pine, and juniper boughs, Gunter Schroeder's carved camels, donkeys, wise men, Mary and Joseph, and Julie Montgomery's doll as the Christ child, wrapped in swaddling clothes supplied by Mrs. Lancaster. To the priest's right, as he stood at the end of the center aisle near the doors, was Titian Reynolds' Madonna and nativity scene within view of the entire congregation. The Irishmen had lowered the flames in the big kerosene fixtures so the big room was now in a half gloaming.

Jesuit Father Demetrius de Mara looked at his silver watch. "Let's light the tapers and prepare for the procession," he announced. Boyd O'Connor and Teague Cosgrove complied. Gingerly, as if it might break, Big Mike Mitchell accepted the Douay Bible the padre had entrusted him with. "Now, Mike," instructed the priest, "as you walk slowly up the aisle, hold the Bible in front of you and well above your head."

"I will, Padre. I will."

"And Pat, try to hold the crucifix steady and straight.

Pat nodded.

Again Father de Mara pulled his silver watch from his vestments. "Just 11:45 p.m.," he announced quietly. Unobserved by him, someone outside gave the cue to ring the fire bell once more. The young priest, hardly a year out of the Old Country, made the sign of the cross, blessed the acolytes, and said a silent prayer. He drank in the scene once more, for it seemed miraculous, this transformation, in so short a time, of a music hall-saloon-gambling den-dance hall into a beautiful Catholic chapel.

Now he glanced to his left to where the organist and young Robert Sungren awaited his signal. Father de Mara nodded; the young singing instructor in turn gave a nod to the cornet player standing upstairs at the back of the balcony, almost directly above where Father de Mara was standing. Clarion sounds shot out over the congregation. When the cornetist ended, Robert Sungren tapped the organist's shoulder. The musician pumped the pedals hard; then the organ played "Hark! The Herald Angels Sing."

The congregation rose and those standing along the wall stood straight, as if at attention. Robert Sungren could contain himself no longer. The music teacher reverted from passenger-express agent to his earlier calling, instinctively raising his arms and leading the congregation and, a bit to his own surprise, singing loud and clear. Christmas carols were the most widely known of all hymns. The entire congregation, including many who could hardly carry a tune, pitched in. Reece's Music Hall had always been raucous, but never had its rafters resounded to the sounds of "Hark! The Herald Angels Sing."

Father de Mara signaled for the procession to begin. He wished the acolytes had vestments, but at least they were dressed in the best clothes they owned. Young Pat Shanahan, straight-backed and tilting his head upward to achieve greater dignity, began the slow march up the aisle. The crucifix he was holding did not waver an iota from its perpendicular position. Then Boyd O'Connor and Teague Cosgrove advanced side by side with the tapers. Next in the procession came barrel-chested Big Mike Mitchell, strutting like a proud rooster as he held the Bible aloft, high above the front of his head. Behind them all, singing lustily, walked the bespectacled padre.

Climbing to the stage, Pat placed the crucifix in the bucket of sand to the right of the altar, Boyd and Teague placed the tapers in the two buckets placed for them, and Big Mike deposited the Bible on the altar. They, save for Pat, walked to the chairs placed for them on the platform, but remained standing as did the congregation. Pat took it upon himself once more to grab the incense burner and swing it lustily, first on the platform, then down to the main floor and up the center aisle, wafting fragrant smoke as he went. Then he returned to the stage, deposited the incense burner against a wall, and joined his Irish brethren.

The music had stopped. Father Demetrius de Mara, S.J., bowed to the crucifix hanging from the ceiling. Ordinarily he would have blessed a vial of holy water and sprinkled the altar, but the vial had been lost weeks ago when Lucifer had balked and shaken off the pack. So now the padre turned and faced the congregation.

In the sea of bearded faces he was reminded of the fishermen of the Sea of Galilee. As he gathered his thoughts he noted the presence of Jack Langford, the man who had killed William O'Bryan just hours ago. He looked into the eyes of Charlton Edwards, the gambler, and had a fleeting thought that he was the man who had approached Robert Sungren about divulging the date of the next gold shipment. He noted lovely Julie and the handsome, protective Barry Millard. There was Titian Reynolds, the painter, and way at the back was Gunter Schroeder, the German teamster and woodcarver. Sang Lee sat respectfully in his beautiful native clothing. Sitting in a row were the painted ladies of Madam Dahlia's. Most of the worshipers, he correctly surmised, were not even Catholic. He would know how many were of the faith when he celebrated holy communion. But no matter. This was the night of the Lord's birth.

Let us pray," announced the priest, stretching out his arms. "*Oxaudi nos, Domine sancte, aeterne Deus...*" (Hear us, O Holy Lord, Father Almighty, Everlasting God...) When the prayer ended, those with chairs sat down.

What was called the Didactic part of the service followed. The padre read verses from the Prophet Isaiah from the Old Testament and from the Book of Luke from the New. Now it was time for him to deliver the homily.

The homily (Protestants called it a sermon): So busy had he been that he had hardly given it a thought. Whatever the padre said had to be impromptu. What could he say to such a disparate gathering of Christians? Well, he better think fast, for the time was *now*. In his clear, low, masculine voice with its slight Italian accent, Father Demetrius de Mara, S.J., began speaking:

"My brothers and sisters in Christ," he began, noting that he had everyone's attention save for the Lancaster children who were mercifully dozing off. "I know that every one of you is in Muddy Creek because of the promise of riches, to obtain gold that buys earthly goods and pleasures. Many of you are separated from your loved ones because of this lust for riches. Some of you have already achieved wealth" (the padre looked at Jack Langford) "and most of you are still searching." (He surveyed the congregation in general.) "There is no mystery, then, of why you are in Muddy Creek. But," the padre added, pausing, "that does not explain why you are assembled tonight in this humble church, hastily created out of a saloon and gambling den and dance hall. It is December and it is cold. Why, my brothers and sisters, have you left the comfort of your snug cabins to come out into this winter's night to attend services in this humble sanctuary?

"What has brought you *here*?

"Wherein lies the profit of closing Reece's Music Hall for an evening so church services could be held here?

"Was it lust for material goods that led a fine artist to work all Christmas Eve so that this temporary church could be beautified with a painting of the Madonna and the nativity?

"Was it for material wealth that led a woodcarver to create, and then loan us, his beautiful carvings of the nativity scene and the crucifix that hangs above the altar?

"Was the quest for earthly luxuries dominant in Sang Lee's mind when he presented us with fragrant incense?"

(The padre bowed slightly as he made eye contact with the young Celestial.)

"Why should a Yankee loan us his product, we who are not of his sect, so that we Catholics can have confession?" (The padre had never met Ebenezer Cotton, but as for Cotton, he lowered his eyes and blushed, as people gave him approving looks.) No one laughed at the irony of an outhouse being used as a confessional.

"Was it the lure of material riches that led several of you to go into the cold, dark woods to collect spruce and pine and juniper bows to decorate the walls?

"What profit lay in a compassionate mother loaning her baby's blankets for the nativity scene?

"And what feeling is it that leads a young lady to loan her treasured doll to play the part of the baby Jesus?

"Why should a non-Catholic loan us the table for an altar, this lectern, from which I am speaking, the packing box for the manger, and the candlesticks and tapers?" (Jesse Tinsley straightened his shoulders and tilted his head upward in pride.)

"And the organist, and the trumpeter, and the young man leading us in song—surely, my brothers and sisters, there was no acquisition of worldly treasures that led them to offer their services. They are gifts from the heart, just as your presence here tonight represents homage, adoration, and faith—all from the heart, to worship" (and here Father de Mara paused and made eye contact with as many of the congregation as possible) "…to worship," he said again, "a babe born nearly two thousand years ago, half the world away, under humble circumstances in a manger filled with domesticated animals." Again the padre paused.

"What, then, is so unusual about the birth of this particular babe?" He paused. "Can it be," he continued, "that there is something lacking in our lives when all we search for is material wealth? Did this babe grow up to offer something to man?"

"Can it be, that—regardless of all the wars and horrors and cruelties characterizing the centuries of Christian man—the world is a better place in which to live because of the birth in Bethlehem of this one babe so many ages ago, a babe prophesied by the Prophet Isaiah, a babe born under a star that led the wise men from the East to the humble manger and there, to bow in worship and leave gifts, for they knew that He was indeed the Son of God. They knew the babe would grow up to show the Way. Surely they were not surprised when He sacrificed His life on the Cross that man would be saved! So that we, here assembled in a converted saloon on the Montana frontier, can share His promise of Salvation and Eternal Life.

"That is why so many of you helped create this beautiful temporary chapel, my brothers and sisters. That is why we have assembled here on this cold December night to honor the birth of our Savior. He is our Hope. He shows the way of life in a cruel and heartless world."

Father Demetrius de Mara raised his head high as he surveyed the celebrants. "It is to worship this babe, who represents the hope of the world but who offers us no earthly luxuries, no riches of gold and silver, no mansions or blooded horses, no power over others, that we have assembled here tonight to give thanks to God for the Savior's birth."

The priest paused, turned, and bowed to the crucifix hanging behind the altar, walked to his chair and sat down. The audience was silent.

After a suitable pause, Father de Mara stood along with the congregation and led them in the confiteor ("We believe in God the Father, the Maker of Heaven and Earth…").

And then it was time for the collection. The good padre, a Jesuit who well understood that a church could not be run on Hail Mary's, had requested some kind of vessel in which to take up the collection and had thoughtfully designated two bearded volunteers to pass the plate. Having spent several months in the mining camps of Idaho and Montana, he was prepared for contributions made from small leather pouches: small pinches of gold dust. He had expressed a fear that some of the precious metal would be spilled. When he saw the container, he relaxed. It was a beautiful white and blue Delft tureen, without the cover. And with it a small, rusted teaspoon to scoop up the gold. He never did learn from whence they came.

The vessel began its journey across each row. Father de Mara did not want to appear avaricious, but his eyes widened as he watched humble working men pull out their little leather pouches, unstring the opening, insert the spoon inside, as if for a spoonful of sugar, and come up with it full of bright, sparkling gold dust. He was amused at the one-upmanship displayed, all to the church's benefit. One miner gave two spoonfuls, the next could not admit to being parsimonious, or perhaps less religious, so he gave three spoonfuls. Two or three spoonfuls were the norm. A few gave much more: one man poured half a pouch into the tureen. Others, men who worked in the hard-rock mines, placed flashing coins of the realm into the pile of gold dust. The priest also noticed that, so far as he could tell, everyone, Catholic and non-Catholic alike, gave something. Even the Lancaster family roused some of its children and had them add small coins to the collection.

That is what Father de Mara noticed. From his seat, Jack Langford observed something else: the blazing, covetous eyes of the gambler, Charlton Edwards, as they followed the glittering golden contents of the tureen as the ushers made their way down the rows of worshipers.

"Why, that son of a bitch," thought Langford. "He's scheming to steal the offering!"

The church remained silent save for the occasional cough or sneeze and the crying of the youngest Lancaster infant who protested when it was taken from its mother's breast too quickly.

Robert Sungren, standing by the organist, felt the silence. He wanted music; music was *needed*. "Do you know the accompaniment to 'Oh, Holy Night'?" he whispered to the organist.

"No," was the whispered reply.

"Then give me a chord."

The organ made a single sound. And, looking over the congregation with a smile, Robert Sungren sang a solo for the first time since he had left Denver as a defeated, sickly tubercular. His voice was as clear as the mountain air.

The congregation was entranced by the beauty of the Gilmer and Salisbury clerk's voice. It had just the right resonance, just the right sincerity; it was in perfect key. And as he sang, Sungren gained confidence. Any music teacher would have noticed the change. Stronger and stronger became his voice, the clear words filling the make-shift chapel with the promise of a world without hatred, pain, and strife. Someone, the padre recalled, once said that music was a prayer twice said. Young Sungren's rendition from memory of "Oh, Holy Night" justified the definition.

Now the two ushers made the rounds of those standing against the wall. Then they made their slow way out the swinging doors onto the boardwalk and into the street where shivering, lonely men gave, even though they could barely hear the service, barely catch a glimpse of the transformed music hall.

When they had completed their rounds, the ushers strode back into the chapel along a path willingly made for them by the crowd. At the back of the church they awaited the cue from the priest. One of them glanced at the tureen, heavy with gold dust and coins. A pointed mound of the precious metal reached to the top of the vessel.

"Good Gawd," whispered one to the other, "there must be a thousand, fifteen hundred dollars' gold in this thing."

Meanwhile Father de Mara, with Pat serving as altar boy, prepared for the Mass, the sacrificial part of the service. Preparations made, the good padre nodded to the ushers. The organist played from memory the notes of "Praise God from Whom all Blessings Flow ." The two bearded miners marched up the center aisle, carefully deposited the tureen in front of the altar, stepped back, bowed, and returned to their seats as if they performed the ritual every week.

For non-Catholics, the Mass was an interesting ritual, and a beautiful service it was, on a Christmas Eve. Everyone found kneeling on the hard, cold floor uncomfortable, but in deference to the Catholic participants, to a man (and woman) the non-Catholics kneeled also. In those days the priest read the Mass in Latin with his back to the congregation, facing the crucifix. Protestants noted the highlights of the service, as when the padre lifted the host—a pie-shaped piece of hardtack, which he later broke into small pieces which were given to each Catholic participant—and said: *Hoc Estenim Corpus meum* (For this is My Body).

"What the hell is he sayin'?" whispered Luke Bassett, the alcalde, to the Irish miner kneeling next to him.

"I don't know," was the reply, "it's said in Latin."

"You're a Catholic and you don't know what the priest is saying?"

"Oh, I learned it in catechism. But that was a long time ago. I've just fergot," replied the miner.

When the time came for receiving holy communion a surprising number in the congregation formed a line in the center aisle and advanced toward Father de Mara who stood on the floor in front of the altar to administer the host. As he placed the wafer in each communicant's mouth he repeated the words *Corpus Domini, nostri Jesu Christi, custodist animan tuam in vitam aeternam, Amen* (the body of our Lord, Jesus Christ preserve thy soul unto life everlasting. Amen.)

Langford, who was observing the procedure with interest, was surprised to see one of the men taking communion: Charlton Edwards. Then he recalled Edwards telling about growing up in New Orleans' French Quarter, most probably in a Catholic environment. "I'll bet,"

Langford mused, "that Edwards didn't go to confession tonight." He was right.

When Mass was over, Father de Mara washed the chalice and, with Pat's help, did other housekeeping tasks. This was still a part of the ritual while the congregation remained kneeling on the cold floor, those outside on the muddy boardwalk and even in the mud of the street. When the padre had finished, he stepped to his chair and sat down. This was the signal for all others to resume a sitting position (if they had chairs) or else resume standing.

For a minute or two the priest sat, saying and doing nothing. Then he rose and spoke, standing in front of his chair. "One day," he began, "there will be a beautiful church in Muddy Creek. It will have regular pews and a permanent altar and a magnificent crucifix and stained glass windows and an expensive organ, and a church bell, and perhaps the Madonna and nativity scene will be hung in a prominent place, and" (he paused) "a fine confessional. But I doubt, my dear friends, *I genuinely doubt,* if ever it will have a service more beautiful for its sincerity, for its devotion to the Lord, than has been held tonight in this humble temporary church.

"To all of you, a Merry, Merry, Christmas."

Father de Mara blessed the congregation, making the sign of the cross. "Go in peace," he said, thus ending the first Christmas Mass in Muddy Creek, Montana.

The organist pumped the Esty organ and played the prelude to another well-known carol. Robert Sungren raised his arms, as a music director should. The acolytes picked up the tapers, the crucifix, and Big Mike Mitchell the Bible after the priest had kissed it, and, in solemn dignity, crucifix, Bible, tapers, and priest began walking down the center aisle. At the proper moment Sungren's arms moved in a signal to begin. The rafters shook with the cheerful singing of "Oh Come, All Ye Faithful" by the Christians of Muddy Creek, Montana Territory, on Christmas Eve, December 24/25, 1865.

Slowly the congregation filed out, people greeting each other, shaking hands, wishing each other a Merry Christmas. Men said hello to men they had never known. Madam Dahlia and her girls filed out like proper communicants, having received instructions from their procuress not to solicit tonight, not under any circumstances. When one of the girls began a flirtation, she received a sharp kick in the shins.

Main Street was silent and dark. Hardly a dim, yellow light punctuated the thoroughfare. The owners of every saloon, shebang, and livery had agreed, almost subconsciously, that when church services began every business establishment would pay homage to the Christ child by closing shop. Any drunks found weaving in the street or lying in the gutter were brought in and laid on saloon floors or billiard tables to sleep off their inebriation in the warmth of the building. And Madam Dahlia, upon reaching her *maison de joie*, ordered the girls to retire, the entrance door locked, and lights out. The night was cold, about twenty degrees, but the sky was clear as the beginning of time, the stars were out in profusion, and the Aurora Borealis (the Northern Lights), as if hailing the birth of the Savior, were in the midst of a magnificent presentation—some said in later years that never since had such a magnificent display been observed.

Once eyes adjusted, one could see quite well in the still night air. A lamp remained lighted at the hotel's front desk; that, and the lamps in the music hall/church awaited snuffing.

Everyone felt better for having attended the service. Some were pensive, others quietly joyful. Father de Mara stood at the entrance dispensing best wishes, shaking hands. It was Barry Millard's and Julie Montgomery's turn to shake his hand.

"Father de Mara," Barry began, already confronting the priest with new obligations, "could you marry us tomorrow?"

"On Christmas day?" was Father De Mara's instant reaction. Then he raised his eyebrows, thinking of Canon Law about marriages on Christmas Day and remembering that this young couple was Protestant.

"Has to be," Julie said. "We're leaving Muddy Creek on the Salt Lake Stage tomorrow. We're headed for Boston. So we need to be married before we start." Then she added, "And the Gilmer and Salisbury Stage is running, even if it is Christmas. It's Monday and, well, I guess Christmas Day doesn't mean much in Montana. Some of the stores will be open too."

Quickly Barry added, "Julie's staying in her room at Reece's tonight, Father, and I'll be at the hotel. And by the way, Father, just walk across the street to the hotel. There's a room reserved for you there. You must be very tired." He paused. "Now, about our marriage."

Indeed, the young Jesuit was suddenly aware that he was tired, more fatigued than he could remember ever having been, but he was still thinking clearly.

"If you can't marry us," Julie added, noticing how the priest had not given an answer, "then we'll have to ask that—that—swarthy, plump little alcalde to marry us in a civil ceremony." Julie paused. "He doesn't have enough religion to marry us."

Father Demetrius de Mara struggled to make a decision. He was a Jesuit. He was a Catholic missionary. This was the wild frontier. There wasn't a Protestant cleric within hundreds of miles. This young couple desired to be married by a man of the cloth. He had noticed the alcalde, and he shrank from the idea of that swarthy, sensuous little man marrying such a fine young couple. The priest stood tall, straightening his shoulders. He decided to stretch Canon Law to the absolute limits. "Of course I'll marry you," he said, "and I hope you will both be very happy."

Julie impetuously stood on her tiptoes and gave the padre a peck-kiss on the cheek. Father de Mara did not blush. It was an impetuous act of a happy young woman, and he accepted it.

While people filed out and left the premises, Jack Langford lingered in his music hall/chapel. Had anyone asked why, his reason would have been that, being the owner, it was his duty to extinguish the lamps and lock up. But he remained for another reason. Unobtrusively he took a position in a shadowy corner near the entrance where he could survey the vacant room. He knew that in a few minutes the Irishmen, probably Pat and Boyd, would return to take care of the tabernacle and fold up the cloth that covered the altar, and so forth, and deposit them with the padre. But right now, the big room was vacant.

Almost vacant, for there was Charlton Edwards quietly standing in a shadowy part of the left wall. The big room was vacant save for him and Jack Langford, whom he did not see. Reece's owner watched as Edwards edged toward the blue and white Delft tureen filled with the offering. It was obvious what he planned to do: grab it as if it was his assigned task to do so, then slowly move to the left, down the hallway by the stage and out to the back entrance, into the fresh air and away with the loot.

As Edwards edged up the left aisle toward the stage and the altar and the Delft tureen, Langford, keeping in the shadows, slowly advanced up the right aisle. Suddenly the gambler lost his caution. A few quick steps and he was at the vessel, reaching for it, when he heard a distinct click—the click, long experience told him, of a pistol.

"Going somewhere?" asked Langford.

Edwards whirled toward him, reaching inside his coat. But he saw that Langford had the drop on him with a Colt six-shooter.

"Leave the pistol where it is, Edwards, or you are a dead man. Dead, right in front of the altar. What a shame to dirty up such a sacred place."

The gambler stood transfixed for long moments then smiled. He shrugged his shoulders. "I was just making an estimate of the take," he said.

Langford did not reply, but waved his head toward the rear door. "Come on out here," he commanded quietly. "I want to talk to you, Edwards. In private."

The gambler paused, hesitated. He did not like taking orders but he saw that he had no choice. He sauntered back to the left aisle and turned down the hall to the back door. Langford was right behind him, his pistol held in his pocket. Edwards turned the knob and pushed open the door. He stepped down the one step into the alleyway. Just as Langford stepped down behind him Edwards hurled the door back in Langford's face and reached for his Derringer.

Langford recovered fast. With his free arm he hurled the door open just as Edwards was taking aim. In a flash Langford had removed his hand and pistol from the pocket and with a lightning-swift sweep of his arm hit Edwards' left cheek with the revolver. Charlton Edwards fell hard. As he hit the ground Langford's left foot came down on the gambler's right arm. Instantly Langford reached down and tore the Derringer from Edward's hand. The gambler lay helpless on the cold, frozen earth.

"Get up," Langford commanded, "and don't try anything." He held his gun menacingly. Edwards slowly got to his feet, dusting off his trousers. "Now you listen, Edwards. There's a vigilante committee in Muddy Creek with a list of names. Yours is on it. If you know what's good for you, you'll leave Muddy Creek now—right now—and never come back."

Edwards held his hand to his bleeding left cheek. "What have I done?" he protested.

"You're a part of the gang. You just may be their contact in town, telling them when the gold goes out."

"Bosh. They can't prove that," Edwards replied.

"And," added Langford, "you've been tabbed as one of that gang that murdered those Chinese at Right Angle Bar in Idaho."

"Can't—prove that—either," replied the man, obviously startled by the revelation that he had been identified as one of the thieves.

"Hmmmm. You are guilty, aren't you?" Langford commented, waving his revolver to indicate that the gambler was to start walking. "Take my advice, Edwards. Get out of town. I'm doing you a favor. Don't come back. If you do, you just might find yourself dancing in mid-air."

A coyote howled far off, and another from an opposite direction howled back. Edwards shivered, rubbing his cheek, and looked around. "Can't I stay until morning?"

"Now," replied Langford. "Let's walk to your horse. I want to see you galloping out of here, *now*."

The two walked to the livery, Edwards slightly ahead of his captor. It was dark inside, but light enough to see. (And dark enough to contemplate making a break, but Langford, holding the pistol and also possessing the Derringer, constituted too much of a risk.) "Here's my horse," Edwards said meekly. "And there's my saddle and saddle blankets."

"Saddle him," ordered Langford.

Quickly the horse was saddled. Edwards led it to the entrance, mounted, and, as if taking his spleen on the horse, spurred it roughly and yelled, "Giddap."

Horse and rider galloped down the street. Jack Langford stood watching for a few moments then pocketed his pistol. "He doesn't know it," he muttered, "but I've just saved him from a vigilance necktie party. That is, if he doesn't return."

He surveyed Muddy Creek. It was as quiet as a ghost town. He noticed that someone had blown out the lamps at Reece's Music Hall-cum-church save for a dim yellow light upstairs. That would be Julie's room. He had seen Julie and Barry make up. That thought made Jack Langford feel better.

"Jest takin' this over to the safe at the Sanborn House," said a voice behind him. "I doused the lights too, and Pat's taken care of the padre's stuff. That ok?"

It was Big Mike Mitchell. Langford thanked him. "Let me accompany you," he said. The two walked together into the hotel lobby and saw the gold dust safely into the safe.

Outside, before heading for his own cabin, Langford looked once more at Reece's. The light in Julie's upstairs room had gone out.

XIV

Gunter Schroeder's Christmas breakfast was interrupted by a persistent knocking on his door.

"Who iss it?"

"It's me. Patrick Shanahan. May I come in?"

He heard Pat fiddling with the latch, watched as the wooden handle rose and the door opened, revealing the young Irishman.

"Vell, come in and close zee door. It iss cold outside."

Pat smelled the fried eggs and bacon Gunter was eating, both of which were rarities in Muddy Creek. Gunter noticed Pat savoring the food. "I bought zee bacon and eggs in Salt Lake City," Gunter said, "and saved zem for Christmas morning." Then, after a pause, he added, "Sit down and haf some."

"I've already eaten," Pat replied. "Mush. And some coffee. But thanks just the same."

"As you vish," answered Gunter.

"Mr. Schroeder," Pat began, "I hate to disturb you on Christmas morning, but—"

"I know," said Schroeder. "Ve need zee wagon and zee oxen. Ve haf to get zee furniture back to zee Music Hall. Zee church lasted less than twelve hours. Vat a pity."

"I know," Pat replied. "To think that on Christmas Day we have to work, moving the furniture back into the Music Hall because they want to start up by ten o'clock. It's—it's—sacrilegious." Pat crossed himself.

"Achh. Sundays and holidays are not much different from other days in zee mining camps," Gunter commented.

Pat agreed. "The shebangs are closed. Most of the stores are closed. But the saloons are all open and the stage runs as if it was just another day."

"It's terrible," said the German, burping, wiping his mouth with a dirty cloth, and rising from the table. "Vell, let's be at it. It von't take long. Help me round up zee oxen."

Schroeder was an excellent bullwhacker with healthy, well-trained beasts. Pat was surprised at how rapidly the oxen were placed in teams of two, lined up, hitched up, and ready to move. In no time at all, it seemed, the wagon was on its way back to Reece's. On the way they passed Big Mike and Ebenezer Cotton slowly advancing down the street. On the horse-drawn stone boat was the outhouse-confessional, bound for Ebenezer's shed.

"They've already returned the bell to the firehouse," commented Pat, "and the Este organ has been returned to the saloon from whence it came, and they've removed the branches and hung up the nudes and the can-can girl placard is already in front of the entrance. Only the tables and gambling devices, which are stored in your wagon, need to be returned. Then it is back to usual for Reece's."

"Vat a shame," commented Scroeder. "Didn't even wait for the gut Father to have a Christmas morning Mass."

At the Music Hall, Teague and Boyd were waiting to help. As Pat walked in the door he stopped short. At the steps to the stage (the altar table and candlesticks having been removed) facing him, was Father de Mara, dressed in clerical garb. In front of the padre, facing him, were a young man and a slender young woman dressed in traveling attire.

"Well, I'll be," thought Pat. It was Barry Millard and Julie Montgomery exchanging vows. Pat paused long enough to hear the priest say, "I now pronounce you man and wife." He watched as the young couple kissed quickly then shook the padre's hand.

"There's one question I want to ask you," said the groom, pausing before they turned to walk down the aisle toward Reece's entrance. "Julie is well-educated and bright, but as you know, she's been a taxi dancer here in Muddy Creek." Barry paused, holding his new wife's hand. For her part, Julie's eyes flashed like diamonds, but the priest sensed a faint shadow of concern.

"Barry's afraid of what his mother will say when she learns I was a taxi dancer," Julie broke in.

"So, Father de Mara," Barrie continued, "Julie and I are thinking of telling everyone back East a permanent white lie."

The padre listened, thinking, why do they ask me if it is all right to lie?

"We're thinking of telling Barry's mother that I was Muddy Creek's schoolmarm," said Julie. "That's about the only legitimate job for a single girl in a mining camp."

A moment of silence followed. Finally Barry said, "What do you think, Father de Mara?"

The young Jesuit looked at the two newlyweds. True, he hardly knew them, but he was a good judge of character and had already concluded that they were good people. The thought, can a lie, a good lie, be lived a lifetime? Appraising the young couple, Father de Mara had already concluded that they would live a happy life together. Possibly, just possibly, a white lie was justified.

"Everyone lives a lie or two in a lifetime," he finally said. Barry and Julie looked at one another. By their faces it was clear they considered the padre's answer an approval. They thanked him, Barry crushed a twenty-dollar gold piece into his hand, and the two turned to leave. "Come, dear," he said, "we've got to finish packing in time to catch the Salt Lake stage." They strode up to and out the entrance.

Father de Mara was not aware until years later, when they were traveling through St. Louis with their children and paid him a call, that Barry had been undecided about Julie until the moments when she descended the stairway singing "Silent Night" and cradling her doll Melissa in her arms. That was the moment when he knew, for sure, that he wanted to marry her, knew he was not mistaken about her. He had risen from his chair as in a dream, stepped to the manger, taken her hand, and led her back to sit next to him. A few minutes later, as the processional was moving up the aisle to the altar, he had whispered in her ear, "Forgive me, Julie. I love you. Let's get married right away."

And Julie, who in later years thought she should have made him squirm a little, had instead burst into tears and, through them, said, "Yes, Barry, yes."

As the two were leaving, Jack Langford, who knew what had happened, stopped to congratulate them. The priest turned to him. "Mr. Langford, thank you for the use of the Music Hall." He swept the room with his hand. "As you can see, the teamster has arrived and we're in the process of restoring the tables and gambling equipment. I think everything else has been returned to its original status. I think you should be able to reopen by ten o'clock. I would have thanked you last night, but you were talking with someone and left by the back door."

Langford frowned. "Oh, him? Yes. Well, he's left town. And he'd better not—he probably won't—come back. Nothing to worry about."

"Was he the gambler?"

"Yep. Why?"

"Oh, nothing," replied Father de Mara, reflecting that the young singer and stage agent Robert Sungren would be pleased to hear the news.

Langford frowned and changed the subject. "First thing, Padre, I can keep the Madonna painting in the living room of my house. It's the finest residence in Muddy Creek and it will be safe there."

The padre thanked him and accepted the offer.

"What are you going to do now?" Langford asked.

The good padre hesitated. "Since there is no church here, I guess I'll head for Last Chance Gulch. There are Catholics there who let me use a vacant storefront for services."

"We need a church here, Padre," replied Langford. "We've got a lot of Irish miners, as I guess you've noticed. They are fine, hard-working men, but they are better citizens when there's a Catholic church and a priest around."

"I know, Mr. Langford," the priest said, with a smile that carried with it an "I understand." "But," he added, "Catholic churches cost money."

Langford pulled a cigar from his vest pocket, pulled a small knife from another pocket, and began clipping the cigar. "As you know, Padre, last night's take—pardon me, I mean offering—is on its way to Salt Lake by today's stage. It will be deposited, as you requested of me earlier, in a good bank."

"Thank you for that favor. It is very kind of you."

"Why don't you use the money to build a Catholic church here in Muddy Creek?"

"Even though it was a generous offering," replied the padre, "I doubt if it would be sufficient to purchase a piece of property and build a church."

"On that score I think you are wrong, Padre," Langford announced, putting away the knife and placing the cigar in his mouth. "Possibly I can give you some incentive to build here. I have a vacant lot down at the end of the street and I'll tell you what: I'll donate it to the Catholic church."

Father de Mara's face brightened. "What?" he asked. "Donate a lot for a Catholic church?"

"Yep." And Langford continued, "I was talking with Ebenezer Cotton—you know, he's the fellow who built the—er—confessional. He says he can build you a nice little chapel for a thousand dollars. And Padre, if there weren't a thousand to fifteen hundred dollars in that tureen last night, I'll—I'll—by Jove, I'll make up for the rest if you'll agree to stay as our priest."

Father de Mara was overjoyed, but cautious. "Wonderful!" he exclaimed, then paused. "But wait, Mr. Langford—"

"Call me Jack."

"Thanks, Jack. What you may not realize is that I am a Jesuit missionary assigned to the Montana-Idaho gold country. I am supposed to make my way throughout the region. Now, I could make Muddy Creek my headquarters, and be here perhaps two out of every four Sundays, but I cannot promise you more than that. And, eventually, I'll be called back to St. Louis and given a new assignment. Of course, a replacement would be sent here."

"That's sufficient," replied Langford, lighting his cigar. "You just plan on staying here, Padre, for half your time. My Irish miners will be delighted. And by the way," he added as he began to walk way, "stay at the hotel until we find a permanent place for you. And one other thing: you can hold Mass every Sunday morning at Reece's until the new church is built."

The Music Hall was becoming noisy. It had been impossible to hold a morning Mass with all the activity going on. For want of anything else to do, at that time of the day, the padre observed the Irishmen and Gunter Schroeder. The German was doing liege service, carrying tables and gambling paraphernalia into the hall and restoring them to their proper places. Over by the bar, Boyd O'Connor was bringing out the barware and the bottles of liquor, and the bartenders were replacing them where they belonged.

Seeing Schroeder working hard on a bulky faro table, the padre said, "Here, let me help." When they had set it down and positioned it, they paused to catch their breaths. Schroeder hesitantly said, "Padre, you know, your Midnight Mass may haf changed my life."

Father de Mara arched his eyebrows. Did this mean he had made a conversion? Converted a German Lutheran?

"You see," Schroeder began, "before zee Revolutions of 1848 I vas a college student in Germany. I planned to enter the Lutheran seminary and become a Lutheran minister.

But zen, being a foolish youth, I got all wrapped up in radical reforms. Next ting I knew I vas a revolutionary vis a price on my head. That is ven I escaped to America."

The padre nodded understandingly.

Schroeder heaved a big sigh. "Ach. It iss quite a story how I ended up here in vestern Montana in zee freight business. But anyway, I've never forgotten the calling I abandoned. I believe in God. I like people. Zey come to me for advice. I'm vasting my abilities being a lonely freighter."

Schroeder saw that Father de Mara was listening intently.

"And so, Padre, I came to your Midnight Mass. And while attending, I made a big decision. A very big decision." Gunter swallowed hard, then drew his meerschaum and a tobacco pouch from his pockets and began filling the pipe. Then he placed it in his mouth, fished a match from a pocket, and lit his pipe. A cloud of fragrant smoke enveloped the German's kindly face. "I'm going to St. Louis to enter the Lutheran seminary there." He looked intently at the padre, who showed disappointment. No convert! "I don't expect you'll like dat news, Padre. Competition, you know."

Quickly the padre composed himself. "Mr. Schroeder, I think that is wonderful. Look at this big America. Look at Montana. There's room for all of us who call ourselves Christians here. I am delighted that you have made your decision."

"Do you tink I vill make a good *Geistlicher*?"

"An excellent one," said the padre. "And if you are in St. Louis for several years, keep your eyes out for me. I will be called back some day, and that means to St. Louis."

Schroeder's eyes lit up. "You vould like to see *me*?"

"Of course. We can have a beer or two. Or I'll take you to a good Italian restaurant and you can take me to a German one. We will recall the first Christmas at Muddy Creek."

"Vell," said Gunter, visibly moved. "By zee way, Padre, you may keep the vooden carvings. Zey are difficult to transport. Zey break easy. Tomorrow I take zee vagon and zee oxen to Last Chance Gulch to sell. I've been offered gut money for it, enough to last me t'rough at least a year of seminary, maybe more. I'll be returning to St. Louis via the Missouri River route." He puffed on his pipe, thought for a few moments, and then added, "And another ting, Padre," he began, "how vould you like my cabin for a parsonage?"

The padre had not seen it, but Pat had told him it was a comfortable little dwelling. It was on the same side of town as Langford's vacant lot. "I am not giving it to you, at least not yet," Gunter added, "but zee title is on file at zee Register of Claims office. Pay zee taxes, vich are almost not'ing, and stay until I return." Gunter paused, watching the delight show on the padre's face. "But I doubt if I vill see Muddy Creek again." Schroeder held out a big, callused hand and they shook hands firmly.

Father Demetrius de Mara sighed and said a silent prayer. In less than twenty-four hours he had performed extreme unction, found a music hall-saloon-gambling den-dance hall and witnessed its conversion into a temporary chapel, celebrated Christmas Midnight Mass, married a deserving young couple, acquired a vacant lot and funds to build a church upon it, been offered a cabin for a parsonage, been given exquisite religious carvings of the nativity and the crucifixion, and acquired a beautiful painting for the church-to-be. Would wonders never cease?

Then Robert Sungren appeared. He was casting his eyes from side to side as if someone was about to accost him. "Oh, Mr. Sungren," the padre called him, "come here a minute."

The padre informed him of how Jack Langford had sent the gambler Charlton Edwards on his way out of town, with a warning not to return. "He won't be playing poker here any time soon, so you can stop worrying."

Sungren sighed with relief, but then added, "I'm glad, Padre, but anyway, I've given up my job."

"You're quitting as manager of the stage station?" queried the priest in surprise.

"Right, Father. Do you know why?"

Father de Mara recalled Sungren's beautiful singing the night before. He knew he was really a music teacher, but tuberculosis had forced him to give up his profession. "Are you returning to Denver? To your career?" the padre asked.

"How did you know, Father?"

"Lots of people can be clerks," replied the priest, "but God grants only a few the voice to sing as you sang last night. You are cured of your illness, aren't you?"

"I didn't cough once," Sungren replied, "and I had space in my lungs for all the air I needed. Did you notice how I projected my voice?"

"I certainly did."

"I do feel bad about quitting the stage company so quickly," added the slim young man, "but I need to get to Denver to start a winter's class." Then another thought flashed through his mind. "Padre, you haven't thought of anyone who could take over my job, have you?"

Just then Pat Shanahan, the frail one of the three young Irishmen, came up. "I heard what you said, and maybe I'd qualify," he volunteered. "I can read and write and cipher. I can do bookkeeping."

Which is how it came about that Pat Shanahan gave up his job at the Sunnyside Mine and occupied himself in employment more appropriate to his physique. His two companions, Boyd and Teague, as well as their boss, Big Mike, were relieved. Pat wasn't meant for manual labor, they all agreed, fine laddie that he was.

The padre was about to leave Reece's, which was quickly reverting to its original condition. Card players were seated at two tables already, and Gus Logan was opening the bar. There were the nudes on the walls. Then Jesse Tinsley, the furniture dealer, entered.

"Hello, Padre," he began. "I guess you noticed that I was here early this morning to reclaim my table, lectern, and candlesticks." He observed Reece's Music Hall, back in business. "Great thing you did for Muddy Creek, holding Mass here on Christmas Eve. I'm not a Catholic, but it sure got me to thinkin'."

"Thank you," said the padre.

"Yep, it sure did," said Jesse, barring the priest's passage to the swinging doors. "In fact, I've made a big decision."

Father de Mara again hoped he had a convert, but such good fortune was not to be.

"I'm writin' my wife, Padre. She thinks I was killed in William Quantrill's raid on Lawrence. But I wasn't, as you can see. I decided while sittin' at your service last night to send for Molly and the girls—I've got three daughters in their teens."

Father de Mara smiled. "I am glad to hear that," he replied.

Jesse frowned. "Know anyone leavin' for the East who I can trust with a letter?" he asked. "Can't depend too much on the mails, you know, Indians and desperadoes and all."

"The geologist, Barry Millard, and his bride, Julie, are taking the stage to Salt Lake," said the padre. "They may be already at the stage station. I'm sure they would be willing to carry a letter, and they can certainly be trusted."

That is where Jesse Tinsley found them. He congratulated Barry and Julie and asked them the favor. "I was always filled with fantasies," he explained. "So when I sent my wife and daughters back to Ohio and stayed in Lawrence, and Quantrill raided the town, I survived and headed west. For more than fifteen months I've been living my fantasies, and you know what? They aren't worth a tinker's dam to married bliss. I just hope my wife hasn't given me up for dead and remarried. Oh, my God! If only the railroad reached here. But it hain't. So please, young people, get this letter to a civilized post office and mail it for me, won't you?"

"Why don't you also send a telegram from Salt Lake?" asked Barry.

Jesse had not thought of that. Quickly he scribbled a few words and handed the scrap of paper to Barry:

ALIVE AND WELL IN MUDDY CREEK, MONTANA. STOP. JOIN ME WITH GIRLS. STOP. LOVE. JESSE

"We'll send the letter and the telegram, Jesse," Julie told him, placing her gloved hand on his. "You'll have your family here before summer is out."

The stage was due from Last Chance Gulch about noon. The weather was good and soon the rattling sound of wheels, the squeaking of leather on leather, the hoof beats of six spirited horses, all gave notice of the arrival of the Gilmer and Salisbury Stage. Waiting inside the stage office were Mr. and Mrs. Barry Millard and Robert Sungren, nervous at informing the Jehu that he had quit and turned the station over to Pat Shanahan.

And now a lone passenger arrived in Madam Dahlia's surrey, driven by the Madam herself. The occupant was the tall, lanky painter, his hat at a saucy pitch, his cape clasped around his neck. "Wait on, my friends," he yelled. Quickly he was out of the surrey, reaching for a carpetbag and a narrow, unwieldy box wherein lay his paints and brushes. The surrey quickly clattered off. He purchased a ticket to Salt Lake City and then Titian Reynolds looked around.

"You're the one who painted the Madonna at Muddy Creek," said Barry, starting a conversation.

"Right you are, my good man," Reynolds replied jauntily.

"It is a beautiful painting," Julie added.

"Bosh. I didn't have time to do it justice. But then, nothing is ever finished on the frontier, is it? I gave it to the padre."

"And now you are leaving?" asked Barry, noting that Titian was dead sober.

"Yep. The painting did it." Suddenly the artist turned serious. "It sure did do it," he added pensively. "You don't know why, my friends, but the painting exorcised my mind of sin and shame. That painting commanded me to clean up and devote the rest of my life to being what God gave me the ability to be: a painter. And so," he said as the stage clattered to a stop, "I'm returning to St. Louis. Going to set up a studio there."

Robert Sungren was leaving Pat Shanahan in charge of the station after an incredibly brief indoctrination. Now he fetched his straw suitcase and stepped to the waiting passengers. He explained how he was leaving for Denver, and Julie complimented him on his singing at the service the night before.

The Jehu spoke to the passengers. "All aboard, folks. We need to be on our way. Need to make full use of what daylight there is at this time of the year, and of the good weather."

"What happens if a storm comes up?" asked Julie.

"There's a stage station every twelve miles," the driver answered. "We can get to a station if it blows up a blizzard." He scanned the sky. "Looks good, though. If we drive all night, we'll be in Salt Lake City by Friday afternoon."

"Any danger from Indians?" asked Robert Sungren.

"Naw. The Bannocks have been quiet since General Connor licked 'em in the Battle of Bear Lake in '63."

Father Demetrius de Mara had left Reece's and was walking down the street to survey the vacant lot and inspect

Gunter Schroeder's cabin. As the Jehu yelled "Hiyaaaa, git!" and the horses jumped ahead and the stagecoach lurched forward, Julie caught sight of the padre on the other side of the street. She waved a gloved hand. "Good-bye, Father de Mara. Thanks for everything."

And Robert Sungren asked Julie, "Is that the padre?" and stuck his head out the window and waved, "God bless you, Padre."

Father de Mara paused in his walk, waved, and watched the Concord advance up the street. Suddenly he found Jesse Tinsley standing beside him. "I sure hope that letter and telegram reach my wife, Padre. Bless them on the way, won't you?"

The padre quietly obliged. Suddenly Jesse's countenance changed and his expression indicated that he had just remembered something important. "I hate to change the subject, Padre, but I've got William O'Bryan embalmed, dressed, and in a casket in my furniture store. Some of the boys are digging his grave. Just thought I'd remind you again. Can you do the obsequies at, say, ten o'clock tomorrow morning?"

Jesuit Father de Mara scowled. Everything had been so positive, so cheerful, so hopeful, and now he was brought back to frontier reality by this. Quickly he regained his composure. "Of course," he replied.

From the boardwalk in front of Sang Lee's laundry, the Celestial also watched the Concord coach disappear. He waved to the padre and Jesse, and then disappeared inside. Jesse, after inviting the padre to have supper with him, said good-bye and headed back to his lonely apartment in the rear of the furniture store.

As for Father de Mara, that high noon of a cold but sunny Christmas Day, he continued his walk until he came upon a vacant lot fitting Jack Langford's description. He sat down on a tree stump and looked far up Main Street, past the fire station—to which, he noticed, the fire bell had been returned—past Sang Lee's laundry, past the Sanborn House and Reece's Music Hall, Tinsley's furniture store, Robinson's café, and even the Register of Receiver's office, until his eyes reached the ridge overlooking the town. It was from there, less than twenty-four hours ago, that he had first looked down upon Muddy Creek.

And he meditated, and finally he prayed. His final words to the Lord were, "Have I done right? Have I accomplished anything good?"

XV

Father Demetrius de Mara, S.J., soon discovered that everyone in Muddy Creek came to him for advice and counsel: Protestants, Catholics, agnostics, storekeepers, a barber, a Chinese laundryman, a local entrepreneur named Jack Langford, and yes, even the fallen women at Madam Dahlia's *maison de joie*.

The first several months he was there, when not making his rounds to other mining camps, events happened that, he reflected, usually materialized over the span of a priest's career. Ebenezer Cotton, a Congregationalist and Yankee if ever there was one, collaborated wholeheartedly with Langford and the padre to build on the Montana frontier a distinctive and beautiful Catholic chapel. Funds proved sufficient to build the basic log structure complete with hewn log pews, a transept, and an apse. Both Father de Mara and Ebenezer Cotton smiled when Cotton, who with the help of Langford and the padre drew up the plans, located a very correct confessional located just inside and to the right of the church entrance.

They wished they had funds for a stained glass window. They wished Gunter Schroeder had stayed in town to carve the Stations of the Cross. His crucifix hung free from the ceiling in the apse behind the altar. The lectern was Jesse Tinsley's gift. Titian Reynolds' Madonna of the Mountains (really a nativity scene) was duly framed and mounted on the wall of the foyer. Much may have been missing, but the total effect, when it was finished, was of a beautiful frontier church.

Father de Mara was amazed at the help from the community. As Muddy Creek made the switch from placer to hard-rock mining the number of families grew, and his congregation, which at first had consisted of Catholics and Protestants about equally, began to take on a more Irish-Catholic strain. Then a Methodist minister settled in Muddy Creek. He was popular with the Cornish miners who had flocked in when hard-rock mining began in earnest. The new preacher, who soon also had a chapel, was sort of stand-offish, but there was never any real animosity between him and the Jesuit.

Some events were happy, some sad. Father de Mara had a warm feeling for the four Irishmen whom he had met that Christmas Eve as, dejected, he had started out of Muddy Creek on Gabriel with the pack mule Lucifer behind. Big Mike Mitchell, Boyd O'Connor, Teague Cosgrove, and Patrick Shanahan became pillars of the church.

Pat thrived at the new job as the Gilmer and Salisbury agent. One Sunday as he carried out the tasks of altar boy, his eyes fell on a new Catholic family in the parish, a family taking up a whole pew on one side of the aisle: father, mother, and a staircase of children right down to a suckling babe. Next to the mother sat a girl in her late teens, blue eyes, dark hair, Irish as an Irish rose, and to Pat, the most beautiful female in the world. Father de Mara had to speak twice, another time three times, about chores Pat should be doing. Finally the padre grabbed a glance at what was diverting the altar boy, and he understood.

The Callahans' oldest daughter was a full-blown maiden pushing seventeen when Pat began his courtship; she was into that age when Father de Mara married them in the first formal Catholic social wedding in Muddy Creek's history. The Callahans accepted Pat as one of their own, and for all of them, the future looked bright, and it *was* bright. When the stage company gave way to the Utah Northern Railroad, Pat simply applied and landed the job as station agent. Until his death in 1917, he was one of the pillars of Muddy Creek's establishment.

One raw, disagreeable day in blustery March, 1866, Father de Mara heard the fire bell ringing and ringing almost histerically, he thought. He ran from the parsonage to see people running up the road toward the Sunnyside mine. He joined, for several parishioners worked there, including Big Mike and Teague and Boyd. Upon his arrival the rumor that there had been an accident proved valid: Gas! Poison gas had struck down several miners. Big Mike, who was working outside the mine, had heard an anguished cry and ran into the mine, hoping to drag the victims to safety, but the fumes were too strong and he succumbed. A flue allowing stale air and gases to escape had clogged. Now workers were cleaning it so they could clear the mine of gas and retrieve the bodies. Among the dead were Big Mike, Boyd O'Connor, and Teague Cosgrove; two others of the eight miners found dead were Catholics.

The funeral at the Church of the Mountain Madonna included three devoted Irishmen who had been instrumental in bringing about the first Catholic services in Muddy Creek. So strange is Providence! The weakest of the quartet of Big Mike Mitchell, Teague Cosgrove, Boyd O'Connor, and Pat Shanahan was the one who had the task of notifying the next of kin. Sending those letters was the hardest task Pat Shanahan was ever called upon to do.

One day in late spring, Jesse Tinsely came to the parsonage with a letter. No, his wife had not remarried. Yes, she had forgiven him—after thinking it over for awhile—for not letting her know he was still alive. And yes, she and the girls would risk the dangers of the Wild West and travel to Muddy Creek to live with him! The days of July seemed to go on forever as Jesse waited for every Gilmer and Salisbury stage to arrive. It was Father de Mara's good fortune to have been at the station on business when the coach clattered up and Tinsley's family, three pretty girls, the oldest about seventeen, and a somewhat lumpy but clearly healthy wife, got out of the coach. Jesse took great pride in introducing his family to the padre, later inviting him to a fried chicken dinner "as only Molly can fix it." And this was but the first of many invitations.

In that same, stormy, blustery month of March when the mine disaster had occurred, Sang Lee informed Jack Langford (who already knew it) that the gambler Charlton Edwards was back in town. The business man and the card shark kept their distance, Edwards frequenting another saloon and doing his card playing with a different crowd from the one that loitered around the Music Hall. Langford asked Pat Shanahan to let him know if the gambler queried him of a gold shipment. This never happened, probably, thought Langford, because Edwards knew that Shanahan had once worked at the Sunnyside Mine.

But Edwards did learn, somehow. Early in April, the Gilmer and Salisbury stage was held up seven miles southwest of Muddy Creek. Not only did the highwaymen get away with several thousand dollars in gold dust, they also killed the Jehu. And the Jehu, Les Warner, was a very popular man in Muddy Creek. Rumors abounded that the vigilantes were going to act.

"Aw," scoffed some, "there ain't no vigilantes in Muddy Creek."

But there were. First came the rumor that four cottonwoods bordering Muddy Creek below town had sprouted strange fruit. The vigilantes, however, were responsible men. Few observed the corpses swinging in the wind because they were promptly cut down by persons unknown and the bodies buried in unmarked graves.

All but one. That corpse lay un-embalmed and in rigor mortis in a crude wooden coffin hastily put together by Ebenezer Cotton. It had been placed on a nondescript wagon that was parked behind a crude barn at the edge of town.

It was a cold, rainy April night, with a foreboding of sleet and snow, the last winter storm of the season. Father de Mara had retired early. He was awakened, and a little frightened, by a demanding, persistent knocking at his door. "Who is it?" he asked, getting out of his warm bed and groping for a match to light his lamp. "What do you want at this hour?" The padre knew these things happened with priests. Even in Muddy Creek he had been awakened by a married couple immersed in a hot but specious argument, asking him to settle it; by some drunks who wanted to confess their sins; and once by a teen-age kid afraid to go home.

"I'm Jack Langford, Padre, and it's important I see you."

The padre groped his way to the door and opened it to face a very serious entrepreneur who was clearly not calling for fear of his immortal soul.

"Father de Mara, I—we—have a favor to ask of you."

"At this hour?" the padre replied, scowling. Then, composing his thoughts, he added, "Of course."

Langford stepped inside out of the wind and sleet and closed the door. He breathed heavily then looked straight at Father de Mara. "Could you show up at the cemetery early this morning, say by seven o'clock? We—I mean, I—need you to perform a Catholic funeral."

Father de Mara scowled, by now wide awake. "Why not at the church?" he asked.

"Padre, please believe me. You don't want a church funeral for this sonofa—for this fellow."

"Why me?" asked the priest. "The deceased doesn't sound like a church-going person. Certainly not a good Catholic."

"He wasn't. He was no good. But the last thing he said before we—before someone—swatted the horse was, 'Boys, do me one favor. Get Father de Mara to bury me with Catholic rites'."

Father de Mara frowned. He studied Langford's face.

"And we said, 'sure will,' and he swung."

For long moments neither man spoke. The wind whistled outside the cabin and one could hear the sleet slamming against the little windows. The padre knew of the vigilantes, had heard about the corpses that rumor said had swung in the wind in the cottonwood grove, knew that

Langford was a Mason and that most of the vigilantes were said to be Masons. He did not argue or question more. He nodded his head affirmatively.

"At seven this morning? I'll be there," he replied simply, and with almost a whisper, Langford replied, "Thanks, Padre."

Father de Mara sometimes wondered why these frontier towns had to choose for their cemeteries such barren, wind-swept places amidst all the beauty of Western America. Muddy Creek's graveyard was at the top of a ridge devoid of trees. Weeds grew amidst the weather-beaten wooden grave markers. On the morning his services were requested a raw, cold wind was blowing with gray clouds occasionally whipping down sleet and snow flurries.

As he approached the cemetery on Gabriel, he noticed beside an open grave a crude farm wagon pulled by two horses. In the wagon bed was an unpainted pine box of sawn lumber. Jack Langford was the only person he recognized, although four other men were present. Father de Mara approached, dismounted, and walked steadily toward the site.

"Hello, Jack."

"Hello, Padre. Er—here's the casket. The boys'll lower it into the ground as soon as you've said—whatever you're supposed to say." Langford did not introduce the other men.

"I must know who he is," said the padre, "although I have a strong suspicion that I already know." He reached up to raise the top of the casket.

Langford quickly reached over and held down the lid. "I don't think you want to see the corpse, Padre," he said.

"I must," replied Father de Mara firmly. "It's all right. It's Charlton Edwards, isn't it? And you hanged him."

The men exchanged glances. "Yes," Langford said simply. "Padre, he's not a pretty sight. We've cleaned him up a bit but, well, the rope slipped and he suffered for quite a spell before we, well, we shot him to end his misery."

The priest again tried to lift the cover, and this time Langford did not stop him. There lay the body of a man dressed nattily in gambler's attire. The cream-colored checkered vest was reddened by dried blood. The searing mark around the neck indicated that he had been hanged. His face was grotesque, as if frozen in excruciating pain. Father de Mara lowered the cover and breathed deeply. Then he said, "Let's get on with it, gentlemen."

The men hammered down the top with just four nails, nails being in short supply at Muddy Creek. Then they lowered the crude, unpainted casket from the wagon bed and set it on two ropes placed on the ground. Slowly, as Father de Mara said the liturgy, the wooden box was lifted over the grave and allowed to bump its way to the bottom while loose dirt fell on and around it. Meanwhile the early morning daylight darkened and snow flurries began whirling around the cemetery. Quickly the men fetched shovels from the wagon and soon had the grave filled and a crude wooden cross poked into the dirt at the head of the grave.

Langford handed the padre a twenty-dollar gold piece. "Thanks, Father de Mara," he said tersely. None of the others said a word, and all five, three up front on the seat and two sitting where the casket had been, clattered away in the wagon. The padre, full of melancholy, was left to make his way back to town on Gabriel.

As he passed Sang Lee's laundry, the Celestial ran out to speak to him. Sang Lee bowed then searched the padre's face. "Pardon, Father de Mara. But—did you perform—funeral services—for gambler?"

Father de Mara was surprised that Sang Lee was so alert to town happenings, or to events taking place so early in the morning. "Yes, Sang Lee. It was Charlton Edwards. He has paid for his crimes."

Sang Lee smiled, bowed, and then made the sign of the cross. "May God have mercy on his soul," said the Oriental, turning abruptly and returning to his dwelling.

After three years as a missionary in western Montana and eastern Idaho, Father Demetrius de Mara was called back to Jesuit headquarters in St. Louis. The city looked strange to him, and frightening. But he was up to the challenge and was soon a cosmopolitan Jesuit, a man of the cloth commanding respect. He was happy in his new assignment teaching Canon Law at St. Louis University. He did chuckle when they informed him of his subject. He figured he had broken more Church law in his three years as a missionary, and especially at Muddy Creek, than any Jesuit since the Middle Ages. In another era and another place they'd have burned him at the stake, he thought.

But he loved his new assignment. One day, a month or so after his return, he was in his office when he heard a low, masculine voice asking for him. Now, in St. Louis, throaty German voices were common, but this one was distinctive. "Ach," it began most sentences, and only Gunter Schroeder's voice made that sound. When the padre stepped into the outer office, he witnessed a transformation. The teamster in frontier clothes now wore the clerical collar and well-pressed black suit of an ordained Lutheran minister.

"Father de Mara," Schroeder exclaimed, holding out his arms for a brotherly embrace. "Since you are responsible for zis," he said, touching his collar, "I tink I should invite you to a fine German restaurant for some real sauerbraten and good German beer, eh?"

Thus continued a friendship that lasted a lifetime. They talked of Muddy Creek and of the first Christmas Mass there. The padre related the deaths of the Irishmen and the lynching of Charlton Edwards and other desperados. On a happier key, Schroeder asked the padre if he had been to the new art gallery. When the priest said he hadn't, Schroeder said he should. "Be sure to look up the director," he urged, "he iss tall, lanky, and vis a Van Dyke beard."

"Not Titian Reynolds!" exclaimed the padre.

"None ozzer. He returned to St. Louis, set up a studio, and has a gut clientele. Zen he married vell—a German-American heiress. And to keep himself busy, he iss a high society promoter of ze fine arts in St. Louis. He iss—vat dey say—a teetotaler. Be sure to see him."

Father de Mara reflected that he had indeed been busy, for he should have known of Reynolds.

A year or two later, one pleasant June afternoon, the padre was looking out his office window when a carriage pulled up at the entrance. He watched as a well-dressed couple stepped out followed by two well-behaved small children, a boy and a girl. Probably relatives of one of the Jesuits, the padre mused. But as he looked more closely, a glimpse of another time and another place came to him.

Could it be Barry Millard and Julie, whom he had married at Muddy Creek on Christmas Day, 1865, in violation of all kinds of religious regulations?

Indeed it was them. They were on their way to Colorado for the summer, where Barry would be a consultant to mining interests. During the school year he was a professor of geology at an Ivy League college. They wanted to show off to Father de Mara their two children, to say thanks to him once again.

"And we're visiting Robert Sungren in Denver," Julie said. "We met him last summer when we attended his church. We heard this wonderful tenor voice that reminded us of Robert, so we searched him out, and it was him."

"Is he in good health?" asked the padre.

"Oh, yes. He's gained weight," Julie replied. "And married. He's music director for the Denver Public Schools."

"And by the way," Julie said demurely, her eyes sparkling, and when their offspring were out of hearing. "The suggestion you gave us that I was the schoolmarm at Muddy Creek has worked. Everyone believes us and Barry's mother—she's the sweetest thing—has accepted me completely."

Father de Mara frowned. "Now, Mrs. Millard. I did not suggest that to you. I just—tried to rationalize its legitimacy—or, perhaps, its inevitability."

"Oh, whatever," the young mother replied, winking at him. "It worked."

And so the years passed. Father Demetrius de Mara was popular with students but when Canon Law became unbearably dull, as on a mild spring day, the seminarians capitalized on the good padre's known weakness. Some students would work around to asking him some questions about Canon Law as it was practiced on the American frontier. It worked every time. He would start to reply, then remove his glasses and lean an elbow on the lectern. The students, with a sigh of relief, would put down their pens and lean back in their chairs. Did the padre know what they were up to? If he did, he cared not. He always began the same way:

"I remember cresting the ridge overlooking Muddy Creek, a boom town on the Montana frontier, on Christmas Eve, 1865…"

Author's Note

"First Christmas at Muddy Creek" is pure fiction. In the New York riots, Quantrill's raid on Lawrence, and any other incidents, the characters and their experiences are fictional, all products of my imagination, as is the town of Muddy Creek. However, even an imagination has to start with a kernel of reality. The catalyst for this story comes from historian Andrew F. Rolle's delightful book, "The Immigrant Upraised: Italian Adventurers and Colonists in an Expanding America" (Norman: University of Oklahoma Press, 1968), pp. 193–194. The pertinent paragraphs follow:

"In 1865, Father Giuseppe Giorda visited one of the wildest western mining towns, Virginia City. He hoped to establish a church at Virginia City. The existence of an atmosphere of violence, prohibitive prices and lawbreakers did not rule out the need for religion. . . . After searching throughout the town, the priest was on the verge of abandoning his efforts when unexpected help came to him.

"On Christmas Eve news of his unsuccessful attempts to find space reached a local barroom. Several of its leading customers, after raising their glasses on high, contacted the forceful Irishman who was acting governor of Montana—General Thomas Francis Meagher. The governor, a striking figure with a bulbous nose and curled locks of hair, agreed to help collect gold so that Father Giorda could rent an already engaged theater at the corner of Wallace and Jackson

Streets. As helpers of every variety began to transform the theater, the actors performing were persuaded that they needed a rest during the holiday season. All the gaudy pictures and signs were removed. A large cross was hoisted over the door, and decorative evergreens were brought into the building. Next, Virginia City's residents constructed an altar, communion railing, and confessional. For Catholics the preparations seems as exciting as the Gold Stampede at Last Chance Gulch.

"A midnight Mass followed. The service was so crowded that worshipers knelt at the door in the inclement weather. After Mass was over, the proprietor of the theater complained that his building had been ruined for future use. Governor Meagher then personally collected another offering of gold dust on a Delft plate with spoons in it to scoop up the gold. The governor, expressing the wish that Father Giorda make Virginia City his home, handed the proceeds to the amazed Torinese priest. By this time Giorda was in tears. The Mass he had celebrated introduced Montanans to their first urban church"